BLOOD OF THE FAE

INTO
FAERLAND

Also by A.J Ponder

The Sylvalla Chronicles

Quest

Prophecy

Omens

The Dragon Society Papers

The Dragon Transport & Pacification Society

The Society for the Prevention of Cruelty to Dragons
& Magical Creactures

Connect with A.J.

PonderBooks.com
Bookbub: www.bookbub.com/authors/a-j-ponder
Facebook: www.facebook.com/AJPonderwriter

Join A.J's mailing list: https://ponderbooks.com/mailing-list/

BLOOD OF THE FAE

1

INTO
FAERLAND

A.J. PONDER
USA TODAY BESTSELLING AUTHOR

A catalogue record for this book is available from the National Library of New Zealand.

Into FaerLand, Blood of the Fae © 2022 A.J. Ponder
Typesetting © A.J. Ponder, 2022
Editor Charlotte Jardine
Cover Art © Christian Bentulan 2022
Map of Kymæria by Rachael Ward of Cartographybird © A.J. Ponder 2025
Phantom Feather Press Logo, Geoff Popham © Phantom Feather Press 2014

EBook ISBN 978-1-99-104716-8
Paperback ISBN 978-1-99-104712-0
Hardback ISBN 978-1-99-104720-5

phantomfeatherpress@gmail.com
www.phantomfeatherpress.wordpress.com

PHaNtoM FeatHer PreSS

Magic, every time you turn the page.

2021 WRIGHT-MURRAY RESIDENCY

The "Blood of the Fae" series was grown within 2021 Wright-Murray Residency. It featured the uninterrupted writing time, an opportunity to contribute the writing community in The Bay of Plenty and to participate with Young New Zealand Writers event held during my stay. It also represented a chance to reconnect with some of the glorious NZ forest that has been so inspirational to this tale.

DEDICATED TO

My husband, Philip, who has not only
supported me throughout
this writing journey,
but was willing to die for this story.

A SPECIAL THANK YOU

Lee Murray & Chloe Wright for sponsoring
the Wright-Murray Residency for Speculative
Fiction. Charlotte Jardine, my amazing
editor, Denika Mead, my beta reader, and
my three heroic red shirt volunteers, Phil
Sirvid, Schuyler Corson and Craig Harder.

UNCHARTED NORTHERN SEAS

THE GREAT LIBRARY
OF ALEXANDRIA

DORNRÖSCHENSCHLOSS
CASTLE

THE
UNDERWORLD

THE
DEADLANDS

WESTERN WATERS

WAYSTOP

CASTLE
CITY

THE
QUILTER
LANDS

THE GREAT LANDS OF
KYMÆRIA

MAJOR SETTLEMENTS ◉
MINOR SETTLEMENTS ◉
NOTABLE LANDMARKS ◆

THE
EYRIE

BROCÉLIANDE

MARKET
TOWN

WÓPBORA
COTIF

THREE
SISTERS
TREE

ABA YAGA'S
HUT

NEW
AVALON

FAERLAND

DRAGON
CASTLE

GOTHEL'S
TOWER

HAMLYN

*"—we never steal children. We only swap them.
An eye for an eye, a child for a child."*

THE SWORD MASTER

1 June 1927

*A*iden tramped down the narrow forest path, careful not to trip on the roots snaking across it. He tried not to think too hard about where he and Corson were going—the crossroads on a desolate pine-encrusted ridge, just past the territory owned by the witch, Baba Yaga. *This Sword Master had better be worth it.* At least Corson was here. A lithe, effective fighter with a solid punch and a way with swords.

Corson grinned. "You think if we run into Baba Yaga she'll refrain from turning me into a frog if I ask nice?"

"If you ask nice, maybe she'll turn you into a prince," Aiden joked. Corson was certainly handsome enough. He always looked like he was coming off a movie set, with his fringe cut long enough to show off the wave in his dark hair.

"Well, that's the dream…" Corson cracked a grin. "Of course, we have to survive first."

Aiden's laughter died. Survival was what this mission was about. Just last week a pack of demons almost got through the village's defences. If the attacks continued, and they couldn't adequately defend themselves against the stone-skinned monsters, the small settlement of New Avondale would have to be abandoned. A blow to Burcham and The Society and all the people who lived there, as well as Aiden and his parents who used it as a temporary base.

"I've heard there's no better fighter than the Sword Master," Aiden replied, changing the subject. "With his swords we'll be less vulnerable to demon attack." He frowned. No doubt this Sword Master would be the tall strong warrior type that would call him Red, or Carrot Top. And be a total condescending arsehole. He shrugged. Sometimes in life you had to suck it up. "I don't know about you, but I'm sick of turning all my swords into twisted hunks of iron on those demons. I'd be better off hitting them with a sledgehammer…now there's a thought."

"Come on," Corson smiled his wide smile. "If you were strong enough, you'd have done that already."

The day passed, footstep by footstep, mile by mile. Carefully quiet, to avoid announcing their presence to demons, the settlements along the way, and the bandits that frequented them. Nottingham Forest and Witch's Place held two of the most notorious stretches of road.

By midday, the thick forest of Brocéliande had thinned revealing the northwestern mountains, dotted with the unmistakable pink of the Dornröschenschloss castle roses. They kept walking until the path was little more than broken rock along a rugged cliff, kept together by the scraggly pines that clutched the barren rock with their wiry roots.

Corson glanced to the left. Down in the gully below was a ramshackle cottage inside a small dirt clearing. "Is that Baba Yaga's hut?"

"I hope not." Aiden shrugged hoping the large creamy-brown shells scattered around the outside of the hut weren't skulls. He walked faster. "Best not to find out. Wait a minute? Do you think this is the spot?" A broken signpost lay on the ground—a fresh hole where it had been ripped out of the rocky ground. The cracked and broken signs had previously pointed the way to Dornröschenschloss castle, Wóþbora cotif and Market Town, and the Deadlands and the Underworld.

"I think so." Corson waved his hand down the escarpment to the sulphurous pools and mountains ahead. "Presumably the track down is to the Underworld, and I don't want to get any closer."

Gravel crunched behind them.

Aiden turned. A massive marble demon towered over Corson. Calcite crystals caught the light in its smooth white-and-grey streaked skin. But however pretty and statuesque the demon was, it was even more deadly.

"Watch out!" Aiden drew his sword and scrambled down the path toward the demon as it threw a marble fist at Corson's face.

Corson turned and ducked, the blow parting his hair. Bobbing up, he smashed his sword into the demon's jaw.

The demon laughed, batting Corson's blade aside as if it were a mosquito.

Skidding on the shattered rock of the steep cliff track, Aiden hacked at the creature's chest. The blade crashed into its stone-like skin with a clang that reverberated up his arm.

"Is that all you've got?" The demon sneered, swiping at Aiden. Aiden danced back.

Corson turned to Aiden, distracted. "Aiden!" he yelled.

The creature lunged for Corson again and hit him solidly in the stomach. He grunted and staggered backward.

"I'm on it!" Aiden kept hacking at the marble demon.

Refusing to be side-tracked, the demon followed up with another blow to Corson's midriff. Corson swerved, but the demon's stone fist glanced his ribs.

"Oof!" Corson grunted. He threw his sword at Aiden like it was a spear.

Aiden flinched as the sword sailed past him and clanged on the resilient skin of a trident-wielding schist demon that had been sneaking up behind him.

I almost walked right into that demon's arms!

Corson's sword bounced off the demon's rock-hard skin, flying over the edge of the narrow path and clattering to the bottom.

"Shite," Aiden yelled as Corson narrowly dodged a right hook from the marble demon. He lunged to join his friend, but the schist demon followed, thrusting its weapon at Aiden's chest.

Aiden jumped sideways and hacked at the demon's face, denting his blade. Then he twirled away from the schist demon's incoming trident and chopped at demon again—putting all his weight into the move. The clang reverberated. Pain numbed his hand, radiating up his arm.

Stone chipped. A tiny fissure. Boiling-hot magma-like blood welled up to seal the crack.

A tang of sulphur split the air.

Aiden shifted his grip and spared a glance for Corson, who dodged behind a scraggly old pine a hairsbreadth ahead of the other demon. *Corson has the right idea. Tire it out. Their speed only lasts so long.*

A roar brought him back to his senses. "Pathetic human," the trident-wielding demon yelled. "Enough playing. Time to die."

Aiden hit the creature on the side of the head with a clunk, chipped his blade and damaged the demon not at all. He darted back again.

A wet thump. Corson cried out.

"Corson!" Aiden risked a glance behind to see his friend scramble over a boulder. *Still alive!*

The marble demon followed.

Dammit. With Corson unarmed and injured, Aiden had to risk everything to get this fight over fast. He blocked the schist demon's trident, stepped inside its reach and swung with all his might.

The blow smashed into the creature's face. Its skin cracked wider, and a gout of hot magma-like blood sizzled against the sword.

The demon clutched at empty air as Aiden twirled away.

Corson cried out again.

Anger flooded Aiden. He raised his sword and made to run at the schist demon drawing a wild attack. Using the demon's own momentum, he pulled the trident from its fingers and ran to Corson, who was backed up against the trunk of a giant pine clinging to the edge of the steep slope.

The schist demon followed Aiden up the narrow track.

"You come to join the fun?" Corson asked, blood pouring down his nose. He threw a rock at the marble demon's face.

Aiden didn't waste his breath trying to be cute. He hammered his sword at the marble demon's arm and stepped next to Corson. He rained blow after blow on the head and shoulders of both demons. Corson grabbed the trident and smashed it over the head of the marble demon until steaming demon-blood ran down its face.

"Sorry." Corson puffed, struggling for breath with wheezing gasps. "I got us a bit backed into a corner."

We need a plan. Sooner or later, one of them is going to grab us. The image of being crushed by the two monsters made him sick.

With a crack, the trident shattered into splinters.

Aiden's stomach sank. His friend could no longer keep the marble demon at bay.

It lunged at Corson.

Corson's arm shot out and grabbed a marble-skinned shoulder. His foot hooked behind the demon's calf. It lurched and toppled forward toward the edge of the cliff. Skidding…falling, the demon's scream of hatred faded as it crashed down the steep slope.

"Nice!" Aiden yelled as the schist demon threw itself at him. Aiden sidestepped and kicked out at it.

"Good try." Corson rushed to shove the demon. It thumped a fist into Corson's stomach, Corson was thrown backward into the tree, and stayed there—slumped over the gnarled old roots. *It'll be a while before he's back on his feet—if he gets up at all.*

It was just the two of them now. The schist demon and himself.

Aiden stepped forward to give Corson some room and battered his mangled sword at it.

It stepped forward, using its strength and weight to get close to Corson. Desperate, Aiden decided to take a leaf from Corson's playbook. He stepped in close, kicked his opponent's shin, and pushed.

Nothing.

The demon swung his rocky fist.

Aiden leapt clear. His hand tingling and numb, he hacked at the demon's head, the clang as loud as any bell. He forced himself to continue—once, twice, three times.

The demon staggered closer. The reek of sulphur heavy in the air as hot demon blood oozed from multiple cracks. It stepped up and wrapped its arms around him, dripping molten magma onto Aiden's shoulders. The molten stone sizzled through his jacket, searing his skin like liquid fire.

Caught in the demon's crushing grip, Aiden screamed and thrashed.

The demon staggered and slipped. Its grip loosened.

With a grunt, Aiden shimmied from the demon's grasp and hit with abandon, gritting his teeth against the pain and inching back to Corson who was struggling to stand.

Again, and again, Aiden hit—the pain from the burns subliming into his own white-hot fury.

The demon slowed, as did the drip and sizzle of its scorching blood. A haze of eye-watering sulphur rising from its wounds.

A.J. Ponder

So close. Arm cramping, Aiden fought to hold the blade and put all his strength into one more blow from his scorched and twisted weapon.

The clash of sword against stone was punctuated with a sharp crack.

My sword?! Aiden bounded back and the demon exploded, shattering into shards of half-molten stone. Pelted by red-hot debris and flakes of schist, Aiden ignored the sting of falling rock to check on his friend.

Corson stood up to survey the steaming pile of stone and magma that had been the schist demon, clutching his stomach and very much alive.

Aiden breathed a sigh of relief. "Hey, you look almost as bad as my sword."

Corson tried to smile. "Me? I'm just winded. Be right as rain in a minute. It's all about the muscles." He flexed an arm. "But that sword of yours is toast. Unless you picked up an iron railing and your sword's fallen somewhere nearby."

"Smartass," Aiden muttered. "You don't think I can fix it?"

"Nah," Corson said, kicking the broken crossroad sign. "We need that new swordsmith to turn up. But we shouldn't wait here any longer, we're like sitting ducks here on the border waiting for him to arrive."

"We can't leave," Aiden said, wincing as he pulled up his sleeve to check his burned arm. "The Sword Master is coming from several worlds away. We have to give him the benefit of the doubt. Besides, we need that expertise." He waved the mangled blade. The cool air passing over his burn helped. Still, his arm was sure going to sting when the adrenaline wore off.

"And if another demon turns up, what are we going to hit it with?" Corson held up his bare hands.

"You shouldn't have thrown your sword down that cliff." Aiden grinned. "Besides, you could always tell everyone you were training with your bare hands because demons aren't scary enough for you."

"I'd rather something more solid than my hands against demons. Or fae, for that matter. You think the fae are ever going to forgive us?"

"No." Aiden sighed. "Although it might help if they'd tell us why us using silver makes them so angry. They're always using silver. It makes no sense."

"Yeah. And if we leave the swordsmith alone here, he'll probably never forgive us either. Then where will we be?"

An ominous crunch pulled their attention. More demons were climbing the path. They were only minutes away.

"I guess you're right." Aiden pointed down the cliff face at the half dozen demons on the track down into the DeadLands. Mostly granite demons by the look of them. Slower than marble and schist, but tougher and very dangerous.

"I guess sometimes you need to know when to fight, and sometimes you need to know when to run." Corson turned back from the cliff. "You think there's—"

"Watch out!" Aiden jumped over a waist-high rock as a dark figure dressed in forest colours sprinted toward them. She had flares of rose-red in her skirt and braided hair down to her waist. Even with a substantial backpack, she was light-footed on the treacherous cliff path.

"Fae!" Corson yelled, joining Aiden behind the flimsy cover.

"Shit!" Aiden held out his pitiful sword. It would do no good against so many demons and a fae—a fae holding the most beautiful sword Aiden had ever seen. Its bright steel flashing in the sunlight was enhanced by ornate silver and gold script that swept up the blade.

"Stay back, Fae," Corson yelled. "We don't want any trouble."

A.J. Ponder

The vision of beauty continued to race toward them. "Demon!" the fae yelled, sidestepping like a dancer—dress flaring into four scarlet petals as she twirled to face a slate-green demon emerging from its hiding place behind an enormous pine.

Flail whistling, the new schist demon charged.

Aiden moved to join her, and face down the massive creature.

Corson pulled him back. Too slow.

The demon's smile told Aiden everything he needed to know. He flung up his battered sword. Also, too slow.

The vision of beauty stepped forward, faer sword sweeping through the demon's flail like butter, then cleanly reversed the blade in a swift arc to remove the demon's head. Steaming gently, the demon's slate-green noggin bounced into the bushes. The body shattered and collapsed in a pool of swift-hardening demon blood.

Corson advanced. Fists raised, he yelled. "I said, 'Stay back, Fae.' We don't want any trouble."

The swords-fae threw faer head back and laughed, faer dangly gold earrings swinging merrily as if they were laughing, too. "I'm no fae. You'd be dead if I was."

Aiden's heart soared and his mind whirred. Fae were supposed to be whip-thin, and eerily quiet. Scornful and distant. This person was none of those things. Substantial and real, *she* was more sunshine than shadow. And although her clothes were unusual, they appeared bright and well-made and not like gossamer down or any of the other strange materials fae preferred. Her face was the shape of a heart. Her lips were like…he wasn't sure…plums? velvet? All he knew was how difficult it was to quell his impulse to lean in and kiss them. And if she was human…. "Where did you come from? We should walk you back," Aiden said, trying to shake the giddy attraction that surged through him like a thunderclap. "It's not safe here."

"You mean, it's not safe for you." She laughed, her smile lighting her eyes. "Do you even know what you're doing? Your sword is more gate-post than blade." She was mesmerising, the spark of her amusement barely contained. "Come on."

Together, they headed up to the ridge back above the creepy hut.

"Are you sure you're not fae," Aiden blurted. "You're so beautiful."

The woman turned to Corson. "Do you think that's an insult or a compliment—I'm really not sure."

"Oh, it's a compliment," Corson said. "Half of New Avalon composes a sonnet every time a fae stops by the forge."

Aiden took a breath trying to stop the blood from rushing to his cheeks—suddenly ultra-aware of his red hair and freckles. *If Corson says anything about fire-engines, I'll....* Instead, Corson winked at Aiden and rushed ahead.

"Alright," she said with a nod that set her braids bouncing as she strode along beside him. "I think I've seen enough. Fire Boy, let's get back to your settlement. It's right next to Myrddin's forge, isn't it?"

What does she mean, she's seen enough? And calling me fire boy? Still, as a nickname, it's not completely without hope. "Yes, King Arthur's forge—or Merlin's if you prefer—is the biggest drawcard in Brocéliande. We're receiving requests for special swords made in its flame already."

A smile played on her lips. He imagined kissing her and shook his head. Brocéliande could play tricks like this. *Love at first sight is for the people who belong here, not me.* According to his parents, anyone foolish enough to fall in love here would inevitably find heartbreak. And besides, being part of The Society meant avoiding entanglements that could compromise the settlement.

She gazed at him, her amber eyes wells of mystery. "I could fix that blade of yours, Fire Boy. Make you a proper one."

"I'm ah…" Heat rushed up Aiden's cheeks. He stopped, frightened he'd make a complete fool of himself and trip over his feet as well as his tongue.

She stuck out her non-sword arm. "I'm Keera, by the way. I also go by the title, Sword Master."

"Oh. Of course. Lovely to meet you." So, she was the swordsmith they'd been waiting for. He should have realised the moment he'd seen her sword in action. "Thank goodness you're here. We desperately need your skills." He patted the pommel of his mangled sword. "Hey, anything's got to be better than this."

Corson turned back. "Yes, that's right. It's lovely to meet you and all, but don't you think introductions can wait, so we can all move a bit faster?"

"You're being ridiculous." Aiden glanced down the slope. The demons were so close he could see their granite faces leering through the twisted half-dead pine trees clinging to the volcanic rock. Some were swinging flails. Others wielded swords that looked more like knives in their impossibly large fists. "It's hardly an army." Aiden said, trying to play it cool. "But maybe we should run."

"Keera Quicksilver, Destroyer," A demon bellowed, shaking its marble fist. "King Hades has sent us to kill you!"

"Hmm," Corson said. "They do look a bit eager. We could slow them down, first."

"No—" Aiden started.

"To that big tree on the saddle. And…**go**!" Corson screamed and brandished a fallen branch. "Death to the demons!" he yelled as if turned into a berserker rage. He ran back along the ridge.

Aiden followed reluctantly until he saw Keera was laughing madly and keeping up with Corson. Wildly flailing with his ruined sword, he joined in.

"Stop now," Corson whispered, coming to a dead halt by the tree—where the demons couldn't see them.

Keeping themselves out of line of sight, they threw rocks into the underbrush down the slope and turned to slink back toward the forest. Keera bounced along beside them, tirelessly springing over the rocky ground until they reached the dappled light of the forest itself.

"Just a minute." Aiden sucked in a deep breath and put his hand on the lush moss growing on the trunks of the trees.

Keera stood opposite, adjusting the huge backpack on her shoulders.

"Come on you two," Corson said. "Stop making eyes at each other and let's get out of here. You know what they say? We're not out of the woods until we get to New Avalon."

Heat crept up Aiden's face. "I'm...um...."

Keera tilted her face up to Aiden. "So, your village is called New Avalon?"

"Given it's a few huts and a wooden fence—and the forge—I'm not really sure it lives up to the name."

Keera smiled, her eyes dancing. "I'm sure it will be amazing, Fire Boy."

"It's Aiden," he blurted like a schoolboy before composing himself. "I'm sorry, Corson and I never introduced ourselves, did we? Well, I'm Aiden, and this is Corson."

"Very nice to meet you." She reached out to shake their hands. "Corson. Aiden."

Aiden opened and closed his mouth, lost for words, before releasing his grip. "Sorry. Ah...so, you're a swordsmith. What made you decide to come and work for The Society?" It was a stupid question, but he wanted to hear her voice again.

"The demons are getting strong, and my people are suffering under their attacks. We've lost a lot of, er, protectors."

"You've lost protectors?" There was so much Aiden didn't know.

"Yes. I thought that if humans had demon-slaying swords, you'd be able to help beat the demons back into the Underworld. Besides, Fire Boy, I wanted to meet you." And there was that light in her eye again. So intoxicating he forgot to wonder about who or what protectors were. "Me? What do you know about me?"

"Nothing at all. Except your sword is completely ruined."

"Yours is so beautiful. Is the silver and gold filigree important, or just for decoration?

Keera pulled out the blade to show him. "It's writing," she said. "Runes. They're very powerful."

"What does it say?"

"*Keera Quicksilver, Destroyer of Demons.* The gold and silver runes give the sword its power to strike true, but because they're unique for the person the sword is made for, it means the sword will only respond to its owner."

"If we're going to make more blades like it, we'll need gold," Aiden said. "That might take a while."

"Never worry. For yours, we can use the gold from my earrings. Surely, you have silver?"

"A little." Aiden's mind raced. He had a literal silver spoon somewhere from one of the settlement's early finds.

"I can't wait to make you a sword. And of course, you, Corson."

Aiden swallowed jealousy as she turned her luminous eyes on his friend. He had no right to be possessive. *What's getting into me?*

"Never mind me." Corson grinned at Aiden with a not-so-subtle raise of his eyebrows, before turning back to Keera. "Except yes, Keera Swordmaster, I'd love one of your swords. And I promise not to throw it over a cliff face."

"You what?"

Aiden coughed. "Truth is, Corson threw his sword at a demon and saved my life."

"A quick-thinking warrior. Good. Lives are more important than swords. Even *my* swords. Besides, my swords have a way of finding the person they were made for—as well as burning the hands of thieves."

Aiden wished she'd called him a quick-thinking warrior, instead of Fire Boy. But Aiden wouldn't have been able to live with himself if he hadn't acknowledged Corson's bravery—even if a part of him wanted all Keera's praise to himself.

I See

Aiden turned to Keera. She was so strong, and so beautiful. He imagined wrapping her in his arms and kissing her soft red lips. Still, he'd happily settle for walking by her side, the warm glow in his stomach a pleasant distraction from his burned shoulder. It had been kind of Corson to rush ahead. It gave them a chance to chat of this and that. Favourite flowers and sword making, and the most dangerous places in Brocéliande.

"Damn it," Keera swore under her breath as they approached the path to *Wóþbora cotif*—the village The Society had dubbed the *Town of the Triplets*.

Three children were sitting on the path, playing one of their strange games of exchanging eyes and ears—for they only had a pair of each between the three and must share them if they wanted to see or hear.

Aiden cringed as the central child picked up an eyeball from each of her brothers and squished them into her eye-sockets, while the two boys slapped an ear each to the side of their heads.

They stood up. The triplet on the left's free hand was pointing to Aiden and the triplet on the right was pointing to Keera.

"I see," the sighted triplet in the middle said. And
the three chorused:
"Gold and silver."
"Life and death."
"Sword and shield."

"I hear," said the triplet on the left
"Sword Master you have found your Fire
"But you anger the fae
"They curse your every breath
"And you, like your swords,
"Will be quenched in the waters
of the River of Death.

"I hear," said the triplet on the right
"Your children will be flowers
"Sweet as nectar and sharp as thorns
"Fae, walkers, demonslayers, witches "All are
friend and foe, hammer and anvil
"Forge their thorns early
"Save them from the fae
"And they may save this world."

Holding hands, the triplets scurried away, back down the crossroads toward their village.

Aiden blinked and turned to Keera. "What was that about?"

Keera shrugged and walked on, shoulders hunched. "Poor kids. They're always running out and spouting nonsense at me."

Aiden got the impression she knew more than she was telling. Unable to put words to his concerns, he walked on, trying to think about what it all might mean before finally giving up and just enjoying the moment—the sunshine dappling through the bush, and the beautiful woman by his side. *What more could anyone want?* he thought, and sighed when they turned a corner to see Corson sitting on a rock ahead.

"What happened to you?" Corson asked.

"We got waylaid by *Wóþbora cotif* triplets."

Corson nodded. "I hurried past. They're always threatening me with death and giant spiders every time I walk by." He shivered. "Still, we're almost at home base, and I didn't want to rush on in case your parents noticed my return and worried that you weren't with me."

"Good call," Aiden agreed as they passed the lookout in a huge oak tree.

Within moments they were at the gate. A crowd armed with swords and axes had gathered near the fence covered in briars that marked the village boundary.

Alice Faulkner had baby Hazel in her arms, and a kitchen knife. Aiden's parents stood beside Alice, twirling their swords, ready to protect Alice and her baby with their lives.

Mayor Harder paced out to the gate with Alice's husband, Prof Brian Faulkner, by his side. While Prof was not a small man, he was dwarfed by the heavily muscled mayor whose favourite sword was so big the point almost dragged along the ground.

"It's just us." Aiden waved, pretending not to notice the scowls and frowning faces. *What's their problem, anyway?*

"What is this?" Mayor Harder humphed. "I mean…"

"Let me." Prof Brian Faulkner waved his arms. "Aiden. Weren't you supposed to get the Sword Master? Who is this? She looks like a wicked queen, or one of those annoying fighting princesses…"

"Don't be ridiculous," Aiden snapped. "Let us through."

"I'm not being ridiculous," Brian humphed in his, *Listen to me, everyone. I'm a professor,* tone.

Mayor Harder took a step back and watched.

What's he doing, letting Prof Faulkner take over like that? Aiden took a deep breath. It didn't help. He glanced back over his shoulder. Keera's jaw was set in a firm line. Corson rolled his eyes.

More and more of the village had downed tools and emerged from their houses. Encouraged by the growing crowd, Brian Faulkner ran out through the gates and stood in front of Aiden. "What are you doing? We have to be careful about who we bring into New Avalon. We've only just created this outpost, and bringing in locals without proper vetting could be catastrophic."

"Stand aside," Corson growled. "You will all treat this warrior who saved our lives with the respect she deserves. Oh yes, and she *is* the new swordsmith we were sent to collect."

Mayor Harder nodded. "Good, then. Wonderful to meet you, Sword Master. When you have a moment, I'd love to see your work. Let them through, Faulkner."

Aiden's father stepped up to Brian's side and looked Aiden and Keera up and down. "This is not good. I knew we should have left you Earthside, Aiden."

Yeah, like that was going to happen. Sometimes Aiden thought his old man lived in the eighteen hundreds and hadn't made it into the 1920's at all.

"Dratted problem with this place," Aiden's father said through his impressive moustache. "Is that it's always doing *this* kind of thing." He shuddered. "Falling head over heels is just bad form." He called back over his shoulder to where Aiden's mother was still protecting Alice and her babe. "Mother? What do you think?"

The crowd parted to let her through. She looked Aiden and then Keera up and down. "Damn, Aiden. Not *true love*?" His mother sighed. "Please, tell me I'm wrong."

Heat flushed Aiden's cheeks. He almost wished he was being buried alive. Anything was better than this. And where was he supposed to look? Back at Keera? He'd known her for all of an hour. But looking straight ahead was worse, with his parents and the village all judging him for falling in love with a woman he'd just met. *If this is love? It can't be.* Blood pounding in his temples, Aiden coughed. "If you'll excuse us. I need to show the Sword Master around." Keera and Corson followed as he cut through the crowd. He envied her composure, showing little reaction to all the accusations except an amused smile that danced on her lips. Although maybe a hint of red flushed her dark skin as she drank him in with her warm, luminous eyes.

"Um, Sword Master Keera," Aiden spoke loud enough for the others to hear. "We should check out the forge. I'm really keen to see how you make swords. I've never seen anything so effective."

Keera nodded, stepping in close. "I've always wanted to see Myrddin's forge."

Behind them, Aiden's mother shook her head and sighed. "It never ends well."

"What? I thought that in Brocéliande, true love always ends well," Alice replied. "Remember that princess bride? All the happily ever afters."

"Have you seen her recently?"

"Well, no," Alice admitted.

"Exactly," Aiden's mother snapped. "It'll all end in tears. And the next thing we know there'll be two orphaned children in these woods, and we'll be left looking after them."

Aiden stomped on, trying to get their voices out of his ears. His mother was worse than all of *Wóþbora cotif's* triplets rolled together with her crazy predictions.

Fae Court

*Humans seem to think fae are either flitting
through the flowers drinking nectar, or stealing
children. Well, only one of those is true—*

*—we never steal children. We only swap
them. An eye for an eye, a child for a child.*

Gather round, my young ones, my darlings, open your beautiful
eyes, and fold your wings neatly, while I tell you a story. The
story of how I lost everything, including my beloved changeling. How
I was banished to the kingdom of mortals and sent to watch over the
human child with red hair.

No, little ones, do not cry. They are not the monsters you think,
and not so very different from us. Yes, they are dangerous, but we fae
are dangerous, too. It's not all fairy godmothers and queens and royal
balls. There is deceit and treachery, and you need to know it when
you see it. I see the silver-fire of the fae in all your eyes. You will grow

strong and powerful. Far stronger and more powerful than I, and that is why I say:

Trust no one.

Hate no one.

You will find what you need when you most need it, and although your hearts will be broken like so much china, you will mend the pieces with your tears—and the burning tears of the sun—for only when you are a spider-work of silver and gold will your hearts be strong enough to break the spell that has sundered our world.

We must make it whole again. And I must save my Nada. It started one spring.

§

The bluebells were ringing.

Lettie's heart fluttered. Fae were coming from far and wide to pay homage to King Hades and Queen Persephone. Many heard the call, arriving in the blink of an eye to witness the commencement of the revelry that would last all summer long. And not just fae, humans and other races also heard the call after blundering through fairy barrows in the deep, dark forest. Dazed and unsure, they spun in circles marvelling at the glamour of Queen Persephone's ball ground.

The elderfae, refusing to recognise Persephone as Queen for long centuries now, would hide and not come out again until winter.

Lettie couldn't imagine it. She loved the summer and the Royal Summer Ball. And she loved the first signs of spring, anticipating the fanfare that went with it. Today was the day. She donned a robin's-egg-blue dress and fluttered her rainbow wings, determined to look her best for Queen Persephone's arrival. And for Nada to look faer best, too. Where was her little changeling?

She searched her tiny treehouse cottage. The nest where Nada curled up to sleep. She threw open the cupboard doors and peered over every square inch of wall and floor. It was so hard to find changelings when they could turn into nearly anything—a skink, a mouse, a bird, a stick insect—anything. "Come on, Nada, where are you?" she called. "We've got to go."

Nada, perfectly camouflaged as a bark-like lizard on the wooden side of the hut, transformed into a flutterby with shimmery blue wings.

"You do know what today is, don't you?" Lettie asked, breathless at the prospect of the ball.

Nada's shimmery-blue wings fluttered and morphed into the darker-blue of a swallowtail—edged in dramatic darkness.

"Nada, the queen's arrival is not edged with darkness. It's a party. And we will both love it. Remember, there will be dancing on the greensward, and twelve beautiful princesses, the swan maidens, the wood nymphs and water sprites. All the sages and mages, the wanderers, the dreamers and fae will be there. Then, after the dancing, the royal entourage will relax on the soft moss-covered roots and we will come home. Quick, now, we don't want to be late."

Lettie popped Nada onto her shoulder and hurried to the twisted wooden balcony made from live wood. "Time to fly, little one." She laughed at her own daring. Queen Persephone didn't hold with flutter-form—*because she cannot do it*. Lettie dropped the thought from her mind. Nothing good would come of thinking ill of the queen.

Lettie stepped up onto the railing, dropped her elegant form, or more accurately her ungainly human-like wingless form, and together, they soared into the woods, rushing through the branches. Above, a thick canopy of leaves protected them from the jealous eye of the sun. Below, mossy roots formed a thick mat above the shallow forest soil.

They flew on, past the giant oak and kauri. Past more types of trees than anyone had names for. Trees that remained solid and unwavering even in all the excitement swirling below. Half the kingdom had arrived to celebrate, and the other half were hidden in the deep, dark woods. *Fools*, Lettie thought. A faint glimmering from the giant glow-worms in the branches around the greensward warned her that she was getting close.

They landed discreetly, just beyond the celebrations, before changing back into elegant form and edging closer.

Her heart soared. The gardeners had outdone themselves. The lush-green ball ground was circled by clamouring bluebells. Glow-worms shimmered, their lights falling on starry silver-white flowers. At the far end loomed Queen Persephone's and King Hades' live royal thrones festooned with tight rosebuds. Their branches were curled around each other to form dramatic spirals, and the high-backed seats were softened by a thick layer of green leaves and rose petals.

"Smell that?" Lettie inhaled the sweet buttery-perfume from the roses and the honeyed notes of ambrosia. "That's the smell of the ball.

Of course Nada said nothing. But to Lettie's delight, her little changeling looked over at the thrones wreathed in buds, and transformed into a fully blooming purple rose—with wings sprouting from either side of the stem.

Lettie beamed with pride and glanced around to see who else was there. She caught sight of a few of Queen Persephone's sycophants burbling about how they couldn't wait to see the queen again. Lettie couldn't help but feel jealous. One day, maybe Queen Persephone would recognise her worth, and then the queen's entourage wouldn't be so haughty. Beyond them was a flash of yellow. It was Zadie, a fellow changeling-nurse, flitting from flower to flower in her trademark sunflower inspired dress. There was no sign of faer changeling.

Lettie rushed over. "Oh, no. I can't see your changeling. Has something happened?"

"Left it behind," Zadie muttered. "I mean, it's not like the things ever grow up, is it? Won't matter if it misses a summer ball to the great and glorious usurper, Queen Persephone.

Lettie gasped and glanced around. Fortunately, no one seemed to be listening to Zadie's treachery. Queen Persephone had sent fae to the Labyrinth for less. She shivered at the thought of the dark, dank pit, and the terror waiting within, and pulled her changeling close. I am no traitor. That fate will not be mine.

Zadie glanced meaningfully at Lettie's ward, and the eerie skull of the death's head moth pattern that rippled over Nada's wings. "Oh, Alette. It's not like yours will become fae, either. And there's no one else here to tattle about my lack of bowing and scraping."

"Just call me Lettie," Lettie said. "You know I'm not one for ceremony, but our great queen is arriving through the Mirror of Tears today. We should—"

"You know how Queen Persephone made the *Mirror of Tears*, don't you?"

"She cried a million tears and—"

"No, that story's a lie. It was the blood of her enemies. She threw their bodies onto the greensward until the moss shone silver...it was only then that she discovered the power and turned the blood of her foes into a fancy mirror."

"But—"

"You know I'm right," Zadie said.

"I know nothing of the sort." *Persephone and Hades were rulers with god-like powers—surely they never resorted to bloodshed?*

A leaden note crept into the welcoming peal of the bluebells as they tired of their call and began to preen for the feast. The fae gardeners helped them by burnishing their blue apparel until it rivalled the slivers of sky above.

"Beautiful," Lettie remarked to the chief gardener as she dashed past. He was moving on from the bluebells to tend a patch of daisies that shone as merrily as the stars in the sky.

"Thank you, Lettie." The old gardener beamed with pride. "Not that that wretched so-called queen of ours will notice."

"I'm sure she will," Lettie said, not wanting to hear any more.

The gardener sighed. "Doing things for the queen never turns out well. I'll be left with a mess when she moves her party on, and that's at best."

"It'll be amazing. You just see." Lettie ushered Nada so they could get a better view of the ceremony, and all the fine noble fae waiting for their most gracious queen. The princesses, swan maidens, dryads and other wood nymphs and water sprites danced, while the sages and mages and noble folk looked on uncertainly— just close enough to observe the queen's arrival.

Trumpets blared.

It's time.

Two Quips—Queen Persephone's soldiers—marched into the clearing, their silver armour shining. They rolled back the blackened rock from the firepit and lit the faery-fire.

Lettie clasped her hands in delight as the blue flame flared to life, dancing joyfully for the appreciative crowd. Then, two by two, six more Quips proudly bore the Queen's famous *Mirror of Tears* draped with silken sheets of spider web and placed it before the royal thrones. "Behold!" they cried, pulling back the heavy silk and bowing low.

Inky darkness rippled in the mirror, but there was no sign of the queen.

Nada startled as King Hades' tall, stone-skinned demons leapt from the fire—the crackling heat swirling around them not fae-blue, but with the red-hot heat of demon blood.

A cry of wonder erupted from the humans in the crowd, but Lettie felt only Nada's fear as she pulled the changeling into her arms.

Where is our Queen Persephone? And her King?

Another cry, this time of welcome, as King Hades followed his demon bodyguards through the fire. He was pulling the shaggy, three-headed Cerberus along on a lead with him. Cerberus howled, glaring around the clearing as he always did. The Quips jumped back as the ancient beast sniffed the air, poison dripping from three sets of sharp teeth.

Hades sighed and let Cerberus jump back into the fire pit. As soon as the creature was gone, two Quips quickly stanched the fire and rolled the blackened-rock back over the pit. Everyone else remained bowing, not daring to lift their heads...but still there was no sign of Queen Persephone.

Time dragged on. Nada, restless on her shoulder, attempted four different forms before settling back into the shape of a rose.

A flash from the mirror.

Pushing her way through the silver mirror as if through the surface of a lake, Queen Persephone appeared at last. Dressed in a red-silk ball gown with pink petticoats and dripping with pink opals and diamonds, she was more regal than ever.

A rush of devotion washed over Lettie as her magnificent queen strode toward her throne, trailed by her entourage of sycophants and Fae-in-Waiting. The elegant fae, scornful as ever, tittered and scoffed, pointing around at the beautiful flowers that speckled the greensward.

When her last attendant had burst through the liquid silver, Queen Persephone yelled, "What is this mess? Who is in charge of the daisies? Where is my constellation?"

Fae backed away. The head gardener was pushed forward.

"My lady?"

"Silence. You shall pay for your failure. This...mess...is not up to my royal standards." Her voice boomed like thunder. Points of red flushed her cheeks as she glowered at the gardener, an icy hatred burning in her eyes. "And so, my final judgement. Thou hast

A.J. Ponder

disappointed me for the last time, gardener. Soldiers, throw that wretched good-for-nothing fae into the catacombs."

But the flowers are perfection, dotted across the greensward like the fae constellation itself. Lettie put her hand over her mouth, terrified to break the eerie silence. *Queen Persephone is distressed. Someone has upset our fair and righteous queen, but not the gardener, surely?*

Demons grabbed the poor gardener, who screamed and squirmed in and out of flutter form. For the venerable old fae, there was no escaping the demon's grip.

Queen Persephone held up a hand that sparkled with diamonds, sapphires and rubies. "Wait."

The gardener paused. The crowd too. Lettie's heart leapt. Of course, Queen Persephone would relent. This was one of her games to keep the gardeners on their toes, make sure they didn't take their queen's favour for granted.

"Before we have our fun," Queen Persephone continued, ignoring the gasp from the crowd. "I have pressing business. Has anybody heard of the Sword Master? Are the rumours true? Has mortal scum desecrated the blood of the fae with cold iron?"

Lettie gulped, too frightened to stand up and speak. This must be why the queen was furious. Even Lettie had heard the rumours. *But can they really be true? And what does it mean if they are?*

Arachne scuttled forward, ignoring the gasps from some of the less civilised visitors. As a glossy-black spider the size of a wolf, it was hard not to draw attention. She flicked an imaginary speck of dust from her midnight carapace with one of her front legs. "There are such rumours, Queen Persephone. But I cannot confirm them."

"Wyrden? Wyrden, where art thou?"

"My Queen." A spry, silver-haired humanoid with a white walking cane and eyes like pools of midnight emerged from within a knot of demons and bowed.

"Wyrden, if this is true, then seek out the abomination and kill them, or better still, bring them to me so they can suffer a fate worse than death."

"Do it," Hades thundered.

"Yes, my King, my Queen. I shall obey." Wyrden sloped off, apparently unaware of Queen Persephone scowling at his insolent back.

He didn't bow!

Persephone clapped her hands. "Now, back to business. Throwing this wretched, insolent gardener into the catacombs."

The poor old fae shivered and glanced toward the entrance to the labyrinth. "My Queen…"

"Silence!" She glared at the old gardener. "For I am not without mercy. Yes, for thy crimes, thou shall be sentenced to the labyrinth. But return my silver axe from the minotaur at the centre of the maze for me, and thou may return to my court. Fail, and I shall banish thee forever."

Lettie let out a breath. Her Queen was indeed merciful. Of course, the gardener wouldn't be banished forever. Even if everybody else the queen had sent to the labyrinth had failed to return, this gardener would succeed. Because he was loyal. And the others had been traitors.

Queen Persephone's musicians struck up a beat, accompanied by the pure tones of ocarinas and other woodwinds. The old gardener was whirled along with the music, pulled and dragged, and kicked and thumped and battered.

The pure sounds of the woodwinds transformed to shrieks and wails that rose to a crescendo as the dancers pushed the old gardener to the iron bars of the wooden door that barred the entrance of the labyrinth.

The music stopped and the dancers did, too. For a moment, the world was still except for the gardener's feeble struggles against the fae dancers who would not let him go.

A trumpet bugled, and a demon shoved the iron-bound door open.

Lettie tried to peer inside, but there were too many people in the way.

The poor gardener was shoved through, and a demon slammed the heavy iron-bound door shut.

Lettie flinched, horrified at the thought of being trapped inside an iron cage lined with stones and bones and filled with monsters. At least that's what Zadie had told her last year when Lettie had failed to get a glimpse.

The dance party was silent.

Waiting.

Listening.

A harrowing scream cut through the wooden door.

A thud…

Then there was silence again, only more oppressive than before.

Lettie shed a silver tear. Her changeling caught it and flew the precious cargo over to Queen Persephone's mirror. A tiny splash, and a ripple, and it was gone.

"Good. Good." Queen Persephone said, turning a sad smile on Lettie.

Lettie's heart was suddenly light. Queen Persephone had noticed. Had shared her pain.

"What a beautiful changeling. Well done." Queen Persephone said with a smile as warm and pure as starlight.

Nada. My beautiful Nada. Lettie's heart soared before she caught a glimpse of Zadie's scowl. "Um. Zadie also has a beautiful changeling."

Queen Persephone raised an eyebrow. "So, Zadie, where is this charge of yours?"

Zadie pointed toward her tree house and shot Lettie a look of hate.

"Well, go fetch faer." Persephone clapped her hands. "Now, where was I? Welcome, one and all, to the dance. Let us be merry today, for soon we shall be at war."

"War?" a soldier asked. "I m-m-mean," the fae stuttered. "Who should we fight?"

"Our enemies," King Hades thundered, blue fire crackling through his hair. "I hope you do not question your queen."

"No, my king. Sorry, my king."

"'Tis the Earthside humans," Persephone shouted. "But we shall not think of their evil today, for today is a celebration."

War with the Earthside humans? Lettie clutched Nada to her chest. *Yes, a sword smith had desecrated fae silver by forging it alongside cold iron, but they would be punished. And the rest of the humans? Yes, they were foolish and blundering, but surely that wasn't a crime large enough to start a war?*

The music resumed—and once again, nobody could escape the dance.

FALLING HARD

*A*iden clutched the ring in his hand so hard that it hurt. *I'm a fool. It's only been a couple of months.* But he couldn't bear the idea of living without her. She was everything.

"Ah, there you are." Keera hurried through the crowded market-place of Market Town, her smile as dazzling as the sun.

Will she say yes?

So many things seemed to stand in his way. He needed to find the perfect place, the perfect moment under the dappled leaves of Brocéliande. Not here in the hot marketplace, with all the people around. And the pick-pockets.

He ran his other hand through his red hair.

"What is it?" she asked. "You get what you needed?"

He nodded. "I um…" He stared into Keera's eyes. "I thought we might have a picnic…go somewhere nice."

A child snatched the ring right out of his hand.

Keera's hand shot out and grabbed the child. "You'd think you would have learned from last time," she scolded, plucking the diamond ring from the young thief's unresisting fingers.

"No harm in tryin'." The urchin wriggled free.

"What's…who's the ring for?" she asked, turning it over and holding it up to the light.

Heat rushed into Aiden's cheeks. *I probably look like a cherry.* "Umm, ahhh…" he mumbled, mortified. "It's an Earthsider tradition."

"Oh?" She tilted her head.

"You're going to make me say it, aren't you?"

Keera bit her lip. "It's just, not all our traditions are the same."

Aiden got down on a knee. "Will you…"

Three near-identical people—with one eye between them—strode in their direction.

Damn.

Aiden bounded to his feet, took Keera's hand and tried to sidestep the *Wóþbora cotif* triplets, but they completely blocked the path.

"You shall have two children."

Aiden blushed. And glanced over to Keera. He'd not even proposed…half proposed at best, and these idiots turned up. All this nonsense about children was a step too far. "That's enough, please." But the *Wóþbora cotif* triplets pressed on.

"A girl and a girl."

"And they shall be as twins though they shall be born two years apart."

"Strong of heart and of mind."

"They will see what no one else can see."

"You will give them everything they need."

"But only if you hurry."

"For in the morning."

"You will be gone."

"I—" Aiden started, remembering their previous encounter with the younger soothsayers.

Keera sighed. "Don't worry. The triplets always come at inopportune times with dire prophecies. This one, they've been saying that to me since I was twelve. It has nothing to do with you. Besides, I'm not the sort of person who wants children. I need to save the people of Brocéliande from the demon incursion. That doesn't leave much time for family..."

Aiden's heart sank. So, this was the rejection. He'd always known...

Her eyes sparkled. "Fortunately, there will be just enough time for you."

Aiden thought his heart would burst. Within moments they'd both forgotten all about the triplets and their embarrassing prophecy. Corson and Keera were right; it did no good to take their words too seriously.

And when they got back to Earth, Burcham offered Keera a permanent contract to use the forge at her discretion.

§

Keera Swordmaster is contracted to forge swords for The Society, with the understanding that demonslayer swords will be forged for members of The Society of her own choosing.

Reimbursement will be at the standard rate, but, due to the value of her work, Keera Swordmaster may use the forge of Arthur Pendragon while part of an official Society mission, even if it is not for official Society business.

§

Years later, the happily married couple moved into Aiden's parents' old house on Earth. Safely away from demons, fae, and the many other dangers of Brocéliande, Aiden and Keera thought nothing of the prophecy when their first child arrived. Born with a shaggy crop of dark red hair, she clutched her parents' hands fiercely. Keera declared that Ruby was the perfect name for this little warrior—the child of their heart, and Aiden agreed.

When the second child arrived and it was a girl, Keera remembered the prophecies. Two children with two years between them. *A girl and a girl.* An urgency gripped her.

For weeks she cast about for a name. The right name. One that might protect her baby and keep her close to her sister, but also set her apart. It wasn't until she was visiting Aiden's parent's cottage in Brocéliande and wandering past the thorny roses, ice clinging to their stems like pearls, that her second daughter's name popped into her head. The name for their dark-haired bundle of fury had to be…Pearl. A dark Pearl full of knowledge and hidden depths. And yet the name could also symbolise a rose. A nod to the red and white flowers of Aiden's mother's garden—and two inseparable sisters who looked after each other through thick and thin.

Keera held no illusions. She'd made King Hades' demons angry. No matter what Aiden said, sooner or later they'd come for her.

Ruby's Sword

1 June 1934

Keera swiped away a trickle of sweat only to find it had evaporated in the heat. The tang of hot steel on her tongue, the charcoal smoke in her eyes and throat, and the clash of metal on metal close to overwhelming as she struggled to keep her rhythm. Her arms ached from pounding and shaping the metal. She should have taken a break before this crucial stage, but didn't want her stay in Brocéliande to be longer than it had to be. Besides, Myrddin's forge was overbooked, as usual, and the many sword-smiths waiting would surely barge in.

Ruby and baby Pearl were playing not so far away, under the watchful eye of Alice Faulkner. Alice was a godsend. Especially as Aiden's parents had gone Library of Alexandria hunting again. Besides, with three children of her own, Alice knew just how to look after the little ones—but when it came to Keera's swords her curiosity was insatiable.

"I wish I could understand how you do it."

"I wish I had the time to teach you, but—"

Alice smiled. "Don't worry, I couldn't do all that hammering even if I wanted to, but maybe there's something in your process I could apply to other things. Your swords can only be used by their true owners. I'd love to know how it works."

"I'm not sure I understand myself. I think in Brocéliande, soul power—or magic—if you will, has to do with intent. And the words. As your motto says, *Verba sunt omnia*."

Alice raised her eyebrows. "*Your?* Aren't you a part of The Society now, too?"

Keera shrugged. "You know how it is." She might be employed by them, but she never felt like she truly belonged. Or that their goals were the same as hers.

Pearl squealed and crawled across the clearing toward her mother, nappy trailing. She was chasing after Alice's youngest, little Tailor who was toddling toward the forge giggling wildly.

"Careful!" Keera yelled. "Hot! Hey Aiden! Can you come and help?" *Where is he?*

"Sorry," Aiden called. "Almost there."

"I've got them." Alice grabbed Pearl, and tucked her under one arm, then snatched up Tailor. "Come on, Pearl, let's give your mum and dad room to think. Thank goodness you're behaving, Ruby. You're the only good child here."

Ruby nodded solemnly, red curls bobbing against her golden cheek. "Bird talked to Ruby."

"Yes, birds do that here." Alice smiled. "Now, how about you and I go and look for Hazel and Arthur and see what trouble they're up to?" She ushered Ruby away to help 'search' for her two eldest children, who were playing in the branches of the old apple tree near the village fence.

"Thanks." Her face covered in smudges of soot, a frown of concentration on her lips, Keera turned back to focus on the steel.

Aiden set down the bucket of water and pulled his mess of red hair back into a rough ponytail, then pumped the bellows again.

His job was keeping the forge hot so Keera could focus on her work, stroke after stroke. With every sparking blow from her drop-hammer, the shape of the sword made itself known. A fine blade… so far.

Ruby raced into the clearing. "Mama, we saw a fairy."

"Fae," Keera corrected without thinking, working on keeping the rhythm of her strokes even.

Alice, carrying a baby in each arm, was close behind. "I'm so sorry."

"It's okay. Ruby knows better than to come too close to the fire."

Alice shivered. "What if your Ruby sees fae when we don't?"

Keera laughed. "It's just a game Aiden plays with her, but I guess seeing hidden fae could come in handy. They can be quite the nuisance."

"Aren't you worried? I mean, if she can see fae when nobody else can, doesn't that mean she's a witch?"

Fortunately, Aiden butted in. "Ruby's going to be a demon hunter like her mum, aren't you, Ruby?"

"She is that," Keera said, holding the new sword up in the air to inspect it. "And here's the sword to prove it." She couldn't be prouder of her work. "Hear how it sings?" She tapped the blade with the finishing hammer along the edge a final time and then plunged the red-hot steel into the bucket of water.

Steam billowed.

Now for the inlay. Keera put her hand on the wooden strips with the delicate silver and gold script inlay and pressed them hard against the sword-blade, carefully binding them to the blade with flax. This was the magic. The moment.

"Almost there, Ruby."

"My sword, Mummy?"

Keera smiled. "If you're good."

She plunged it into the centre of the forge until the twine and wood were nothing but smoke. The blade glowed silvery-red in the heat of the forge.

Aiden glanced at the blade and grinned. "I think this is your finest work ever."

"Don't speak too soon." Keera inspected the blade minutely. "But I do hope so." She plunged it back into the water.

At last, with Aiden's hands over hers, they declared over the hiss of water and the roar of the fire. "I name you Heart of Ruby, Demonslayer and Protector of the Righteous."

The sword stayed true, gleaming in the sunlight.

Ruby clapped and held out her hand. "Mine."

"Yes," Keera said. "The sword is yours and will respond to none other." *If only she had the time and energy to make Pearl's today, but the sun was already dipping below the horizon. And Aiden's parents had been suspicious enough, given Ruby was nowhere near old enough to wield a sword yet.*

"Careful." Aiden guided Ruby's hand to the exposed metal where the pommel would be.

Ruby grasped it and smiled. "Sword. Mine."

A.J. Ponder

WYRDEN RETURNS

Spring 1934

Lettie brushed down her bird's egg blue dress, fluttered her rainbow wings and settled on the nursery rocking chair near the nest where Nada was supposed to be sleeping. One instant, Nada was in the form of a butterfly—fluttering verdant wings— and the next, faer was kicking legs the colour of autumn leaves out of faer nest.

Lettie pulled on her favourite bluebell cap. "Are you ready?" she cajoled, happy that she finally had a moment to sing to Nada. Nervous that she was deliberately missing Queen Persephone's arrival this year—fear bubbled through her, as it had every year since the death of the gardener.

Nada transformed into a sparrow and opened faer beak.

Lettie's heart skipped a beat. Hoping beyond all hope that today would be the day that Nada would sing along, she began singing *The Song of a Zephyr on a Summer's Day*.

Rustling echoed around the small chamber.

Was that a note? Or was it the wind? Lettie's heart thundered in her chest. "Nada," Lettie whispered. "You're going to have a true name. You're going to *be*. I just know it." Hoping against hope this bundle of twigs, wishes, and precious stones would manifest as fae, she burst into song again.

"Oh, dreaming fae, the sun of day will stab you.

"But in the twilight, you will delight and scare the nasty sun away."

A silly song. But curiosity about the sun had killed many a young fae as its glitter and shine drew them to fly to their deaths.

"Lettie! Lettie! Where are you?" Zadie burst in through the nursery door. "Queen Persephone is asking for you. Come quickly."

"Darn it all." Lettie sighed, imagining all the reasons the queen could possibly want her. *She doesn't want me; she wants my changeling.* The thought shot through her like a lightning bolt.

"Stay safe," she whispered to her charge fluttering around the tiny tree house where she'd made her home.

"Hurry, hurry." Zadie wrung faer hands. "The queen is in such a temper she's threatened to send us both to the Underworld, and our changelings with us."

"But she can't," Lettie spluttered. She thought about carrying Nada with her, but her little changeling was exhausted. So, instead, she called Nada back to bed. Grabbing for Nada's spider-silk throw, she grazed her palm on the hook. A spatter of silver blood splashed the wall.

Lettie grabbed a fuzzy leaf to clean the mess.

"No, no, we don't have time," Zadie insisted, hurrying to drape the spider-silk net over the crib herself.

Lettie wiped the wall angrily, but only smeared the silver further. "Boggarts and beasties!" she swore. Maybe the neighbour could help. She ran out and knocked on her neighbour Rose's door. "Hey, Rose! I've got to go out."

"There's no time." Zadie grabbed Lettie's arm and dragged her out onto the ledge of the balcony.

"What is it?" Rose poked her peachy-pink head out the door.

"Keep my Nada safe," Lettie yelled as Zadie pulled her over the ledge. Together they flitted out through the dark forest toward the glow-worm lights of Queen Persephone's Great Summer Ball.

Today, the musicians stood silent.

Instead of dancing, the king and queen were draped decorously on their living-wood thrones. Even smothered with spring roses, the living thrones radiated an aura of sorrow, as if they were also mourning the gardener who was surely dead. Lettie shuddered at the idea, her stomach turning at the way the roses' sweet honey scent saturated the air.

All the queen's fae, in their fancy suits and ball-dresses, clung to the trees around the outskirts of the clearing, their faces twisted in disdain.

Shame coursed through Lettie like cold iron as she shifted from her shimmery blue and rainbow flutter-form to the heavy humanoid, so-called elegant form, the followers of Queen Persephone preferred.

"There you are!" King Hades thundered, lurching himself upright. His dark hair swirled with power as he glared at Zadie and Lettie.

"Finally, thou art here." Queen Persephone snapped. A brittle, porcelain smile on her face. "But at least *you* are not seven years late."

Seven years? Lettie swallowed back her confusion.

"The Queen's drunk her nectar from the wrong side of the flower today," Zadie whispered.

Fortunately, Persephone didn't notice. She'd turned to glance back at a silver-haired man with a white cane. Wyrden! He clutched his white cane in one hand and cradled some kind of long stick in an oilskin under his other arm.

"Now, show everyone what you have," Hades demanded, pointing to the oilskin.

Failing to hide a mocking grin, the man threw down the bundle. It fell open, revealing a silvery, glimmering…something.

Lettie leaned in to see.

It was a brightly burnished sword with elegant gold and silver writing flowing down the blade. Exquisite flowing writing that glowed with power. She shivered. The silver wasn't just any silver—

Queen Persephone turned back to the man and roared, "Seven years! This desecration hath been happening for over seven years, and thou only get back to us now!"

Lettie clenched her jaw, mind spinning at the horror of the fae blood decorating cold iron.

"If only Persephone had downed all twelve persimmon seeds, then maybe King Hades, Persephone and all the highborn would be living it up in the Underworld the whole year round," Zadie whispered. "Then the fae kingdom wouldn't have to put up with these endless tantrums. And the unseelie court could have put this sacrilege to rights a long time ago."

Lettie swallowed, glancing about to see if anyone else had heard. *Zadie's shocked. She doesn't really mean what she's saying about our noble Queen Persephone.* Fortunately, nobody was paying them any mind.

"Wyrden, my Queen is right," Hades thundered. "Why have you waited so long to come hither with this news?"

The trench-coated man stared him down with eyes that glistened oily black.

Lettie smothered a gasp. *Wyrden is a skin-demon! Does anyone else notice? And he stands mere steps away from Queen Persephone. This should not be. And yet the queen herself called for him.*

The queen's court rustled nervously. Lettie risked a glance. Queen Persephone was unruffled by the soulless eyes, and King Hades' smirk was downright terrifying.

The skin-demon Wyrden licked his lips. "I got here as soon as I could get my hands on one of the swords. And I come with not just a sword." He pulled a folded square of paper from his pocket. "This map has everything you need to find the Sword Master herself, and her children—if you hurry."

"Wyrden, don't try me. You are *my* minion!" Hair crackling with power, Hades bunched his fists.

Lettie jumped. Hades' glare alone was enough to turn an ordinary fae to flame—but Wyrden barely flinched.

"Of course, my lord." Wyrden bowed low. "I am troubled by being unable to be in two places at once. If you will excuse me, I'll get back to that other urgent job you suggested..."

Hades narrowed his eyes further.

"...the whole spider thing on the border with the humans. Remember that?"

"Yes, yes, of course." Hades rubbed his hands together. "Overrun their pathetic new settlement before the mud-humans get a foothold in Brocéliande and send any survivors to the demon mines."

"Good, we have been waiting a long time," Persephone agreed.

"Yes, my love, and that is why we are going with your plan."

What plan?

Hades shooed Wyrden away with the flick of his hand.

The spry, silver-haired humanoid stepped toward Lettie, forcing her to jump out of his way. A bully to the bone. He smirked at her before striding off, leaving the sword in the centre of the clearing.

Persephone, Hades and all the fae stared at the sword still lying on the grassy moss.

Hades bent down to pluck up the sword only to drop it again. "This," he yelled, "is an abomination. Take it away."

Wyrden, having disappeared into the forest, did not come back. Instead, fae after fae tried to touch the blade. One wrapped spider-silk around the handle only to have the silk burst into flame.

"Lettie," Zadie whispered, tugging at Lettie's hand. "I have a bad feeling about this. Why would Queen Persephone specifically ask for you? For us?"

Lettie pulled her hand free, determined to stay and find out what was going on. Angry fae flittered around the clearing, voices rising in anger.

"The blood of the fae." Persephone's voice cut through the clearing. "The humans dare too much. Do not worry, I *shall* deal with this."

"They slaughtered *my* demons," King Hades protested. "I should be the one—"

"What are a few demons?" Queen Persephone arranged her gown with care. "The blood of my fae hath been defiled with cold iron and scolded with the gold…I mean, the tears of the sun. I shall have my revenge."

Hades' hair crackled with power. "Only if I don't have mine first." He pounded the side of his throne and screamed with anger— Lettie hoped it was because he'd hit his hand on a rose-thorn. "You think your fae's silver blood is important, or that I care one whit if it is mixed with iron or gold. But it is *nothing. My* plans are all that matters. This court is but a distraction."

"Enough," Queen Persephone grated. "Without me, thou wouldst be rotting in the Underworld. Now, let me talk to my two fae nursemaids so we can deal with the Sword Master once and for all."

"It's what the humans would call a pissing contest," Zadie whispered. "At least what the male humans would call a pissing contest. We have to go, we're only *nursemaids* to them. What if they threaten your precious Nada?"

Nada? Queen Persephone doesn't want me. She wants Nada. Lettie gulped, betrayal ricocheting through her gut. This time she let Zadie take her free hand. Together, they started to back away.

Persephone's gaze landed on them, heavy as a mountain lion and twice as self-satisfied. "And where are you two going?"

"My queen?" Zadie asked, although how fae could even speak at a time like this, Lettie wasn't sure.

Persephone smiled radiantly upon them. "Zadie and Lettie, I have a job for your changelings. Dost thou think they're up to it?"

Lettie shivered. The thought of Nada placed in the hands of humans was too awful to contemplate. "My queen…"

"They'd better be ready," Hades growled. "Or I'll feed you *and* your changelings to Cerberus myself."

"Don't listen to the old grump." Persephone's voice was pitched so sickly sweet it would make bees vomit. "Take this map. Find the Sword Master and swap her children for your changelings. You can do that for your queen. And tell the changelings to do a proper job on the torment and murder before they return."

Lettie took a deep breath. "My Queen—"

"That had better be a yes, because Cerberus will be the least of your problems if the Sword Master survives."

"Yes, my queen." Zadie stepped in front of Lettie and took the map with a bow. "At once, my queen." She turned to flutter form and zipped up into the sky.

Lettie bowed lower still, trying to give herself time to think of a way out of this.

Hades' hair still crackled with power. A threat for sure.

"Wait," Queen Persephone said. "This swap cannot go wrong. To ensure everything happens according to plan, I will send Arachne to the border. Do not fail."

Reluctantly, Lettie rose and followed Zadie, zipping through the giant trees and dappled evening light. "Wait up."

Zadie turned on her. "Frigus ferrum. This is your fault, Lettie."

"Please, tell. How could the fault be mine?" Lettie asked. She didn't need an answer—she was blaming herself already. *Zadie was right, we had every opportunity to run.*

If only I could take my beloved Nada and flee now. But after seeing the blood-script on the sword, no fae will forgive me if I don't make this sacrifice.

CHANGELING

3 June 1934

"Hello, squirrel," Ruby called out to a red squirrel. It bolted up into an oak tree.

"Bye, bye, squirrel," she said, disappointed that the creature hadn't answered.

"Never mind." Aiden took Ruby's hand in his, careful not to hold too tight. "Come on, little one. We're falling behind your mum and little sister. Now we've crossed the border, it's well past time we were home."

"Hungry," Ruby grumped.

"We're all hungry," Keera called back. Pearl was snuggled up against her chest in the baby pouch, noisily sucking her fingers and drooling down her white dress. "The picnic tables are just ahead."

"Ooh, look!" Ruby cried—finger pointing to a circle of red-capped fly agaric mushrooms. "Fae."

Aiden glanced back. "Yes, they're fairy mushrooms. Don't touch, you'll scare the fairies."

Ruby nodded; eyes wide.

"The fae will be fine." Keera pushed Pearl's beanie up. "But you won't be if you touch poison mushrooms. Stay away."

"Keera, come on. It's just for fun. When I was little, Mum and I would look for fairies everywhere we went." He smiled that infectious smile of his. "Look! Someone's even made little fairy houses along the walk."

"They're not real fairy houses, Aiden."

"Didn't you ever think fairies were the cute creatures in books?"

Keera bit back a grin. "No. I don't think so. When *I* was little, I thought fairy stories were horror stories. This whole cutesy fairies thing is weird."

Ruby laughed, pointing at the snails and their silvery trails, before discovering a "village" of tiny pretend houses that had been artistically hidden among the trees and shrubs along the side of the path. "Fae, fae. See Mama?"

§

Lettie hugged Nada tight and looked out from behind the fly agaric mushrooms toward the family. The adults seemed ordinary enough humans, but the eldest girl, Ruby, was pointing right at her and Zadie with an enormous chubby finger.

"I didn't know humans could see us here, like this," Zadie muttered.

"It's unusual even for children," Lettie replied. Because that's what the old gardener had told her. He'd had a soft spot for this Earth place. She couldn't see why—the trees were sickly, and it smelled weird.

Still, the little girl was charming with her red-autumn leaf hair and gold-brown skin.

"Are you sure these are the ones?" Lettie asked Zadie.

Carelessly holding faer changeling by the heel, Zadie shrugged faer green speckled shoulders. "It's them. You know it is. We've been chasing their trail through Brocéliande to this forsaken place. I can still smell the sword the woman made, the cold iron, the tears…"

"Yes, they're very pretty," Aiden said. "Ruby, come and see."

Like Ruby wasn't tired and hungry enough already. "Shall we make it to the picnic table? Have some lunch?" Keera said.

"Soon, Mama." Ruby crouched down to better see the little painted clay toadstools clustered near the base of a tree that had tiny fake windows and a green and gold door placed artfully on the outside, as if it were part of the tree trunk.

It wasn't the only one. It would have taken time and care and a certain sense of humour to place the miniature village of fake fairy houses along this quiet forest walk as an attraction for the families walking through. Small and cute. This is how ordinary people thought of fae. Diminishing them by adding wings and pretty dresses. Aside from the penchant for gorgeous clothing, they couldn't be more wrong. Fae, at least the fae people could see, were as big as humans, as dangerous as demons, and fickle as the wind. Wiry, quick-witted warriors with no mercy for anyone who stepped into their territory or got too close.

"Come on. Lunch time." Keera hitched the straps of the baby pouch.

"Big fae," Ruby said. "Not fit in houses."

Keera's heart dropped until she saw Ruby was trying to open one of the tiny fake doors.

"No." Keera took Ruby's hand. "We have to be careful. We don't want to break the special houses."

"But look," Ruby said, pointing to a butterfly flitting through the trees. "Fae. Look!"

"Not here." Keera let out a nervous burst of laughter. "Still, keep an eye out and warn us if you see any silver-clad warriors."

Pearl was slurping her fist with gusto. *If she didn't get fed soon, she'd burst into tears.*

"Come on, your sister's hungry, Ruby. Aren't you hungry, too?"

"Why are you being so pathetic?" Zadie scraped a handful of puddle-slime and raced ahead to the picnic table. "We have a job to do. Let's get it done."

"I don't like this," Lettie shook her head. Nada squirmed in her arms.

"Who are we to argue?" Zadie replied. "The crime was committed. The King and Queen have made their ruling, and the price must be paid."

"And the Myrddin Pact?" Not that Lettie cared a jot for the treaty with the humans—except that it outlawed exchanging changelings for human children, and she was all for that.

"Void, I guess." Zadie shrugged. "But there's nothing we can do now. We follow the queen's plan, or we die."

Lettie's heart felt like it was being stomped on. The queen did not know what she had asked. Persephone had never spent hours making faces, or waving her hands at the wind, listening, hoping, begging for a changeling to Become. "I'd condemn Persephone to the Underworld if Hades hadn't done that to her for half the year already. *And* it's going to be so hard on Nada and…your wee one."

"Eh, we lived through this. Our changelings can, too.

"Not me," Lettie said. "I was never sent to be raised by humans."

Zadie gritted her teeth. "You were one of the lucky ones, then."

§

Aiden's stomach rumbled.

"Pretty." Ruby pointed past the picnic table under the great willow tree to the burbling brook meandering beyond it.

Aiden felt a weird pressure from there, as if someone or something was watching.

"Look, the fae's got a baby." Was there a glow in the air where Ruby was pointing? *Can't be. Fae don't come to Earth, there's not enough magic*. Except now he felt like second-guessing everything he knew. Everything he'd learnt.

"The children love the forest here," Keera said. "But all this talk of fae is making me feel nervous. Like we're back in Brocéliande."

"I know what you mean." Aiden shivered. Talking about fairies didn't feel quite like a game anymore. "Maybe we should picnic closer to home."

"Picnic, Mama? I'm hungry now."

"So am I, sweet pea. So's your sister. She's going to swallow that hand if we're not careful." Keera sighed and rescued Pearl from the baby sling. "And this is a lovely spot." The willow's drooping leaves offering just the right amount of shade. Keera eased the front pack off her shoulders and sat down at the picnic table. Then, fast as lightning, jumped up, clutching Pearl. "Oh, no."

"What is it?" Aiden asked, accidentally touching the slimy table. "Ew." He wiped his hand against the nearest tree. "Can you watch Ruby for a moment?" He raced down the grassy bank to the stream. In a nervous hurry, he half-slid down to the rocky edge. He glanced back, but could see nothing.

They're fine, he thought, rinsing his hands in the cool running water. *Keera can more than look after herself. There's no reason to worry.*

§

The pale red-headed man approached the slimy table.

Zadie laughed as he jumped away, wiping his hand repeatedly on a nearby tree before rushing off to the stream. "See how silly they are? Fussing over a little slime. Quick! Tear a fragment of the child's dress while they're distracted."

Lettie didn't think it was so funny. She rushed to Ruby and snipped a fragment from the older sister's dress while Zadie sneaked up to cut a thread from the baby's bib. Not that the Sword Master was going to notice. She was too busy watching the man nearly fall into the stream.

"There. Happy?" Lettie muttered, waving a fragment of Ruby's red dress.

Holding a piece of white fabric with her fingers, Zadie shuddered. "Humans are so gross. The babe had spit all down it."

Lettie stifled a giggle. "I thought you were the one who didn't mind a little slime?"

"Slime's different." Zadie huffed. "Come on. Arachne is waiting for us."

§

The instant they'd passed into Brocéliande, the change from flutter form to elegant form hit Lettie like a brick.

Arachne scuttled toward them, clicking angrily. "How long must I wait for you? Here, take these." She thrust a blue butterfly-wing pendant into each of their hands. Two tiny threads, white and red, from each of the girl's dresses were knotted around each chain. "Put the Queen's Talismans on now. They'll keep you in elegant form, even on Earth—and keep you and anything you're holding, shielded from the humans. Well, all the humans except the girls themselves… that's what the cotton's for. You, and even the children, will be able to walk past other humans screaming—and they won't notice a thing."

"Queen Persephone's so clever," Lettie murmured. "She's thought of everything."

"Yes, yes," Zadie snapped, while Arachne rolled her eyes.

Reverently, Lettie pulled the iridescent necklace over her head and smoothed it against her skin. Nothing happened. Of course it didn't.

Muttering, Arachne sewed replicas of the children's dresses, her eight legs clicking in her haste. "I hate it here on the border," the old spider grumped. "That dead world is no place for someone like me, and here is little better. By the Underworld, I thought the queen had finished with these games of hers."

"Our Queen commands, and we must." Lettie piped up.

"Don't listen to me. I'm just an old spinner who wants to get back to Faerland where I belong."

"I won't breathe a word." Zadie turned to give Lettie a sly wink. Fae was such a gossip. There was no way fae would be able to resist telling everyone up and down FaerLand of Arachne's lack of respect for the queen's orders.

"Almost there," Arachne said, picking up Nada and pushing faer into the dress.

Nada wriggled and rustled by way of laughter.

"Is Arachne tickling you?" Lettie asked, listening so hard for an answer she imagined Nada had replied with the softest, *yes*. But of course, neither changeling said a word. It was nothing more than the wind. She was silly to hope, especially now that her Nada was about to become Changeling Ruby.

"Arachne's work is amazing," Zadie said. "Do you think if I ask nicely, she'd make me a gown for the queen's ball?"

"I can hear you perfectly well," Arachne said. "And no. Bad enough being at the queen's beck and call. Ask someone else to make your dress, or make it yourself."

And with that, Arachne was done. Lettie swallowed. The change-lings were not only dressed in replicas of Ruby and Pearl's clothes, but they appeared exactly like the human children. Changeling Pearl's chubby baby limbs kicked, just like a human child's. Changeling Ruby put faer hands on faer hips. Only now, Nada could no longer become a butterfly and hover over Lettie, or turn into roses or reptiles. She was stuck as Changeling Ruby.

"And remember, the talismans' protective charms mean you can hold the human children and they will not be seen. But you cannot fly away, and I would not drop them. The queen values these talismans more than most fae lives."

Lettie nodded somberly, and Zadie grasped Changeling Pearl under faer arm like a bundle of wood. "Weird human thing."

Lettie didn't think Pearl Changeling was so weird. Faer hair was beautiful, black as ebony, shiny as silk. Faer chubby cheeks held a delightful scowl. Fae kicked out her baby limbs, opened faer mouth...

...and shattered into an assortment of precious stones, argentite, and other oddments.

Zadie burst into tears. "My darling. My precious. I never thought I wanted a changeling. Why break now? Why?" She pushed silver tears aside with the back of her hand.

Lettie didn't know what to say. Zadie had never wept before. Or at least Lettie had never seen it. But much as her heart was breaking for her friend, it hurt to see her own changeling immutable and unchanging.

Lettie's treasured changeling, Nada, had lost something precious—but at least fae was still here, snuggled close in her arms—if not for much longer.

Lettie had to harden her heart.

Only it felt like breaking as Nada...no, Changeling Ruby, blinked. Her green eyes accusing.

"Maybe we could run away? We could keep my changeling, reverse this enchantment and find somewhere the king and queen will never find us."

"Where would that be?" Zadie said between sobs. "No, we have to work with what we have. And it'll be easier now with just the one."

Lettie clutched Nada tight while Zadie wiped away faer tears.

Faer chin set, and eyes narrowed, Zadie pulled a red jewel out of faer pocket. "I have the perfect lure."

§

"How about we have another little rest here and finish our picnic?" Aiden pointed to some exposed tree roots, the perfect size for a bench. "Much better than that slimy table." He pulled his backpack down with a sigh of relief and rolled his shoulders. Even if they did really need some family time together, walking back from Brocéliande with the children and all Keera's sword-smithing equipment hadn't been the best idea.

"Picnic!" Ruby giggled and pulled a face for baby Pearl. Pearl giggled back, kicking her chubby legs, and drinking in the forest as if it were sunshine.

"Uh. Uh!" Pearl flung out her arms.

Keera pulled the baby out of her sling and sat her down on the mossy carpet. But Pearl wasn't in the mood to stay still. She clambered over the roots and pulled at Aiden's pant legs as if she was trying to stand.

"Not yet, you don't, rabbit," Aiden cautioned.

While he picked up Pearl, Ruby toddled over to a mossy bump under an elm tree. "Get away from there!" Keera called, a note of panic in her voice. Elms were treacherous.

Aiden's eyes met hers, and she relaxed. *This is Earth. Not Brocéliande. Keera needn't always be on guard.*

Raising her chubby hands up onto the rough bark, Ruby called out, "Look a soft."

"No," Aiden said. "Bark's rough."

"Ruff, ruff," Ruby said. "I like doggies."

Aiden laughed, only to be confronted by the cutest chubby-cheeked scowl from Ruby. He glanced away to smother his mirth and unpacked the boiled eggs.

It was good to stretch his legs out in the shade. Keera leaned in and pushed a strand of hair back. She kissed his nose. "It'll be good to get back home."

Aiden couldn't agree more.

"Alright, I think it's past time for lunch," Keera said. "Come and wipe your hands. Ruby? Where's Ruby?"

"Ruby!" Aiden called. Guilty he'd lost sight of their daughter, his heart thudded, a single beat of concern before he saw Ruby's hand reaching out for something red and sparkly within the elm's branches. Aiden frowned. *Maybe it's a trick of the light—or maybe it isn't.* "Ruby, what are you doing?"

Ruby returned; her chubby little hand clenched in a fist.

Keera reached out a hand. "What have you got there?"

"Nothing."

"Open it," Keera insisted.

Reluctantly, Ruby opened her fingers one by one, but there was nothing inside.

"Let's eat up," Keera said in her no-nonsense voice. "I'll feel much better when we're home."

§

Zadie snatched the gem back and turned on Lettie. "Alette, you missed. That was on purpose."

Lettie shook her head—but it was true. She had no intention of letting Nada go.

"Fine," Zadie growled, grabbing hold of Changeling Ruby's hand and pulling her away from Lettie.

"No!" Lettie cried. "Give faer back."

"Don't make me hurt it!" Zadie warned, clutching Changeling Ruby tight.

Lettie whimpered. *Should I free faer? Will fae break?* She tugged a little, but Zadie only held Nada…Changeling Ruby tighter.

"Let faer go. Queen Persephone doesn't need to do this. *We* don't need to do this," Lettie begged.

Zadie ignored her, hurrying toward the family with Changeling Ruby clutched in front of faer.

The child, Ruby, waved and walked nearer, an egg clutched in one hand. She waved with the other. "Hello."

Nada waved back. It was eerie, like watching a child with a wayward mirror reflection.

The baby, Pearl, burst into tears and the parents glanced away from Ruby to offer the bawling baby food. Seeing faer chance, Zadie rushed in.

Lettie lurched forward…too slow to stop Zadie as fae pushed Changeling Ruby away and snatched up the human child. In the rush, Ruby's half-eaten egg dropped to the ground.

"No," Lettie cried. The changeling she'd cared for, for so long, walked toward the strange people like they were faer parents. Like they'd looked after faer for a hundred years.

"You knew it was always going to come to this." Zadie thrust the human bundle into her arms. "Queen Persephone doesn't tolerate failure."

"And what about you?" Lettie asked, holding the squirming child, Ruby, tight to her chest. "Your changeling failed."

Zadie let out a strangled cry and wrapped faer arms around faerself.

How could I have been so cruel? "I'm sorry."

"No, you're not," Zadie snapped. "And it was a good point. So, what am I going to do? I'm going to wait a hundred years or so for the queen to calm down." Zadie ran, leaving Lettie alone with the human child.

"Mama, what about me?" Ruby said, watching her parents pack up their picnic and continue on their way. Strange that neither seemed to notice that their talkative child was now apparently silent—oblivious of their real child only footsteps away.

What have I done? Lettie felt as if iron was running through her veins, even as she did her duty and held the child. The pain of losing Nada made worse by this human horror that stank of stale egg and talcum powder. "This way," Lettie insisted, pulling the little girl away.

"Ruby's hungry," Ruby said.

A.J. Ponder

"Is she?" Lettie replied, flashing her sharp teeth. "What if Lettie is hungry?"

Ruby didn't seem to notice the threat. "Ruby wants to go home," she said. "Take me home."

Lettie sighed. "Well, come along. The faster we move, the faster you will see your new home. It has been a long time since we had a child at Queen Persephone's Court. Tell me, do children eat spider-silk or ambrosia?"

"Food," Ruby licked her lips. "Chocolate. And pancakes." In her hand, she held Zadie's red jewel.

"Now, when did you get hold of that?" Lettie tried to take it.

"Mine!" Ruby shrieked. "Mine. Mine. Mine."

Lettie clamped a hand over her closest ear. *I am cursed to have lost my beautiful changeling for this ghastly creature.* The last thing Lettie wanted was to leave Nada behind and take a human child through the border into the Fae Kingdom, but an upset, crying child was worse. After her sacrifice, she still had to hope one child was enough to curb Persephone and Hade's wrath, but she couldn't imagine the queen being impressed with this one. The little girl screamed in a voice even more piercing than most humans, "I'm hungry and I want my mama."

"Human child. You will be the death of me." Lettie threw Ruby over her shoulders and trudged onward, determined to offload this annoying creature as quickly as possible.

"Hungry! Hungry!" Ruby cried tears of saltwater down Lettie's dress.

Lettie sighed and pulled out her personal stash of food. "Hi, Ruby. Maybe we should start again. I'm Lettie. Would you like some nuts and berries?" It wasn't ambrosia or anything fancy, but it would have to do.

Nut by nut, and berry by berry, she passed her entire month's supply of food up to the child, whose struggles slowly eased. At last, battered and bruised, Lettie felt safe enough to put the child down. "Move, Ruby. You are most annoying. I do not like you."

Ruby looked up and smiled. "I like you. And I like my pretty present." She turned the red stone over in her hands so it flashed with light. "Are we going home now to see Mummy and Daddy?"

Lettie wiped a silver tear from her eye. It was all she could do not to break down on the spot and cry herself to death.

"Don't cry." Ruby wrapped her chubby arms around Lettie's legs. "Do you want the jewel? Here."

Lettie shook her head and pulled herself together—for Nada's sake. *Why is the human child being so likeable? It's only making this worse.*

She closed her eyes and imagined it was Nada hugging her tight.

§

"So, what do you think, Ruby?" Aiden asked when they'd finished eating. "Are you ready to go yet? Are you sure you don't want something else to eat?" After all her complaining, Aiden hadn't seen her touch a thing since she'd run off with the boiled egg.

Ruby shook her head.

"Was that a nice picnic?... Ruby?"

Ruby shook her head again and lay down on the mossy forest floor.

"Of course you're tired. It's been a big day." Aiden picked up his little girl. She didn't cuddle in, but lay stiff in his arms.

Keera flashed him a worried glance. "Maybe we should've asked Corson to help."

"Maybe," Aiden replied, his gut churning. He shook his head and tried to get the idea of fae snatching Ruby out of his head. *So, Ruby isn't talking. It's been a long day. She'll be right as rain in the morning…*

LETTIE WITH QUEEN AND RUBY

Lettie arrived at the Fae Court, exhausted from carrying the small and grumpy child, and hungry after giving Ruby all her food.

Music swelled, triumphant and achingly beautiful.

Lettie sighed. Her arms ached. And every dew drop she passed reflected her image, so totally inappropriate for the queen's court. Her skin, instead of glowing a healthy green, was the colour of pale-mustard. And her beautiful blue dress was spattered with mud and salt.

King Hades and Queen Persephone were sitting on their thrones under the towering green of the elder trees. King Hades' tousled hair proclaimed his anger, swirling like a storm cloud with lightning that arced into the twilight.

With a wave of the queen's hand, the music was silenced, the fae musicians motionless as if frozen mid-note. The string players' bows hovered over the strings as if paused on a knife's edge, and the ocarina and flautists' lips remained pursed over their decorative instruments.

"My Queen, I have the child," Lettie announced, pushing Ruby in front of the throne. "Now, please, I…" Lettie's throat burned.

She needed Queen Persephone to understand her sacrifice. And Zadie's. *Maybe the Queen will relent, and I'll be able to rescue my changeling and bring faer home.*

Zadie's head popped up from behind the royal thrones, smirking maliciously.

Zadie didn't run away at all.

Lettie's throat seized. *What's Zadie told the queen? She can't have told her the truth, or she wouldn't be sitting right there, smirking.*

"What hast thou done?" Queen Persephone roared.

Lettie flinched. "I...I brought the child." She pushed Ruby in front of her. "I've done everything you wanted—"

"So, I see. And still you backstab me, and all fae. Zadie has warned me about your perfidy. That thou should do such a thing... 'Tis beyond forgiveness."

Zadie's smirk widened.

What? Lettie opened her mouth. "I..."

The fae court pressed in close. Closer. Waiting for Queen Persephone to pronounce her judgement.

The child, Ruby, looked up at them all with big brown eyes. "I'm hungry."

Still?

"And that child looks tatty. Hast thou been dragging it through the mud?"

No thanks to Zadie. "Yes, my queen. I'm sorry, my queen. I only did—"

"Do not lie. I know why thou hast only one child. You destroyed Zadie's changeling in a burst of jealous rage. And now we are bereft. We may never get the revenge our people need."

"What? No! I never! Ask Arach—"

"Thou destroyed the balance. A life for a life. That is the bargain. A child for a changeling. It has been so since the beginning of time. By—"

"Zadie is…I would never…" Zadie's betrayal was like a blow to her wings. And in her shock, the words she needed to exonerate herself would not come. Seeing Persephone's rage, Lettie's stomach fell and her head whirled as she waited for the awful moment where the ground would swallow her up.

"…and that be not the worst of it," Queen Persephone continued as if Lettie had said nothing at all. "One changeling alone cannot serve the revenge the defilers deserve, and we have no more changelings. Now thou must tell Wyrden to finish thy job and kill both the Sword Master and her husband and child before they make more trouble."

"Wyrden?" Lettie repeated, dizzied by the speed of her calamitous fall. No favour would be granted, no quarter given. Her heart sank as her hope of a speedy reunion with Nada melted like summer snow.

The child Ruby appeared equally perplexed. Looking over the gathered fae, she inched closer to Lettie.

Queen Persephone grabbed the child's arms. "Wonderful to meet thee, Ruby." She turned to her husband. "Let us dress this child for a ball. She shall have nothing but the best spider silk. And husband, thou send this miserable fae to sort out your half-demon." She turned to the still-smirking Zadie. "And thou be little better than Alette. Didst thou even bother to get Arachne to sew this child a ball gown for my summer festivities? What was thee thinking?"

Zadie said nothing.

Queen Persephone waved a hand and two of her attendants left, dragging the sobbing child with them. Then the royal musicians struck up a sombre chord.

"Don't worry, Ruby." Lettie called after Ruby. "They'll look after you, you'll be like a princess in the prettiest gossamer silk dress." *And I'll still be wearing this old thing.*

A Fae-in-Waiting beside the Queen frowned. "She has my pendant. I need it back."

Queen Persephone nodded, and before Lettie could reach up to remove it, the fae tore it from her neck and hugged it tight. Whyever she wanted it so badly, Lettie didn't know, and wasn't sure she wanted to.

"Right, you," Hades snapped at Lettie. "You'd better hurry. Through here." He pointed to a mirror. *The Silver Paths of the Dead.* Lettie froze. An old rhyme from her own nanny returned unbidden.

Do you fear to tread,
The Silver Paths of the Dead.
Good. Then, do not go.

Bad enough leaving the child with the queen who seemed to care more for Ruby's looks than her happiness, but travelling the paths of the dead was dangerous, as was going anywhere near the skin-walker, Wyrden. That creature was more terrifying than all the paths combined—even the labyrinth with its minotaur.

She shivered, thinking of the poor gardener thrown into the lightless hole, while his carefully tendered plants were trodden into the soil. Maybe the labyrinth was worse, after all.

"Do you really think I should be the one to tell Wyrden… anything?" *If he was dangerous enough to give the king and queen pause, he'd think little about snuffing out an insignificant fae like me.*

"And tell Wyrden," Hades thundered, "tell him he should have dealt with this himself from the beginning. And if he can't, I will find someone else to do his job."

"Yes," Queen Persephone backed him up. "We are at war, fighting for the very lives of the fae against the perfidious humans. Thou wilt not fail us again."

Lettie hesitated in front of the rippling surface, dreading her mission with every fibre of her being. The horror of war sweeping through FaerLand the only thing stopping her from flying away. She needed to harden her heart and do as her queen commanded. It was so difficult.

All these people, all gathered around watching her, and she'd never felt so alone—not for a hundred years.

"I said, GO!" King Hades roared. He shoved Lettie through the liquid surface.

It was like being pushed through fire.

Lettie screamed. It wasn't just the suffocating metal blinding her and clogging her nose; she was changing against her will. Despite doing everything in her power to stay in elegant form, she was pushed into flutter form. She'd face Wyrden small as a tiny bird. The prospect was terrifying, but at least with the wings she could fly. A myriad of hellish reflections and fiery landscapes flashed by. A murder of crows appeared. Their eyes glinted like daggers, their claws as large as swords, they flew at Lettie.

Where is Wyrden? Not in FaerLand or Brocéliande.... Earth! Lettie screamed—crows' claws raking her skin as she was thrust into the magic-dead world.

Not-Ruby:

5 June 1934

Pearl was in her high chair, throwing gobs of porridge on the wood floor. In between cleaning up the mess, Aiden tried not to stare at the too-quiet Ruby sitting close to Pearl, pushing food around her plate.

"That will do," Keera said, taking the porridge away from Pearl and wiping her hands. Before she released the wriggling baby, she glanced over to Ruby, a frown creasing her forehead.

Is she as worried as I am? "Keera? Have you heard Ruby talk since we got back?"

"Do you think…?" Keera left the question trailing like a thread.

"I don't know." Their eyes met in sudden realisation. They'd both been thinking the same thing while telling themselves that this couldn't have happened on Earth. Yes, in Brocéliande, maybe, but to have fae follow them over the border—Aiden would have thought it impossible.

They moved out of the kitchen, to the corridor. "There must be some other explanation," Aiden whispered. "And even if it's a changeling, what do we do?"

Keera frowned. "In the old days…"

"No. Even if it did work, we can't torture children." Aiden shuddered. The tales he'd heard of throwing children into fires, and other cruelties, to discover if they were fae or not, were unthinkable. No wonder fae thought humans were barbarians. "And, anyway, what about Pearl? She's too young to be talking. What if she's a Changeling that's doing a better job of hiding? We'd never know. Not for sure."

"Yes, there is." Keera rummaged through the closet for her travelling backpack and pulled Ruby's new sword from its scabbard.

Aiden took a deep breath. "We're probably overreacting."

"Best to be sure." Keera stepped toward Ruby.

"No!" Aiden shouted.

"Not like that," Keera said. "I'd never. This is Ruby's sword. If the child is Ruby, the sword will recognise her."

"Ruby, my heart. Do you want to see your sword?"

Ruby shook her head. She placed her hands behind her back.

The sword swirled so that the pointed edge faced Ruby.

"It's reacting to her. That has to be a good sign," Aiden said.

Keera frowned. "It should find its owner, pommel first."

"I'll try," Aiden said, unwilling to give up.

"Don't bother." Keera wrapped the sword in oil cloth and put it away. "It's not Ruby."

Ruby...Not-Ruby looked up at them with knowing eyes, hugging her arms around herself.

"It's alright," Aiden said, his mind spinning. "Why don't you get the blocks out and play with your sister?"

"Uh," Pearl held up her arms, determined to be released from her highchair prison. Aiden rescued her and plopped her onto the floor. Once they were busy building, Aiden drew Keera aside and whispered. "If that's not Ruby, we have to go, rescue the real Ruby. Maybe we can ask Alice to get us into FaerLand through her portal mirror. Otherwise, we could be caught on the border and trapped there for a hundred years."

Keera shook her head so her braids bounced on her shoulders. "No, there are better ways into FaerLand. Less dangerous paths that won't take so long." She smiled. "Your soul is precious to me. Besides, we have to see if Pearl's a changeling, too. Which means I need to go back to Brocéliande and use the forge again."

"And make her a sword? But it will take too long."

"Luckily, time moves very slowly in FaerLand. So, much as it breaks my heart, it's better we do not rush in to get Ruby back but wait until we know if we are looking for one child or two."

"But if Ruby's eaten anything..." The thought that they might get there and not get Ruby back was horrifying.

"That's the Underworld," Keera said. "FaerLand is...different. Not so cut and dried... Pearl? How did you get over there?"

Aiden swivelled around. Pearl was shuffling along on the carpet, determined to get to the cupboards—and into trouble.

"Ugh, so we have to go to Burcham's office and tell him we're going back in sooner than we thought.

"When will we ever be able to disentangle ourselves from The Society? I joined because I thought we had a common enemy. But I just don't know any more."

Aiden nodded. Keera had argued passionately about the damage The Society was doing. And no one had listened. It was the least they should've done. Keera knew the world of Brocéliande better than anyone else from New Avondale. And now she was going to have to swallow her pride and beg to go back in.

§

Aiden turned to Keera, hesitating outside Burcham's heavy oak office door with its officious brass nameplate stamped with Burcham LLB. Inside, he could hear voices.

"You ready?" Aiden asked.

Keera pushed her braids into a wide hair-tie and nodded. "Yes. Are you?"

Aiden flashed a grin. "My ancestors were Scottish. I know how to fight."

"Yeah. Losing causes," Keera replied. "But we're not losing this one. No matter the cost, we have to convince them to let me into the latest mission so I can forge that sword. Let's go." She knocked.

"Come on in," Burcham called.

The office was already full of people. Sitting alongside Corson and Professor Brian Faulkner was an academic in a tweed jacket held together with patches. Opposite them was a silver-haired gentleman wearing dark, dark glasses and gripping a white cane.

Corson grinned welcomingly.

"Perfect timing," Burcham said. "I'm so pleased you wanted to come on board."

On board what?

Burcham leaned over his oak desk. He looked like a badger that'd been stuffed into a business suit two sizes too small. "You're just in time to meet everyone else who's going on the expedition tomorrow."

What expedition? Aiden glanced around the crowded office.

This isn't the plan.

Not that he could tell anyone that. He couldn't let The Society, or anyone, know of Ruby's condition. *Condition* sounded better than changeling—*anything* sounded better than changeling. He'd not even mentioned the possibility to his parents, who were no doubt wondering right this minute why their talkative grandchild had turned silent.

In the corner, a sliver of silvery green light peeked out from a green velvet cloth—a glimpse of Alice Faulkner's infamous silver mirror. A dangerous and tempting artifact for those who knew how to use it. The only time Aiden had ever seen it uncovered, it had reflected a variety of scenes, forests and rivers, and tiny rooms. *Fortunately, Burcham would never risk travelling the Silver Paths of the Dead himself. He's more about rarities and curios than risk.* According to ancient law, the risk was possession by demons. The idea made Aiden's skin crawl—but if it came down to it, he'd be willing to risk everything for his family.

Focus. Keera's right—there are other ways into FaerLand.

Burcham waved over to the patched academic. "Dr Philips here is an arachnologist. He's coming on this trip to bring back spider specimens and the famous Brocéliande spider silk."

"Delighted to meet you." Philips stuck out a hand. A solid handshake. "Have to say I'm excited about this place Faulkner's been talking about. It could have some real potential to create innovative materials."

"Lovely," Keera said. "But what's this about spider-silk? Wasn't the policy to stay well away from the creatures?"

Burcham leaned over his desk, casting a furtive glance—not at the scientist, but at the elderly gentleman with the cane—before turning his attention to Keera. "You must understand, this mission is important to me. We've spent years setting up New Avalon and we need the operation to pay its way. So…" Burcham steepled his fingers. "We're taking on a commission."

Aiden's eyebrows rose. Somehow, he stopped himself from saying, *surely this is a recipe for disaster.*

Beside him, Keera cast her "I told you so," glance. She'd warned that The Society's, and Burcham's, studied ignorance about Brocéliande would get them into trouble.

There's no choice. We have to get onto this expedition, whatever the cost. And Keera had to use the forge, which meant she had to be officially invited.

Oblivious of their reservations, Burcham nodded. "The scientific part of The Society wants us to bring experts on missions, and they're paying, so we're not really in a position to say no. Not to mention the exciting knowledge we'll be gaining."

Not that Burcham cares as much for knowledge as he does about treasure and cold hard cash, but I guess he has to finance the settlement and the expeditions somehow.

"For this mission, Corson's going to be taking point. He'll be monitoring the project and keeping our experts out of danger." Burcham turned to Alice's husband, Brian. "And, of course, you know Professor Faulkner."

Aiden nodded.

"Hmm. And this is Dr Wyrden, our sponsor."

"Delighted to meet you," the elderly gentleman said. "This is so very exciting." He clapped his hands. "And I have something I wanted to give you, Aiden."

"Me?"

"Yes, you. I'm so pleased to have caught you here today. You're a very important part of our strategic plan going forward. To understand Brocéliande better, I think you should have this." He pulled out a heavy tome bound in old leather and passed it to Aiden. Demonologie, by the High and Mighty Prince, James & c was stamped on the outside in faded gold ink. A collector's piece for sure.

"I've killed a few demons in my time," Dr Wyrden said. "And this book opened my eyes to the world I was getting into."

"But—" Aiden frowned.

"No buts," Dr Wyrden lifted a hand. "There are truths hidden within, if you dare look. But I'm very late. I really must be going. If someone will see me to the door." He grabbed Aiden's arm in a vice like grip.

"Thank you, sir." Aiden stood and helped him through to the corridor.

"I'd be careful if I were you," Dr Wyrden whispered once they were out of ear shot of the others. His breath was hot on Aiden's ear. "You should never have married an outsider." Aiden's blood felt like it was boiling as the old man left, walking with an uncanny accuracy, never changing direction even once. If it wasn't for the dark glasses and the cane ringing on the ground, Aiden would never have thought he was blind. Even Brocéliande seers had more trouble negotiating their surroundings.

He shrugged and returned to Burcham's office. It was a problem he hoped he wouldn't ever need the answer for.

"Such a kindly old man. We're so lucky to have him as a sponsor," Burcham said when Aiden returned.

Keera's hand jerked as Aiden murmured a non-committal, "Indeed."

"So, it's sorted. Corson, you're taking my dear friend, Philips, in to check out these spiders. And I'll give you a bonus for keeping our generous investor, Dr Wyrden, happy."

"I'm not sure about going out of our way to see the spiders," Corson said. "They're hardly the garden variety that Mr Philips is used to. Begging your pardon, I mean Dr Philips."

Dr Philips shrugged. "Large spiders don't bother me." He glanced at Faulkner. "I don't know why everyone is making such a big deal of them."

"Dr Philips, Mr Burcham, you don't understand. They're not ordinary spiders. Going into their territory will be dangerous," Prof Faulkner said. "And we're so close. If we find the famous library, we should be able to open a path...then everything will be back on track. There's no need to take risks."

"Professor Faulkner is right, Mr Burcham," Aiden said, pleased for once about Prof Faulkner's obsession with finding the Library

A.J. Ponder

of Alexandria. It made him an ally against this interfering with the FaerLand spiders nonsense. "Messing with the giant spiders would be foolish."

"This is not a democracy," Burcham muttered. "It's non-negotiable. Take it, or stay home."

Keera coughed. "Um, we were planning to bring the children."

"Yes, and they'll be perfectly safe. Always have been, you said so yourself, before…" Burcham trailed off.

Keera bit her lip, clearly finding it as difficult not to inflame their previous disagreements as he was.

Burcham frowned. "Believe me, we are where we are. If you like, we need not put you on this mission at all. You could wait for the next one."

"Not at all," Aiden said. "Keera and I are very excited to be going back in. And you know nobody can make a sword like Keera."

Keera leaned over the table. "And I wouldn't take Aiden's reputation so lightly. Or his parents."

Burcham wiped the sweat from his forehead. "It's good to know you're on board."

Aiden stuck out a hand. "It is indeed. Thank you, Mr Burcham. And, if that's all, then I guess we'll be going." He turned to the others.

"Afternoon, Philips. I have to say, I'm looking forward to working with you." He wasn't, but it was hardly Philips' fault. The man seemed nice enough. Finally, he turned to Corson. "Good to see you, old friend."

Burcham handed Aiden an envelope. No doubt it was their usual retainer.

"Afternoon, Burcham."

"You forgot your book."

Aiden grabbed the leather-bound *Demonologie, by the High and Mightie Prince, James &c.* and stalked out.

"That didn't exactly go to plan," Aiden said. "Wyrden gives me the creeps, and this stuff about spiders.... What are they thinking?"

Keera shrugged. "It went better than I thought. And as I'm going in officially, my original contract comes into play. They have to let me use the forge."

"But they're planning to go into the spider territory on the FaerLand border. Why don't they just go around poking the fae with sticks? It's not going to end any better."

"Don't worry, that spider expert will think again when he sees a spider the size of a car. Right now, he probably thinks he's going to be flown to some island. Or that we're certifiable. One or the other. It's always hard to tell with English academics." She laughed. "They always like to act as if nothing fazes them."

Aiden grinned back. "Come on, we better rescue the children before Mum realises Ruby's a changeling."

Keera's smile dropped like a hammer blow.

TEETH AND BOOKS

6 June 1934

The faries exchange a life for a life.
Bring your changeling with you if you
want to see your child again.

Aiden turned the pages of *Treatise On Fae* back and forth, desperate to find an answer.

§

The Myrddin Pact

From this day, no child of mortal born
may be exchanged for a changeling.
Break this pact, and I shall return.

Signed:
Myrddin
Queen Persephone

(In the Earth year 573)

§

The section on the Myrddin Pact was particularly frustrating. But he should not be surprised. Persephone was unlikely to lose sleep over breaking it. After being dead so long, it wasn't like the old wizard was going to come back to wreck revenge on her immortal self.

Aiden sighed and dropped the book on Fae and hefted *Demonologie, by the High and Mightie Prince, James &c.* again. It made his teeth itch. But maybe it was simply his distrust of Wyrden. An unreasoning distrust could be keeping him from the very answers he needed. He opened the old tome to where he'd left off.

§

…. The fearefull aboundinge at this time in this countrie, of these detestable slaves of the Devil, the Witches or Enchanters, hath moved me (beloved reader) to dispatch in post, this following treatise…

§

Beloved reader, indeed.

A treatise of fear, but also Aiden was beginning to suspect, of jealousy. The prince had been in Brocéliande, for sure. But as a spoiled royal brat, he'd come expecting to be lauded and got his nose in a twist. At least, that's how Aiden saw it as he flicked through page after page of half-truths and lies designed to turn people against magic users. All presented as a discussion.

Maybe that is the point. If the creepy Wyrden thought it would turn him against his wife, he was wrong. And if it gave insights Aiden's other books didn't show more clearly, he couldn't see them.

Aiden shook his head. *Demonologie, by the High and Mightie Prince, James &c.* looked impressive, but the truth was, for all its hints and warnings, all he could find within its pages was an unreasonable dislike of any people with the ability to keep demons at bay. The man appeared more deranged than anything. *Likely with his nose out of joint for not being welcomed at the fae court.*

The prince even seemed to respect the strongest and most evil of the demons. Aiden shivered. He'd be happy never to see one of the terrifying creatures ever again.

A bookmark half-fell from one of the pages. A chapter headed:

Faries and Changelings. Supplemental.

There was an extra proviso written in faded ink in the margin: The first part was smudged, but the rest was clear:

*...invite yourself to the dance—not
even the queen herself can hurt you
until after the dance is over.*

Interesting. Then, amongst the usual rules:

*Don't eat the food, or you may be
trapped in Faerland forever.*

*Don't touch what is not yours, for it all belongs
to fae, and the fae have no mercy for mortals.*

*And don't stand still—time
disappears in FaerLand*

There was one rule, and a particularly vile one, that stood out as being a rewording from other texts:

*The faries exchange a life for a life. Kill
the changeling and the pact is broken.*

He shivered.

"Aiden," Keera called from the kitchen. "I've packed. I've organised the girls. Are you ready?"

Aiden slammed the book shut, raising a century's worth of dust. Disgusting. How could anyone endorse a book so cold-blooded as to promote this evil myth? *No. Why am I second guessing my decision now? Even if I did kill the changeling, and the pact is broken, the text says nothing about a live child being returned.*

"In a minute." He found his shoes and pulled them over his thick walking socks.

A page had fallen from one of the other ancient books. He glanced at it before tucking it into a drawer.

> *Daemons can walk through fire—their*
> *paths often leading strait from the*
> *Underworld to hot pools, fiery pits,*
> *and volcans both large and small.*

"I hope you're not reading that cursed book the creepy old guy gave you," Keera said.

"It's just…never mind." Aiden threw off his worry, plastered on his best smile and hurried to shrug on his enormous backpack and meet his family by the back door.

Changeling Ruby was standing there, sucking the end of her hair.

Pearl, trapped inside the canvas front-pack he'd made, wriggled and kicked her chubby little legs against the side. The bag pitched sideways.

Aiden lunged and grabbed the bag before it fell. He struggled to pull the font-pack up and strap it securely, with Pearl, their chubby nine-month-old, wriggling like an eel. Even then, it wouldn't be so bad if he wasn't carrying a sword and a week's worth of supplies on his back.

"Looks like a perfect day for it." Aiden leaned in to kiss Keera's worried frown away—but Pearl thrashed her arms and legs.

Aiden lurched sideways to avoid falling over. "Oops! Sorry." He adjusted the sheepskin shoulder protectors and tightened the straps. "I've got to get used to this."

"Do you?" Keera's eyes lit with some of the old sparkle as she grazed his cheek with her lips. "Come on." She lifted half an armoury onto her back. "We'll be late to meet Brian and Alice Faulkner and the rest of the expedition at the Sister Tree."

She glanced down at Changeling Ruby. "You ready, Champ?"

The silence was deafening.

Stomach lurching more than when he almost fell, Aiden forced a smile.

"Ruby, you're a stout young walker. A real trooper. But today we're going to have to walk fast, no stopping to look at snails or squirrels, alright?"

Changeling Ruby nodded.

"Good. Let's go." Keera opened the door to reveal a clear autumn day with a pale-blue sky that promised the day would get hotter.

§

Grumpy at having been sent to Earth, let alone having to find the creepy Wyrden, Lettie emerged through a mirror into a greenish twilight created by a green velvet cloth—it created quite the barrier for her in this tiny form.

I have to get out.

She battered her way to one side, finally freed her wings, and heaved a deep sigh.

Ugh. Earth. It even smells wrong. Of oil and dead wood and metal—so much metal it made her teeth itch.

And the room was awful. Large and echoey and made from some kind of horrible-smelling dead-shiny wood. Even the chairs, reminiscent of King Hade's and Queen Persephone's thrones, were dead.

Her attention turned to the green of the world outside. She rushed to the window and almost flew into the glass. She kicked the pane in disgust. Despite being transparent, it was pretty solid. Luckily, one of the windows was open a crack. She flitted through it and over black solid tar mixed with gravel—*a human road*—and onto a lawn with a peeling-green park bench and a few sad rose beds. Even the trees behind the low-mown grass lawn seemed gloomy, lacking the vivid greens of FaerLand. Or maybe it was the thin morning light, and the old fae enemy, the sun peeking its head over the distant hills.

Wyrden was sitting on a park bench in the middle of the grass. He was wearing dark glasses with his trench coat and fedora and throwing food at the pigeons. The more they ruffled their feathers in indignation, the more he smiled.

She expected the birds to say something about the rude person throwing food at them, but the most they did was caw at the sky.

What in Hade's name is the skin demon up to? she wondered, sneaking closer.

Wyrden turned and stared right at Lettie in a way that made her want to run and hide. "So, little fae. What brings you here?" Wyrden's smile was worse than Zadie's. Empty. He pulled off a large hunk of crust. "You're smaller than one of these birds, and your wings are so gossamer fine you'd be lucky to survive a hail of stale bread."

He raised his hand.

Lettie hesitated. She hadn't meant for him to see her yet. And she still didn't have a plan. *How do you convince someone like Wyrden?*

He threw, and she whirled away—lumps of stale bread barely missing her.

Wyrden pulled out some more, lining up the shot.

"Persephone…"

A.J. Ponder

"You're not very good as a spy, and useless as an assassin, so why has Queen Persephone sent a slip such as you to me?"

"The thing with humans is that they're so annoying," Lettie said. Almost as annoying as Queen Persephone. Why couldn't she see how much I loved her, how I threw my life away to obey her? But it was best not to say such things out loud, not if she wanted to keep her head. "Our, ah, kind and benevolent queen—and of course, King Hades, well, they've decided they're tired of playing games. They want you to deal with the Sword Master problem."

"Do they?" His lip curled. "And what if I am also tired of playing games, and jumping to their every whim? What if I want a little more out of my arrangement with them?"

"You'll have to talk to King Hades about that yourself," Lettie called, determined not to cower for his entertainment. *The only reason I'm here is because I'm disposable, unimportant to the great Queen Persephone and her retinue. Still, there was no point advertising that fact by cowering like a fugitive.* "What do you think I am, your personal messenger?"

Wyrden lowered his glasses, revealing eyes like pools of midnight. They seemed even creepier here, under this yellow sun, than they had in the soft light of FaerLand's forest.

"What sharp teeth you have, little fae," Wyrden murmured. "But I don't think they'll do much to hurt me."

"I'm sure that's true, but King Hades and Queen Persephone would not be amused if you disobeyed her or anything should happen to me," Lettie said, flitting up close. "You know Queen Persephone objects to the demon-infected on principle, let alone ones that threaten her personal staff." *A ridiculous bluff.*

"Are you saying she wants me to kill the Sword Master without destroying her first? It's so blunt. Still, I suppose needs must. We don't want any more of those very dangerous swords of hers lying about, now, do we? They infuriate Hades so."

Lettie shook her head. There was just one more thing to brave. For herself. And more importantly, for her infant. "And that is not all the queen asked. Changeling Ruby must be kept safe."

He nodded. "I thought I remembered you. You're the timid little changeling-nurse. Look at you out in the big wide world, acting all brave and powerful like you wouldn't blow away in a strong breeze. Like your beloved queen would care about one useless changeling." He steepled his fingers and barked a mirthless laugh. "I could help with the mess you're in, but instead you're asking me for favours— for a pile of barely sentient sticks. It's pathetic."

Lettie wanted to scream. How dare he? Nada was everything. One day, and soon, faer would prove herself and become a fully-fledged fae with a true name. *If faer survives. And I have to do everything I can to make that happen—including threaten a demon.*

She stifled a shiver. "I could go to a certain witch; tell her of this little visit to Earth." *Baba Yaga might even care enough not to kill me for my insolence.*

He smirked. "You would not dare. It would break the bargain."

She fluttered up, out of his reach. "I have no bargain. Whatever bargain Queen Persephone has signed with you, I can do as I please. Do not try me."

"How dare you!?" Wyrden dropped the bread and picked up his cane, whipping the stick up—as if it were a blade. "Your queen will be furious with your little games. But not as furious as I."

Lettie flitted out of its reach. "Queen Persephone is already angry with me, with you, with all the worlds. So, she can choose to dance her fury away, or bring it down upon the both of us. You choose. I will have what I want, or I will take you down with me." Her heart skipped at her audacity. *I will stop at nothing.*

"Fine." His oily gaze unreadable, he lowered the cane. "We don't have all day to argue. They're off to Brocéliande now. If we dawdle, we'll miss them."

A.J. Ponder

"We?"

"You're coming along too, little fae. Otherwise, how will you know for sure I did as I was asked." He shrugged. "I could have the Sword Master spirited away to make swords for me. Imagine that power."

Lettie stifled a gasp.

Wyrden chuckled. Brushing the crumbs off his jacket, he strode ahead. "If we're going to catch up with them, we'd better hurry."

She followed, flying a safe distance behind him as he strode down a gravel path through the park, passing close to a cluster of women in white dresses and strange caps. Wyrden was heading toward a scrubby trail of half-grown trees that led into the heart of the dappled earth forest.

Voices rustled through the forest ahead. The gurgling of a baby. The footsteps of a child.

Lettie's heart leapt. She was about to see Nada again.

§

Within a few hundred yards of the house, Aiden was already backhanding sweat from his forehead. Carrying Pearl felt like carrying a mini-sauna around. Fortunately, they'd soon be deep in the forest where the autumn sun would struggle to filter through the leaves. And Brocéliande would be cooler still, with dense foliage that had never seen an axe.

As Aiden was day-dreaming about cool breezes and ice-cold drinks, Keera whispered, "I think someone's following."

A twig snapped behind them in the otherwise eerie silence.

We've been through here so many times. Why does it feel so different today? He glanced down at Changeling Ruby. Maybe that was it. He laughed at his own nerves. "I'm beginning to wish we decided to meet the others on the way in."

"We'll be at the Three Sisters tree soon enough if we hurry." Keera took Ruby's hand.

Changeling Ruby stopped and sat down.

"Come on, Ruby," Aiden cajoled, "we'll be late to meet your friends. Hazel and Arthur and the other one."

"Tailor," Keera prompted.

Ruby shook her head, her hands waving in flat denial.

"Ruby?" Aiden whispered.

The changeling shook her head.

"We have to hurry." Aiden took the changeling's other hand. "We can play one, two, three jump! But quietly. Ready?"

Changeling Ruby nodded. Together, they forged on along the forest path, swinging her every fourth step. The gathering unease lending speed to Aiden and Keera, to the delight of the changeling, whose grin got wider with every jump.

Another stick cracked behind them, followed by the ring of metal, like a sword being drawn.

"Someone's definitely following us," Aiden muttered, checking the sword at his hip. "Nobody except The Society uses this track."

"You don't think it's one of the others?"

"Maybe, but we're running so late—everyone should be waiting for us."

They picked up the pace again, the soft thud of footsteps behind them getting closer and closer.

Tangled roots tumbled over the path. All around, the ancient trees covered in moss and thick, tangled lianes, loomed. "We must be almost there."

"Shh." Keera pulled Changeling Ruby close. They listened to the curious resonance of the footsteps. The last time Aiden had heard footsteps like that, he'd been in Brocéliande—with demons after him.

Behind them, loud voices echoed, and the thud of the footsteps grew nearer.

Changeling Ruby took a step backward and tried to wrap herself in Keera's tramping skirts.

A.J. Ponder

"I've got you." Keera scooped Ruby up like she wasn't already carrying a heavy backpack. "We're close now."

Pearl wailed.

"Sorry, bubs," Aiden wrapped his arms around Pearl and the awkward front pack, but he didn't slow. As Corson always said, sometimes you have to know when to fight, and sometimes you have to know when to run. Keeping his knees bent so Pearl wasn't bounced around too much, he sped after Keera who leapt nimbly over the path despite the child and heavy backpack.

Old oak trees spread their golden leaves above, like offerings to the sky. They were close to where they were supposed to meet the others. *We'll be safe soon—unless it's a trap...*

It can't be, he thought. *I need a moment to think.* But his brain was spinning as he loped along.

Keera handed Changeling Ruby over to Aiden and pulled her sword from its scabbard. At least she seemed calm. *Calmer than me.*

"It's all right, bubs." Aiden's lungs were burning as he tried to smooth his stride. He was really hot now, carrying Ruby Changeling on his hip as well as Pearl and the pack. "We just need to be quiet— like hide and seek. Okay?"

Changeling Ruby put her finger to Pearl's lips, and the baby stopped crying, although her bottom lip still quivered.

Aiden picked his way over the roots and the half-buried rocks of the trail as fast as he could.

Not fast enough.

He put on a burst of speed over the stony path, but he couldn't keep it up. He stubbed his toe and almost fell. Scared he might hurt the children, he slowed again. His arms ached, and his back and shoulders throbbed. Maybe Keera could take Ruby for a bit. He glanced back, but Keera wasn't there.

Where is she? He peered back through the dense forest. A bright light flickered in his vision. Keera's sword? It slashed through empty air. "Run!" Keera yelled, not turning around, but slowly backing toward them.

She swung again, her sword clanging against another, but whoever was wielding it was behind a twist in the path, obscured by the dense forest.

Aiden, caught between wanting to rush to Keera's side or taking the children to safety, stood rooted to the spot.

Sword Master," Wydren said, "prepare to die." He lunged at Keera, flicking the narrow blade at her throat.

§

Lettie's anticipation grew as she trailed after Wyrden. She imagined bringing Nada back home in triumph. That Nada would speak faer first words, play faer first trick, spoil faer first bowl of milk…

Lettie couldn't wait. She zipped ahead to see Nada, past emaciated beach trees with shafts of morning sun piercing their tiny leaves. It had nothing of the grandeur of the lush forest of FaerLand, or the ferny understories of the forest of Brocéliande,

A footstep ahead crunching on rock was the first sign they were close. The second sign, an endless babble from one of the parents.

She flew fast, determined to get a glimpse of her changeling. She could see the parents trudging over roots and… there faer was, caught up in Aiden's arms, smiling. Her heart swelled to see faer. But so did her throat. Lettie swallowed to stop herself from crying. *I should never have let Nada go.*

A stick cracked next to her. *Wyrden.* He was running fast now. And so were the family.

"When I attack, you distract them!" Wyrden whispered over the wind.

"How?" Lettie asked. "Even if I flit up to them and say boo, they might not notice me. You know how blind humans are." *And I'm not sure I want to help him, anyway. I'm here to save Nada.* "Besides, the queen asked me to pass a message onto you, and I've done that. Or—"

"You know," Wyrden said. "I don't think Hades and Persephone would have sent you if you weren't disposable. So, if you don't help, after I have fun killing all of them, I'll kill you."

"You think they have sent just any fae to deal with you? They need me."

"What? A nursemaid who lost their changeling?"

His words were like needles. "I haven't lost faer. The Queen ordered her on a mission. Fae's right there."

Changeling Ruby was clinging to the man and pressing her head against his chest.

Pain squeezed her heart.

Is that love? Or jealousy? Her blood felt like cold iron running through her veins. Besides, Aiden was hugging her Nada too tight. *What if she breaks? What if Nada doesn't love* me *anymore?*

No, Changeling Ruby was clutching Aiden, terrified of the skin demon she'd brought here. And Aiden was patting her red hair, reassuring her without words. *Does he think the changeling's his own child? Does it matter? They are protecting the youngling Queen Persephone has endangered...I have endangered.*

Ahead, Wyrden trod on another stick. "Humans," he cursed, pulling a sharp sword from his cane. Cold steel. It had been hiding there all this time in protective wood so she wouldn't be able to sense it. But now, the taint of cold metal filled the air.

Wyrden was bold, she'd give him that much. He'd brought that white cane right up to King Hades and Queen Persephone themselves. Which meant that they were not the all-powerful beings she had believed, or they would surely have struck him down for his daring.

"Come, do your duty and fight!" Wyrden yelled at her. "Or I shall have all the glory myself." The old man's smirk was reflected in the hollow emptiness of his eyes—as unremittingly lightless as a starless sky.

Would the father keep her changeling safe? Why isn't the man running? Can he not see Wyrden is about to deliver a mortal blow to his wife? He has to run. Lettie held back a scream. She should wish the humans both dead for their crimes, but as always, her treacherous heart wanted something she couldn't have. And so, Lettie watched, indecision tearing her apart.

"Sword Master," Wyrden said, "prepare to die." He lunged at Keera, flicking the narrow blade at her throat.

Lettie, in fright, fluttered back and forth on the knife of indecision—and impotence—as Keera parried and the battle raged on. Wyrden was good with a sword, but his gloating had cost him his chance to end the battle quickly, and his weapon wasn't as sturdy as Keera's. He had to be careful not to over-extend. And she had to be careful to watch his unnatural speed.

Lettie caught sight of Changeling Ruby and abandoned the fight. *What do I care if they die, so long as it is not my dear Nada.* She fluttered over and landed on the changeling's shoulder. "Don't be frightened. I'm here to protect you."

Changeling Ruby burrowed deeper into Aiden's chest.

"I'm sorry," Lettie said. Not that it made any difference. She'd abandoned Nada, and now Nada was bonding with these humans. Becoming more and more Ruby every minute.

It shouldn't happen. What happens when a changeling bonds with humans? Nada will disobey Queen Persephone's orders at the least. And then what? Will I lose my beautiful, whimsical, changeling altogether? Will faer become nothing more than a pile of mementos and sticks? Like Zadie's?

Even thinking of the loss hurt so badly she wanted to tear her hair out and cry—and to hurt all the people who'd hurt her. *Is this what Zadie had felt? Is this why she'd lied? To patch up the pain in her heart with poison oak?*

"Get back over here and help," Wyrden snarled at Lettie. "Or, by Hades, I'll kill you and scatter your bones to the wind!"

The old gardener's words, "*doing things for the queen never turns out well,*" echoed through Lettie's head as she dived into the fray. *No.* She shook her head. She couldn't think that way. It was wrong. *The old gardener must have deserved his fate. Somehow. Queen Persephone must have seen his treachery. That was it.* All she had to do was bring Nada back home in triumph as a full-fledged fae and Queen Persephone would recognise both of them. Maybe even throw them a ball in their honour. Buoyed with new hope, Lettie screamed and threw foliage at the Sword Master.

The Sword Master jerked backwards and stumbled on the rough ground.

§

Aiden lurched toward Keera, and stopped himself. Keera was already back on her feet, and parrying away Wyrden's blow.

More leaves fell while Wyrden argued with a fae they couldn't see. He glanced down at Changeling Ruby. But the child, or fae, or whatever she was, snuggled deeper into his chest. Whatever was going on, she wasn't to blame.

More footsteps. Aiden sucked in his breath as a man crashed through the foliage toward them. "Stay back!" Aiden warned, putting his free hand on his sword-hilt and hoping against hope he wouldn't have to fight.

"Hey!" The newcomer burst into the clearing.

"Corson!" Relief sucked the wind from Aiden's stomach as he recognised his friend. He pointed over at Keera's attacker. "Get him!"

Eager for a fight, Corson ran to where Wyrden had been, but the spry old man had already disappeared into the forest.

"Are you alright?" Corson asked Keera.

Keera nodded. "Did you see where he went?"

The forest was silent in both directions. There was no other trail than the path they'd been walking on.

"Thanks for turning up, Corson," Aiden said, putting Changeling Ruby down. He sighed in relief. "My hands were a little full." The child clung onto his leg until he picked her up again.

"I can see that," Corson replied. "And of course I'll always help you, my old friend." He held up the sword so the ornate silver and gold writing shimmered in the sun. "Look at this blade your wonderful wife gave me. Where would I be without you both? But what do you mean, Wyrden attacked you? You can't mean the blind man we saw yesterday?"

"Yes, Wyrden, our sponsor," Aiden insisted.

"What?" a voice said behind them. Professor Faulkner—wearing his usual patched tweed sports jacket. He also held one of Keera's swords at the ready. "You didn't say you were fighting Wyrden, did you?"

Burcham was just behind him, his business suit replaced by a tweed walking jacket-and-trousers. Somehow, the lawyer still managed to look like a badger stuffed into a size-too small clothing. "Hmm. Were they saying the blind old man attacked them?" Burcham asked Faulkner.

When Faulkner nodded, Burcham turned to Keera and Aiden. "You have got to be joking?"

"Do we look like we're joking?" Keera demanded.

"It was definitely him," Aiden agreed. "And he's not blind."

Burcham glared. "That's enough. Wyrden couldn't possibly have come here, let alone attacked anyone with a sword."

A.J. Ponder

"Mr Burcham…" Aiden stopped. Riling his current employer wasn't going to get them where they needed to be. Instead, he floundered to say something that would put Burcham in a better mood. "I have to admit, I'm a little surprised to see you here."

Mr Burcham shrugged. "I decided you were right. I can't run this part of the business from behind a desk." He clapped his hands together. "Isn't this wonderful? There's so much to see."

"Wonderful." Aiden parroted, trying to make the word sound enthusiastic. Keera raised an eyebrow.

The silence hung uneasily until Burcham broke it. "Corson, my man." He thumped Corson's shoulder. "Did you see who it was?"

Corson glanced across at Keera. "No, but if Aiden and Keera say…"

"Pish. Heat of the battle and all that."

Changeling Ruby wriggled. She poked her head over Aiden's shoulder and waved.

Aiden held her tighter. "Are you alright, Ruby? Is there someone there?"

"Not that I can see," Corson replied.

"Thanks, Corson." *At least someone on this mission has their wits about them.*

"Anyway, everybody, even though we're still Earthside, we should stay close together. We don't know if Wyrden was working alone."

"No more of that. You know it couldn't have been him." Burcham laughed. "I know what it is. You think all old men look alike. I know I used to. Come on. Let's get back to the others."

The look Keera gave Burcham should have burst his bonhomie, but it slid right off.

Aiden gritted his teeth.

They didn't get far before the rustle of the forest gave way to children's laughter. The Faulkner children were waving sticks and declaring themselves king of a moss-covered tree stump.

Keera took Ruby from his arms and the changeling buried her head in Keera's shoulder.

"Are you ready to walk yet? You can see your friends."

Changeling Ruby shook her head, clinging in a way Ruby never had.

"It's alright, little one," Aiden said. "We'll get you home, soon. See, we're almost at Brocéliande. There's the Three Sisters right in front of us." Aiden pointed at the ancient three-trunked tree, dripping in green lianes and glimmering with a soft-green portal light.

"Hey, you made it," Alice yelled from in front of the Three Sisters. Aiden blinked. In her muted green jerkin and brown full-circle tramping skirt, she was easy to miss. "Children! Time to go," she called.

The two boys waving sticks jumped off their moss-covered tree stump and Hazel, their older sister, clambered down from her hiding place up in the branches of a large overhanging sycamore tree.

"Are we ready?" Alice Faulkner straightened the eldest boy, Arthur's, collar. "Hazel, Arthur, Tailor, it's up to you to look after Ruby and Pearl."

"Yes, Mama," Hazel said with all the solemnity of a seven-year-old. Her two younger brothers giggled and turned to run back to the tree stump.

Alice grinned. "Not so fast. Come and say hello before we go."

Burcham stomped up to the tree. "Good, we're all here. Brian and Alice Faulkner, Corson," Burcham rattled off names, barely waiting for a response. "The Faulkner children; Hazel, Arthur, Tailor. Philips…uh…where's Dr Philips?" Burcham demanded.

"Here." Philips stopped poking around in the leaf litter long enough to wave. "Sorry, I was a little distracted." He lifted a half-rotten branch.

"Good. Shall we be off?" Burcham stepped toward the sacred tree. "Let's go."

"What?" Aiden said. "Hold up a minute." A cold sweat rippled down his spine. "What if Wyrden follows us?"

"Don't be ridiculous, man. Like I told you, Wyrden is blind. Such a generous, kind man…besides, whoever you saw is more likely to follow us if we hang around, so let's get moving, shall we?"

Aiden shook his head. There was nothing he could do but walk on—and keep his wits about him. "Has everyone been briefed?" Aiden asked. "Faulkner, did you warn Philips about what he's getting into? You both work at the university. Surely you had a moment to warn him about the danger of riling the spiders. And Philips, do you even have a sword—something to defend yourself with?"

Philips laughed. "You're not frightening me away that easily."

"Man after my own heart," Faulkner said, slapping Philips on the back. "Besides, we all know what we're doing, don't we, children?"

"You have my sword," Arthur said, having returned from the mossy stump.

"And my bow," Hazel added. "That's even better than a sword."

Aiden bit back a laugh, determined to be diplomatic. He couldn't exactly ask Philips to leave the party, not with Wyrden back there with who knew what on his agenda. *So, what should I say?* "Of course, we want you to come along. I was thinking that after all our…excitement…I'd appreciate it if we focussed on getting to New Avalon before…" *annoying the giant spiders* "…looking for any spider-related adventures."

Burcham stepped forward. "We'll see how it goes. Sometimes you have to seize the day." He chuckled as if he'd said a joke. "Let's get going. We're already late."

"Yeah, sorry about that," Aiden said. "I was distracted by some last-minute reading. And then we were attacked."

"Oh, was the book any good?" Philips asked.

"Certainly didn't have the answers I was looking for," Aiden replied.

"Pity," Philips said. "This one is rather good." He pulled a copy of *The Sword in the Stone* out of his pocket. "Not sure why the Prof thought it would be useful, but it's an interesting read."

"Great," Keera muttered, adjusting her sword-belt. "He's going to get us all killed."

Alice's eyes met hers. "Children, one last thing before we go. Corson's a warrior and a martial arts champion, so Hazel, you and Ruby and the boys need to listen. If Corson says jump, you jump. Understand?"

All the Faulkner children nodded.

"Ruby?" Alice prompted.

Ruby glared at the ground.

Alice raised her eyebrows. "What's up?"

Keera shrugged.

Corson, Philips and Burcham were on another round of hand-shaking. Aiden, his hands full of children, couldn't exactly join in. "Enough of this, let's go," he said. Careful not to scrape the ancient bark and verdant green moss on the three-trunked Sister Tree, he stepped through the westernmost gap and into the bright, leafy forest of Brocéliande.

INTO BROCÉLIANDE

Keera held her breath as they made the transition from the Earthside forest to the wilderness that was Brocéliande. It was beautiful, the sun shining through the leaves above and forming a speckled canopy of light and shadow. Her heart soared to smell the clean, fresh air and hear the birds chattering. Half song, half scolding the travellers for entering their territory.

Moss clung to either side of the narrow path and up the nearby trees.

Gravel crunched underfoot. A large greywacke stone marker heralded that there was 10 1/5 M to Avondale and 5M to Market Town.

Keera startled, drawing her sword as she waved her other hand for silence.

The shock of Wyrden attacking while they were vulnerable still on her mind, Keera waited a moment longer listening for danger.

Nothing…except the chatter of birds.

They moved on, Corson and Brian Faulkner taking the lead, with Burcham and Philips close behind.

The trees hanging over the path held no untoward shadows, and nothing seemed out of place, except every footstep pierced her soul like a warning. She needed to unwind, but the leaden weight of responsibility would not let go. Not just concern for Ruby, lost in FaerLand, but for everyone here. Aiden and Pearl. The changeling. The academics. And especially the Faulkner children, Hazel, Tailor and Arthur, all striding along with sticks in their hands and pretending they were warriors like Corson.

Here I am, prepared to risk everyone, and everything we've built, by bringing a changeling into New Avalon. She glanced across as Aiden slipped Not-Ruby back down to the ground.

Not-Ruby picked up a stick and followed along behind the older children. A perfect imitation.

The thunder of an approaching horse jolted Keera out of her thoughts. Aiden held a hand up and pulled Not-Ruby back to safety.

A young woman riding a speckled white stallion passed them, a rich cloak around her shoulders, and the glint of a gold tiara under her battered brown hat. "A beautiful morning. Have you seen the Captain of the Watch?"

"Which court?" Keera asked.

The young lady shrugged and continued on her way, singing. A handful of birds fluttered around her shoulders, adding their voices to her melody.

"Another princess in hiding," Keera said.

Aiden grinned back. "Yup."

"You should pay up, Philips."

"I don't know about that," Philips said. "How could you possibly know that was a princess?"

Aiden laughed. "Were you blind? Did you not see the gold crown? You think every waif in Brocéliande wanders around with one of those gold things on their forehead?"

Grudgingly, Philips passed a bundle of notes to Corson and Aiden.

"That's enough of that," Burcham spluttered. "Fleecing the newcomer is hardly fair."

Alice glared at her husband.

"Fine." Prof Faulkner sighed. "I rescind all further bets. Corson?"

Corson shrugged. "I was only trying to warn him. Anyway, see those enormous trees to the right." Just steps ahead, giant trees marked the fae border—their gnarled roots like writhing snakes poking out of the emerald moss that surrounded them like blankets. Their massive trunks were the width of a tennis court, and their spreading canopies reached up into the clouds.

In the shadows, something was moving.

§

Lettie took a deep breath as she contemplated following the humans through the barrier. She could feel the power humming through the tree that stood as a gateway to each of the sister territories. Right would send her back to FaerLand. Left, and she'd follow the humans.

A hand grabbed her by the scruff of the neck.

Wyrden.

"Listen, fae, I'm going to go and get the spiders. With that fool scientist on board, the humans are sure to make a nuisance of themselves. You keep an eye on them and report back to the Queen when you can. Understand?"

Lettie nodded.

He shook her so her head whipped back and forth. "Good. And if you get the chance, little Lettie, kill them all and let us be done. I'm tired of being the queen's pawn. I have better things to do, even if you don't."

"So, somehow, all by myself, I attack all these humans, kill the Sword Master and get my changeling back?"

Wyrden scowled. "So long as the Sword Master and her husband are dead, I don't care what you do. But if you're thinking what I think you're thinking, you'd better remember I have Persephone's royal ear. Now flutter off and get to work." He released her, and Lettie dove for Brocéliande.

Pain lanced through her. Her arms and legs growing tall and willowy and annoyingly all elbows and knees. *Elegant form.* If there was one thing worse than being stuck in flutter form, it was being forced into elegant form, knowing she couldn't change back. Not while in Brocéliande, anyway. Her flower cap, designed to hide her in the bluebells, stood out like a blue beacon. Everything was outsize and ugly. *Hardly elegant at all...a total mess and a laughingstock if Zadie, or anyone else, sees me.*

She shook herself. *At least I'm in a whole different realm to the skin-demon. And now that I'm as large as the humans, I've a much better chance of completing my mission. Killing people might not even be that difficult—no more difficult than spoiling milk.* Lettie's stomach lurched at the thought. *I can't be soft. Not if I'm to save Nada.*

§

Does anyone else notice how tense Corson and Keera are? Aiden thought and bit his tongue. Anything he said might give away the changeling in their party. Still, both Aiden and Keera kept glancing over to the FaerLand border like they expected attackers to jump out at any moment. But whatever had caught their eye, Aiden couldn't see it. On the other hand, a gossamer thread of spider silk was hanging in the branches, footsteps away.

At last, Corson spoke, focussing on Philips and Burcham. "See the FaerLand trees over there? They're an extra-good reason for staying on the path. Who knows what is moving under the shade of those great trees. Also, the Fae don't like people touching anything they consider sacred. Go in, and you're not likely to come out again, understand?"

"And even if you make it out alive, it'll likely take a hundred years or so and everyone you know will be dead," Keera added.

"We'll be fine," Burcham replied. "Nobody is talking about going over the border. Let's all get a little closer to see what we can see."

Not-Ruby ignored the adults and swished her stick sword from side to side, striding determinedly after Arthur and Hazel. Keera inched closer to her, placing herself between the child and the FaerLand side.

"The fae?" Philips echoed, oblivious.

"Just go with it," Faulkner said. "The name is not important, but the warning is. It's not safe to get too close to those trees. And keep your eyes peeled for anything moving."

"Fantastic, I can't wait. You know, other countries have spiders as large as a human hand. I'd love to find one at least that big."

"Just don't blunder into any spiderweb," Aiden muttered.

"Yes, and I must collect spiderweb." Philips nodded. "Wyrden was very keen on a sample. There's some there, not so far off the path."

Keera flinched and did a poor job of hiding it with a smile. "It's best to stay on the track. Maybe come back later when the children are settled."

"True," Aiden said. "Besides, there's no point in killing all of us, when we have Burcham and Philips as volunteers."

Philips and Corson didn't miss a step, but Burcham turned scarlet. "That's a bit much."

"Ha," Faulkner fake-laughed. "It's not as bad as that. We're all on edge after the attack on the Earth border. We'll feel better once we've made it to Avalon."

At least he's admitting there was an attack.

Philips coughed. "I'm not sure what the fuss is about. Dr Wyrden didn't say anything about the spiders being dangerous."

"Nobody's been stupid enough to get that close," Alice said. "It's just common sense."

"Besides, Dr Wyrden just tried to kill us," Aiden muttered.

"And he didn't say anything about being a murderous skin-demon either," Keera agreed.

"And now you're saying the sweet old philanthropist is a demon as well as an attempted murderer. *Really*." Burcham tutted. "He's blind, and you're a warrior. What's he going to do? Rap your knuckles with his cane? Come on. What do you say we sneak a little closer to these spiders while we're here and get a good look? The old path's not so far out of our way." Burcham pointed to a faded wooden crossroads marker. "See, this way is even shorter." He wiped moss from the marker to reveal a 9 1/2M burned into the wood—along with a skull and crossbones dabbed in red paint. "See, nine and a half miles versus ten," he enthused, completely ignoring the skull and crossbones.

"Shorter and slower," Alice muttered. "There's good reason nobody takes that path any more."

Prof Faulkner nodded and glanced over to his children. "Mr Burcham, be reasonable. The spiders can wait."

"The children should be perfectly safe." Philips pointed to a brown, long-legged spider, smaller than a thumb, scuttling over a mass of web. "See, it may be big, but it's not dangerous to humans. If I'm not mistaken, it's a new species of Cambridgea. I wonder what she's doing here on the wrong side of the world." He pulled out a collecting jar with a flourish. "Let me just grab this little beauty."

Keera sighed, scrambling through her brain to find the right words to convince him to cease and desist. By the way he was scratching his jaw, Aiden was trying to do the same.

Corson cracked his knuckles. "Don't get me wrong, I'm happy to provide backup. But that's a tiddler. The spiders we're worried about are bigger than we are. If it comes down to a direct confrontation, there's not a lot I can do."

Philips stepped off the track, scooping the spider into the collecting jar with one hand and using a large furry leaf to guide it in with the other. Deftly, he dropped the leaf in and screwed the lid on. "See, that wasn't so hard, was it?" he said, oblivious of the growing tension.

"Small spider." Little Arthur stretched out his arms. "Big spiders stay over there." He pointed over at the hazy mist enveloping the FaerLand border.

"Impossible." Philips waved his arms. "Creatures with exoskeletons simply can't grow much more than this." Philips' hands stopped a shoulder width apart. "And that's at most. It's all about weight and oxygen diffusion. You see, arachnids don't have the lungs we do…"

"What about book lungs?" Prof Faulkner asked. "I mean, there has to be a way, because I've seen them."

Aiden nudged Keera. "Books might be useful for research, and some magic, but they'd make very poor lungs."

Keera's lips quirked into a half smile.

"Book lungs are found in many spiders," Philips began a clearly-well worn lecture. "They consist of a series of thin plates…"

"I think we need to get moving," Burcham snapped, ignoring the fact that their path was less than a stone's throw away from the misty border of FaerLand.

Faulkner turned to follow Burcham. "Can't a person have a stimulating academic debate?"

Alice put a hand on her husband's shoulder. "Wait, we can't go that way."

"We can't leave him by himself." Faulkner said. "He's got no idea."

"And we shouldn't split the party," Corson agreed. "It'll be easier to keep the children safe if we stick together."

Keera clutched Not-Ruby's hand as the forest closed in over the path, becoming denser and denser as they forged down this old trail where the sun barely pierced the leaves above.

Aiden nudged Keera. "There," he whispered.

Keera nodded, her heart skipping a beat as she saw the huge greenish-blackish spider perched on the massive trunk of one of the FaerLand border trees. She swallowed and kept on walking, but Philips stopped in his tracks. "Wow! That's gorgeous!" he said. "It's very realistic for a model. Well done. Even I thought it was real for a second, there."

Gorgeous was not the way Keera would have described the chitinous creature staring at them with cold-multifaceted eyes— even if it was only the size of a small cat.

It moved.

The party jumped. Keera clutched her sword and hoped she wouldn't have to use it.

"That's really interesting," Philips whispered. "Give me a moment." He pulled out a camera.

"Don't use that!" Faulkner grabbed for the device.

Philips pressed the button. There was a small pop and a whiff of burnt metal.

Faulkner blew a sigh of relief.

"That could have been worse," Aiden said. "Surely someone told you modern equipment like cameras have been known to explode here."

"Mmm." Philips looked at his camera and put it back around his neck. "Damn, Faulkner. I thought you were having a laugh at my expense. I didn't think for a moment any of it was real."

"Ugh," Faulkner said with a shake of revulsion. "I'm not sure what you see in spiders. They're the creepiest things in Brocéliande, and that includes the demons."

"What?" said Burcham, his stride as stiff as a show pony's. "Not more drama about demons. Surely that's going too far."

"Right." Philips was still examining his camera. Keera didn't have the heart to tell him it was never going to work again. That was the thing with Earthsiders, they thought everything should work here the way it did at home.

The spider was still watching them with its cold-multifaceted eyes.

"Okay, fine," Philips said. "There are giant spiders. But there's no such thing as demons. I'm not falling for it."

"Ah," Faulkner corrected him in his self-proclaimed expert voice. "I very much want to assure you that there are demons. But no need to worry, we're keeping well away from their territory today."

"Did you see the red mark on the abdomen on that black spider?" Burcham interrupted, pointing to another human-sized spider on the side of the track. "I think it's rather—"

The spider jumped.

ATTERCOP GIGANTICUS

The shiny black giant spider swung closer on a thread of spider-silk to land on one of the huge oak-like trees that overhung the path on the FaerLand border.

"Stay calm. We're all alright." Keera's heart fluttered as she pulled Not-Ruby up into her arms and the party stumbled to a halt. *Aiden's fine. Pearl's asleep. The Faulkners…they were also good.* Hazel, unruffled, had her bow out, while Alice carried the two boys.

"We need to move away slowly. Please stay on the path," Keera ordered.

"Yes, if there's one rule when you're anywhere near Faerland," Prof Brian Faulkner said, "it's stay on the path."

Hazel nodded. Readying an arrow, she strode out to her father, who was looking back and forth as if unsure whether to stay with Burcham, Philips and Corson, or to inch back to the rest of the party.

We're too close.

"Don't panic. The spider can't possibly be that big—it's just a trick of the light. Besides, most spiders have very poor eyesight. They rely on webs to catch their prey. We'll be perfectly fine so long as we don't act like dinner." Philips pulled out a pad and began

A.J. Ponder

sketching a decent rendition of the approaching spider under the scrawled title *Attercop giganticus*.

"Um." Corson took Dr Philips' hand. "Let's not assume too much, shall we?"

"Not an assumption, old chap," Dr Philips said, expounding on how spider metabolism worked, including facts about the diffusion of oxygen and the difference between haemoglobin and hemocyanin.

Not-Ruby struggled in Keera's grasp, peeking up over her shoulder and waving a hand, before cuddling close in an attempt to burrow into Keera's chest.

Keera held her tight, heart hammering at the thought that someone else might have noticed. It felt like holding Ruby—but it wasn't Ruby. *It feels like I'm keeping my child safe, but I'm not.* Her heart sank as her thoughts went to Ruby all alone, and in terrible danger, somewhere within the trees of FaerLand—so close, and yet a world away.

§

Lettie couldn't believe her Changeling was waving at the spiders. Did she think they were all Arachne? *What is my too-clever-for-faer-own-good-changeling doing?*

Lettie ducked back into the bush and ditched the wretched white sheet. Lucky the humans were so blind, or they'd have seen her when she almost crashed into them.

Slowly, slowly. It was stupidly dangerous wandering into the territory of the spiders. You might as well wander into Mirkwood.

§

Keera clutched her sword as another spider appeared. Black as a shiny new kettle, and large as a horse, it scuttled along the path toward them.

The red-spotted spider swung closer, landing on a huge, liane-encrusted tree. Its fat body swayed on spindly legs, chelicera waving like arms in front of its mouth.

Arms outstretched, Alice gathered Arthur and Hazel. "Back off slowly."

Faulkner joined them, taking the path back the way they'd come.

Corson grasped his sword. "Burcham. Philips. Move, or die—those spiders are hunting."

Philips dropped his pencil. "Maybe, on second thoughts, we should back away—slowly. Has anyone got any fire?"

Burcham fumbled in his pockets and struck a match as they backtracked along the trail.

The spiders jumped down from the trees near the misty Faer-Land border and raced closer.

"Here," Corson called, holding out a brand. "You got a light?"

Aiden pulled out his tinderbox and struck a sulphur-tipped match. It burst into flame and tumbled to the ground, smoking and threatening to set the leaf-litter afire.

The spiders hissed.

Aiden poured water from his drink bottle and stamped on the debris. Then he struck another, determined not to fumble it again. The match lit with a puff of sulphur and, in moments, he'd lit Corson's brand. Corson shoved the brand into Keera's hands and pulled out another. He held the second brand against the first until smoke billowed, catching in Keera's throat and drawing tears from her eyes.

The spiders reared back, but did not move—two terrifying sentinels guarding the trail ahead.

With the two brands between them, Corson and Keera shielded the front and the back of the party, respectively.

Safely back at the crossroads, the spiders out of sight, Burcham coughed and puffed out his chest. "I think we might have overreacted

A.J. Ponder

back there. Let's go back and gather a stray shred of silk from one of the larger webs."

"Maybe not now," Corson muttered. "Apart from the spiders that might eat us, we also have the children to worry about." He waved an arm at Keera and Alice carrying the young ones. Even stoic Hazel was sagging, her bow drooping low as she leaned on a large stone to the side of the path.

"Perhaps you're right." Burcham peered back thoughtfully.

Thank goodness. He's finally realising how crazy it would be to annoy one of the giant spiders.

"Hmm. Maybe tomorrow would be better."

Keera blinked. "Tomorrow?"

Aiden placed a hand on her shoulder, and their eyes met. Living until tomorrow wasn't their only concern.

A flash of black chitin slipped through the thick woods behind them. "The spiders are trailing us, aren't they?" Brian Faulkner said. "And the torches? Do we have enough?"

"Sorry," Corson said, "I only brought the two. But we should be able to get to Market Town before the brands burn down."

Keera's gaze danced between the flickering light and the spiders moving through the forest. *Why are the giant spiders so worked up? Surely, it's not the one tiny spider Philips captured? Or are they still angry that we were walking along the border of FaerLand?*

The brand burning down to her fingers, Keera gripped the very end and peered into the sun-dappled trees, trying not to imagine the spiders with their long chitinous legs scuttling over the forest floor— darting closer and closer—their fangs eagerly dripping poison.

As her brand flickered, flashes of brown and black erupted from the trees. Her nightmare becoming reality, she stifled a scream. "Get ready. They're coming."

THE MARKET

Aiden backhanded a trickle of sweat with his sword hand and glanced down at Pearl. She was fast asleep and blissfully unaware of the oncoming spiders. They shied back as Corson, his brand also near the end, hurried to back Keera up.

"This makes no sense." Philips shook his head. "Spiders are solitary hunters."

Beside him, Burcham was shivering with shock.

"Damn, and we're almost there." Corson waved his sword at a lichen-encrusted sign. *Market Town 5 mins.* "Swords out. Children in the middle."

The party bunched tighter and tighter as Keera's brand guttered and died in her hand. And then Corson's was out, too.

The ground-dwelling spiders lunged, and just as they did, a new spider swung across the track in front of them, leaving a trail of silk dotted with sticky glue in its wake.

"Stand clear." Keera pushed Ruby into Aiden's free arm and swiped at the web with her sword, then dodged the falling strands. A faint, but unpleasant, smell of burned nails accompanied the web's fall.

Changeling-Ruby waved at the spiders.

Is she greeting them or asking them to stay away?

The spiders seemed to hesitate, swaying with their whole bodies. For a moment, Aiden thought they were talking to her, but then the distant rumble of hoofbeats and jingle of harness bells pierced the forest and the spiders slipped back into the woods, out of sight.

"Quick! This side." Corson helped the Faulkners move their children to the side of the path furthest from FaerLand.

"Right you are," Philips said, pulling Burcham with him and taking special care to stay away from the fallen web.

Aiden jumped to the side to avoid a horse carrying a cloaked noblewoman, or maybe a red-riding hood, thundered toward them— her scarlet cloak trailing behind her. The horse slowed fast, hooves caught in the sticky web, and she tumbled onto the stony ground.

"Brigands!" she yelled, picking herself up and running for the village.

"Not at all," Burcham said. "We're—"

She was gone. Her horse neighed and thrashed on the ground.

Worried about a hoof clipping Ruby or Pearl, Aiden legged it, but turned back when the Faulkners and their children rushed past, but Keera hadn't. She'd stopped to pick up a handful of moss from the side of the track.

"Keera," Aiden called over the thrashing hooves and frantic cries of the horse. "We can't muck around. The spiders will be back any second."

While he was distracted, Not-Ruby wriggled out of his one-armed grip. He took her hand.

"Go, protect the children. I'll just be a moment." Keera used the moss to scrape at the sticky mass of web coating her sword with reasonable success and strode over to the horse.

A bulbous black spider crept back through the trees. It tugged on a line of silk, dragging the web-ensnared horse closer.

"Keera, watch out!"

Keera nodded, taking a moment to walk around the sticky silken trap.

"Come on," Aiden encouraged Not-Ruby. But the changeling refused to budge, watching with wide eyes as Keera threw clumps of moss onto the web and sliced through the resulting mess.

With a triumphant neigh, the horse rocked back onto its feet and galloped past the rest of the party, off after its mistress. Keera sprinted after it, the spider on her heels.

Aiden swung Not-Ruby back into his arms and pelted right into the middle of a group of travellers making their way to Market Town. Along with the rest of their party, there was a boy leading three goats to market, a woman cradling bundles of brown paper tied up with string, and some silver-haired wizards strutting along importantly.

"What the heck?" Corson said, glancing behind—sword in hand and ready to protect them from any pursuers—but the spiders had melted back into the bush.

Three wizards glared at them, muttering into their long silver beards.

Burcham mopped his forehead and pretended he hadn't been running, despite sucking in deep breaths of air. Aiden pulled himself together and placed Not-Ruby down on the ground again. "You'll like it here," he said. "Listen."

The noise of bartering and children's laughter rose to meet them along with the smell of hot cooked food.

Aiden's mouth watered from the tantalizing aromas and exotic spices wafting through the air, and the memory of eating hot-cooked pies from one of the many stalls.

"Now this is more like it!" Burcham exclaimed.

Aiden nodded. Through the trees, brightly coloured stalls and billowing tents made his heart soar.

"Everyone, meet you back in an hour," Corson said.

Burcham glared at him. "Yes. An hour. Keep an eye out for brands or anything that'll keep those spiders away. Now, I have very important things to do. Don't be late." He strode off.

The party fractured, with the Falkners, Corson, Burcham and Philips all going in different directions.

For an instant, Aiden felt free of the weight of responsibility and fear. Laughing, he pulled Keera into a half-embrace—little Pearl fast asleep in her pack between them. "Remember the first time we came here? Don't you love it?"

"Thanks for the hug," Keera said with a winsome smile. "But I guess I have a lot of memories of here. Which ones in particular?"

"The first time we came here together. I remember you loved the stalls, and there was that sweet old lady selling jewels and silks. It was magical. Didn't you think so?"

She smiled. "Hmm, I'm not so sure. Didn't a child pick your pocket?"

Aiden blushed scarlet. He recalled the moment vividly. Keera's fierce grin as she grabbed the kid by the ear and shook a king's ransom out of his pockets. Then she demanded that Aiden only take what was his, letting the boy keep the rest.

"And then there was the time one almost stole our wedding ring."

"You were so beautiful—how could I keep my eyes off you?"

"I'm sorry. What was that?" Keera cupped her chin in a hand, her sharp gaze softened by the dimple of amusement that creased her cheek.

Aiden bit back a grin. "Yes, I'm such a fool. You're so much more beautiful than the day I met you."

"Don't think I'm going to kiss you now," she said—and kissed him anyway.

"I don't deserve you."

"Ah, but I deserve you," she said. "And so do our children."

Aiden's heart skipped a beat.

They both turned to look at Changeling Ruby. She was staring at them with wide eyes that drank everything in.

Aiden forced a smile. "And for you, little one. We'll just have to do our best."

Not-Ruby nodded sagely.

"Would you like something to eat?"

She nodded again.

Aiden shrugged and passed her a handful of raisins. One by one, with the happiest of smiles, she let the treats slip through her fingers.

Distracted by the birds swooping down to gather Not-Ruby's abandoned raisins, Aiden wandered close to an old lady selling tinderboxes. She leaned on her cane and held the ornate box out in her crooked fingers.

"No, thank you," Aiden said. "I already have one." He smiled politely, determined not to be mixed up in any tinderbox nonsense.

"Well, aren't you a polite one," she muttered. "If I told you there was treasure—"

"Then you should keep it somewhere safe," Aiden replied. "I have a strict no-treasure policy." Also, a strict no-buying-tinderboxes policy. Both lessons had been passed down in the family's records.

"Very good," she muttered and waved him on. "Off you go, then, sonny, before I change my mind."

§

"Look what I got," Burcham said, waving a bundle of torches. "It's quite the ticket. More firebrands for everyone in case those spiders make another appearance."

Corson took four. "Never know when they'll come in handy." He glanced around. "Um. Just be careful with them. We burn down this forest and the spiders will be the least of our problems."

"Come on," Keera said. "Let's get going. I'd like to push on for New Avalon. It's a couple more hours and the children are already tired."

"Hmm. I'm not so sure," Burcham prevaricated. "We could—"

"That's why we're here. To forge the swords."

"But there's no need for all this hurry. I'd like to take a better look around." Burcham edged back toward the market.

Aiden swallowed. If he dared to say something about Ruby, they might get some help—but he couldn't risk telling Burcham anything. "Come on. Let's go. We, ah, don't want to be travelling in the dark."

Brian and Alice joined in the call. "The quicker we get there, the quicker we can get comfortable," Brian said. "I know I'd love a whiskey."

"Now you're talking." Corson turned to Burcham and raised an eyebrow. "What are we waiting for?"

"Hmm, I guess, nothing," Burcham said, and trailed after Corson as he set a brisk pace through the last of the stalls. Burcham eyed the silk and jewels on display as they went past. A gaggle of children appeared. "Give us a copper, Guv," one said, grimy hand extended to Burcham.

"Ignore them and they'll go away soon enough," Keera advised, failing to follow her own advice and discreetly falling behind the others to hand each child a biscuit and tell them to buzz off.

They eyed her hand on her sword, and all but one of them disappeared. A skinny girl wrapped in an old cloth that looked in even worse condition than the dirty blue dress beneath. She trailed along at enough of a distance that Aiden was happy to ignore her as he slowed to join Keera.

"We can't let Burcham throw his weight around like this," Keera said. "What if he stops my work? We have to bring our Ruby back from FaerLand before—"

Aiden had heard the stories. The idea of Ruby never coming home or succumbing to madness was unthinkable. There was only one *skerrick* of hope for Ruby and for them. "We're both doing everything we can, and time doesn't work quite the same in FaerLand. She might not even have noticed we're gone yet."

"Every second trapped with the maddening fae is a second too long."

Aiden nodded. That Ruby, and possibly Pearl, were trapped with fae was something he'd rather not face right now. He glanced down at baby Pearl and hoped she was indeed their daughter. She was eating, so that was a good sign. *Probably eating*, he corrected himself. With all the banana smooshed over her face, it was hard to tell. Not that that was unusual. On the best of days, most of Pearl's food ended up smeared over her face or dropped on the floor.

Their every decision was so difficult, like it might be their last. Coming to this place he loved and searching for certainty had felt right. And even now he was having second thoughts about the expedition, he still felt the need to verify that the love in his heart was not misplaced and Pearl was really Pearl. *Maybe because there will be no certainty once—and if—we cross the FaerLand border.*

Fortunately, the changeling who'd taken Ruby's place had been easy as pie, nothing like the horror stories he'd grown up with. He glanced down at Not-Ruby and smiled. "Thank you."

She nodded and kept on walking…far longer than the real Ruby could have.

They Know

Lettie shuddered at the revolting stench of all the humans in the crappy little town with its lingering aroma of decay, burned food, and astringent human magic. But the Sword Master and her husband were here, and if she was going to get Nada back, she had to find them and kill them.

People stared at her dress as she traipsed down the gravel road. Tatty beggars, their hands out, demanded coins she did not have. She shook her head, slipped around the back of the township and found an old sheet hanging from a clothesline strung out between two houses. Once it was wrapped around her tightly and tied over the shoulder, she rubbed some mud into the makeshift garment. Happy that she looked as tatty as the rest of the beggars in the village, she found a small group of half-starved children, and offered them her blue cap and a handful of nuts to follow the Sword Master and her party.

Except for Keera and her paltry biscuits, the humans refused to give even the tiniest gift to the younglings, and just kept on walking. *Fae would never allow their younglings to run around half-naked without feeding and clothing them.*

The Sword Master whispered to her fire-headed husband. "We have to bring our Ruby back from FaerLand before—"

Our Ruby? FaerLand?

They know! The stubs of her wings shivered as cold terror ran through her bones. *Is that why they're here? To murder Ruby*

Changeling? No, they could have done that Earthside. What are they going to do to Nada in Brocéliande, that they couldn't do on Earth? They could steal her magic or use their evil human magic against her. The possibilities were as endless as they were terrible.

And then Aiden leaned over, showing his teeth to her changeling. She wanted to tear him apart. *How can he threaten her so? She's a child. An almost child.*

Lettie needed to rescue Nada and hold faer tight and carry faer far away to safety. *My child. Not Queen Persephone's. I should never have done this. I should take her back. I should…* Plans chased through her head. Dreams. Nightmares. Nothing that would work.

A child for a child. Unless the Sword Master died and the bargain was broken, she couldn't just take Nada back.

How do I kill them?

The answer did not arrive. Not all the time they were walking through the forest of Brocéliande. The other beggars long gone, she dropped back, out of sight. And, too soon, they arrived at New Avalon.

The gates shrieked open, and Nada was carried through the threshold of ivy and iron.

Lettie watched the archers in the stone bell towers. Made from the earth's bones chipped and laid bare and stacked high for the humans, the towers stood to either side of the settlement overlooking the front gate. *A perfect vantage point. If humans weren't so blind they might have spotted her.* Lettie remained hidden in the brush. Merlin's rules still worked in Brocéliande.

Does that mean Merlin's alive?

The gate clunked closed with an eerie finality. Nada was gone—passed through a threshold that was closed to her, and into a world that stank of iron and paint and humans—their ugly houses squat along the ground in unnatural lines and colours. Her eyes brimmed with silver tears as she cursed the stone dust and all things human.

New Avalon

A iden waved up to the archer in the closest of the two stone bell towers standing vigil over the front gate of New Avalon. The archer didn't wave back. "Open the gates!" she yelled, and went back to staring out into the distance.

The ivy-covered gate shrieked open, and the weary group trudged through into the village. Newly thatched homey wooden cottages were set in neat rows to either side of the welcoming beige-stoned town hall that stood like a mini-castle behind a cobblestone courtyard.

The villagers, mostly newly settled Earthsiders, boiled out into the town square to greet them. Ruddy cheeks glowing, Mayor Harder had turned up to welcome Burcham with a firm handshake.

"Whose job is it to oil that gate?" Burcham demanded, strutting inside like he owned the place.

"Burcham, is that you? I never!" the mayor said. "You come to check up on me?"

"I'm impressed. You're doing a fantastic job running New Avalon," Burcham said in a voice that could melt butter. "This place is even prettier than I imagined."

He wasn't wrong. With all the thatched roofs and cobbles, the place had a nostalgic old-timey village look.

"It's like watching two peacocks in a yard of hens," Keera muttered.

Aiden nodded. He was less interested in the two men than in finding out if his mum and dad were around to help look after the kids. They said they'd be here. But maybe they were already off on an expedition somewhere. He'd just about given up when his mother emerged from behind the roses sprawling over their porch. "Alice! It's so good to see you!" she called.

"Hi, Mrs Andersen," Alice replied.

"Have you seen Aiden?" his mother added quizzically.

Aiden waved.

Mrs Andersen's jaw dropped. "Aiden! Keera! My goodness, how did I miss you? And our lovely granddaughters. Ruby, you get prettier every day."

Not-Ruby turned to stare at Aiden's mother, and then back at Aiden.

"Aren't you going to talk to your favourite grandmother?" Mrs Andersen said, gathering the changeling up in a hug.

Not-Ruby wriggled free and rushed back to Aiden. Her eyes wide, she stared at the people who thought they were her grandparents.

Aiden and Keera exchanged a glance. *The changeling fooled us. She should be fine for a few hours—hopefully.*

He'd not even mentioned the possibility to his parents, who were no doubt wondering right this minute why their talkative grandchild had turned silent.

"What is it? I know that look," his mother said. "I told you this whole relationship would end in tears." Her voice rose. "What is it?"

"It's nothing, Mum. Don't make that face. We've done nothing wrong. Just taking a break."

She frowned, casting about a piercing glance—but then nodded and ushered them all inside. "Well then, now you're here, let's get you settled in."

A.J. Ponder

"Thank you." Relief flooded Aiden. There was no way he could answer his mum's questions, but he sure appreciated her help. "That'll give Keera a chance to get started." He glanced around, but she'd already slipped away, leaving him with his parents and the children.

"I'm so pleased you're here." His mother watched Not-Ruby intently. "All the fresh air. It's so good for the children."

"Just for a while," Aiden said by way of agreement.

His mum looked at him sideways. She knew avoidance tactics when she heard them.

His father appeared from behind the cottage. "There you are." He strode up and clapped Aiden on the shoulder. "Good to see you, son. Pleased you made the cut. But do watch that tongue of yours, son. People talk, and it's never a good idea to bite the hand that feeds you. We have to earn a living, too, you know."

Great, so Keera and I can't even make the tiniest bit of constructive criticism about the Society. Aiden bit his tongue. If he talked, the only thing he'd get from his father was a blazing row. He had other priorities. "Mum, do you mind if I leave the children with you?"

"Of course, you go and help Keera set up the forge. I'll look after my lovely grandchildren."

Pearl gooed. *Surely that's a good sign?*

Here I am second-guessing myself again. Besides, Keera is right— going into FaerLand once is dangerous enough.

Changeling Ruby sucked her fingers like a baby, her expression unreadable. Aiden ignored another sharp glance from his mother and fled along the cobbled walkway down the side of the village hall to the tents and temporary housing clustered around the forge. People from all around Brocéliande came to the village to use it, most of them not staying long enough to set up home.

As Keera's fame had spread far and wide, so had tales of the famous swords she'd created on the iconic forge. From being a forgotten curiosity, now, it seemed every hero wanted a sword forged in the fires of King Arthur. Gnomes, goblins, warriors, men, women, and even children sat with their supplies bundled up around them. Some had pop-up tents and deck chairs to lounge in; others were lying on the grass, or propped up against large river stones picked up from the River Des Os that ran behind the settlement. A simple wooden suspension bridge, hanging from thick twisted steel cables, spanned the gorge.

Keera, keen to get started, was confronting Burcham not so far from the queue, their voices gravelly and low as though they were trying to stop their conversation from carrying on the sultry late-afternoon air.

"Keera, you must be exhausted. Why don't we get you settled in first, while I sort this?" Burcham waved his hand at the sweat-soaked smiths working the forge behind him.

Keera stepped forward. Hands on hips, she glared over Burcham's shoulder at the forge. "Tomorrow then."

"We have a lot of people working. I thought a day or two…"

Aiden burst into the conversation. "We only have limited time—you wouldn't want to waste that. Keera is the best. And you know it."

"You don't understand—the forge is booked."

"*You* don't understand," Keera said, pulling out her contract. "I'm here. Therefore, I can use the forge whenever I want. See that. So long as any swords I make are intended for people with *a close and friendly relationship with The Society.*"

Burcham gaped as he stared at the creased and battered paper carrying his own signature. "What? You're pulling that old thing out now? You can't be serious?"

Aiden stepped in. "Serious as a sledgehammer." *How long has Ruby been in FaerLand? Minutes? Hours? Every second she's in that place, she's in mortal danger.* "What about all your talk about never breaking a contract…" Aiden began.

Burcham sighed and walked over to the line of people who were waiting at the forge and watching the discussion avidly. "I'm so sorry about this, everybody. I know you've paid for your slots, but Keera's contract must stand. She'll be using the forge in the morning. Those of you who can't get your work done today will just have to wait a little longer."

From the not-so patient queue, a groan rippled through the waiting smiths and angry glances were directed at him and Keera.

Tomorrow? "But—" Aiden started.

Keera shook her head in defeat. "It's okay. Morning will be soon enough. I'll finish the design on the long table in your parents' workshop tonight. All being well, I'll be able to complete the sword tomorrow."

And then what? Sneaking through the Sister Tree and into FaerLand at night?

Behind them, agitated smiths clustered around Burcham, their voices raised in anger. Biceps were displayed and knuckles cracked. "She's just going to barge in tomorrow? That was our day. We've been waiting all week—"

Then, from the middle of the queue, a raven-haired princess stood up, gold crown askew. "Awesome. Let's learn how to forge like the master herself. We can watch, can't we?"

Keera nodded.

The princess grinned. "I can help if you like."

"I would very much appreciate that," Keera said, and was suddenly inundated by a deluge of offers.

Loud wailing pulled Aiden's attention away from Keera and the forge. Coming down the path by the town hall, red and angry, Pearl was crying in her grandmother's arms.

She's a fae.

She's not a fae…

The thought hurt, even as a small someone pulled at his hand. *Changeling-Ruby.* Her fingers wrapped around his.

"Yes, we're going to have a bit of a rest. Let's go make pancakes."

The changeling nodded and dragged him back to his parents' cottage.

"And when we're inside," Aiden's mother snapped, "we're going to have a little word about your…situation." She glanced down at Ruby and then back up at Aiden. "Understand?"

Damn.

"Pancakes first," Aiden insisted, suddenly realising how hungry he was.

Not-Ruby clapped her hands together joyfully. Strange child. Like she cared about pancakes she wouldn't eat.

SACRIFICE

Lettie crept as close to the ivy as she could bear, the wretched leaves' stinging itch crawling over her skin. She tried not to scratch as she listened through the iron railings—her ears close enough to the cold iron to feel their frozen burn.

So, the humans were going to be making swords. They could so easily kill her changeling. *Did they plan to sacrifice her on the altar of human greed?* Altars of human greed were a thing, apparently. Another reason Nada shouldn't be so trusting of the humans.

Lettie paced the settlement's perimeter, looking for gaps in their defences, but the humans had placed cold steel the whole way around, even into the river itself. Night fell, and she curled up in a hollow beside a mossy tree trunk. *If I do this right, Keera will be dead soon, and it will be all over.* Sleep was fleeting with this thought and worse, chasing through her mind.

In the morning, Lettie woke, cold and wretched. She wished she'd kept the sheet from the village yesterday—even if it would have made her easier to spot. People in the village were moving. She leaned in to see what was happening. A looting party, by the look of the people milling around in the courtyard with swords and bows. Aiden was in the middle of it, with Nada on his hip. *So many swords surrounding faer. If they'd wanted to kill Nada, they could have a hundred times over.*

An older lady, with the same determined jawline as Aiden, strode up to him and grabbed his shoulder. "I don't like to leave…." She looked askance at Changeling Ruby. "But after all these years, we're so close to the Library of Alexandria. And who knows what wonders it contains. It might even help with your current predicament."

"We'll be fine," Aiden insisted. "We have a plan."

A plan? Lettie's ears pricked up. *Making a sword is hardly a plan? What are they up to?*

"Just don't get into any trouble while I'm away," Aiden's mother said. "And please don't leave without me."

The humans with Nada only just got here. What are they up to? Are they planning to make a sword and murder Nada outside FaerLand?

"If Pearl is alright," Aiden was saying, "we'll leave her with you. But only if you get back in time. We can't wait."

Who cares about that mewling brat? What about my changeling?

"Perhaps you're right." Aiden's mother nodded. "Alice is here. She'll do almost anything for you. You know she still talks about how Keera gifted her husband that sword. You know, I've never seen her so proud of anything in her life—excepting her children, of course. Oh yes, and remember not to breathe a word to your father. It's best he doesn't know." Mrs Andersen inclined her head toward two gentlemen hurrying toward them.

Aiden turned and waved. "Hello, Burcham. Father."

"I'm so pleased you're coming with us, Mr Burcham," Aiden's father said.

Pleased? Lettie huffed. *Could Aiden's parents look any less happy?* Watching them, Lettie daydreamed about killing them all, saving her child, and being rewarded by the great Queen Persephone with a ball in her honour. And, more importantly, her changeling Nada being recognised as the first young fae in a thousand years.

The dream was so beautiful, her blue spider-silk gown all flowing and clinging in just the right ways. The music a triumphant crescendo as the Queen acknowledged her success, and her bravery.

"You're going to love flying," Mr Andersen was saying. "We're going to be taking the griffons out over the water.... I can't describe how thrilling it is to take to the air on one of the majestic beasts."

"It's just so freeing," Aiden's mother said, a fierce glint in her eye. "I love the way they swoop over the ocean."

"Well, that is exciting." Burcham cradled his stomach. "Maybe, I um..."

Aiden's father patted Burcham's back with considerable vigour. "Yes, very exciting. I love the way griffons make me feel alive, knowing I could tumble from the saddle at any moment."

What a strange man Aiden's father was. Could he not tell that Mr Burcham felt sick at the thought of riding griffons? And only sensible, too. Griffons stank. And more than that, they had a penchant for plunging into the salt spray of the ocean, avoiding dashing themselves on the rocks below by less than a hand-span. Lettie shuddered. In her opinion, the only thing worse than the ocean was cold steel.

Three more human males sidled toward the growing cluster. Burcham waved them over. "Faulkner! Corson! Philips! You got everything you need? I mean, I'd come and investigate the spiders, too, but I'm going to—"

"That's a good idea. Why don't you go and see the spiders?" Aiden's father interrupted. "I'm sure it'll be fascinating."

Burcham choked back a laugh. "No, no, I couldn't, possibly. Although I have to say I'm terribly sad I can't be in two places at once. Still, my knowledge of law is somewhat greater than my knowledge of spiders. I'm sure it will hold us in good stead if we find the Great Library."

"I don't think it's right," Faulkner snapped. "I should be going on the Library of Alexandra expedition. It's my calling. I've been working on finding it for just over a decade now. The Andersens…"

"And what about us?" Aiden's mother asked. "We've more than put in the work."

Prof Faulkner glanced at Mrs Andersen. "Ah, I was only saying that you and I are the experts, unlike…" They all looked askance at Burcham. "Anyway, I'm sorry. That's not fair. It's, ah…. I really don't see what help I can be with the spiders, and you know exactly what Dr Wyrden was looking for."

"Oh, dear me, no," Burcham jumped in. "I don't have the experience here. It's got to be you." He performed a wide-armed shrug, as if it was all beyond his authority.

Lettie didn't blame either of them for not wanting to go anywhere near the spiders. Arachne was nice enough, but some of her progeny were touchy, to say the least.

"You could leave the poor spiders alone," Aiden muttered.

A good point. But Burcham didn't answer it. Maybe he didn't hear. Then Aiden turned to Corson. "I really don't like this. You know how dangerous riling the spiders on the fae border is. Every village has warned us that the fae are brutal if people stray too close to their border."

Brutal, says the human. Lettie rolled her eyes and wished, despite everything, that Zadie was here to poke fun at the humans, not to mention lending a hand to rescue Nada.

"Don't worry," Corson whispered. "We're going to be keeping a safe distance. I've got everything to live for."

Aiden raised his eyebrows. "Who's the special person?"

"That'd be telling." His cheeks tinged pink, Corson stared into the distance.

Burcham pulled out his notebook. "I do hope that nobody here is about to disobey a direct order." He glared at Aiden, Corson and Faulkner.

A.J. Ponder

"No, it's fine." Faulkner hefted a day pack. "Aiden, give my regards to your lovely wife."

"I will," Aiden said.

Lovely? Humans are crazy. Surely, they are aware of Keera's many crimes, even if they're not aware that she's so hated that Queen Persephone has broken the Myrddin Pact to punish her.

Keera appeared, carrying Pearl. She reached over to take Nada from Aiden. "There we are." Her words were soft and kind in a way that made Lettie doubt Nada had been doing her job. Still, Lettie had to admit to herself, that for all the energy channelled into breaking the woman, Keera was neither broken, nor apparently worthy of the trouble. Except for her abominable metallurgy— mixing blood of the fae with cold steel and the tears of the sun— she appeared pretty decent for a human. *But others have killed fae, and worse, and Queen Persephone has done nothing. So why is she incensed about Keera's misuse of fae blood? She cares not that her soldiers are practically encased in it.*

Changeling Ruby's eyes flicked toward Lettie before going back to staring up at Keera with a hint of a smile, her dark eyelashes framing luminescent brown eyes.

Lettie's jealousy surged, crushing her chest. She struggled to breathe, acid burning her throat with the words she did not dare to yell. *"Why aren't they dead already? Can't you see you're putting our lives in danger by not killing either of the parents like you were ordered?"* Instead, Lettie swallowed the tide of anger and settled back into her vigil.

The older Mrs Andersen picked up Pearl. "You stay strong and healthy and stay away from fae, hear me?" The baby gurgled. Changeling Ruby flinched, but Mrs Andersen didn't seem to notice.

Lettie shivered. Keeping her head down, she watched Aiden and the defiler Sword Master wave goodbye to the explorers from her hidey-hole under the thorn hedge.

"Don't worry, we'll be back before dark, dear." Mrs Andersen handed back the human baby, who was kicking her cute, fat little leg, drooling and murmuring "ba, ba."

"We've got an encouraging lead that the library's on an island. It may only be an hour's flight from the griffon eyrie that overlooks the beach." She waved and joined Burcham and John, who were already striding out through the gates not so far from Lettie's vantage point.

"Good luck!" Aiden called.

Mrs Andersen's eyes lit up. "Today's the day we're going to find it. I just know it in my bones. A lovely smithy said they'd been there, and I believe him."

Mr Andersen frowned. "We've had tips before."

"This one is credible. We said they could use Merlin's forge for free if they helped us find the library."

"And if we do find The Library of Alexandria," Burcham piped up, "it's going to open up all the wonders of Brocéliande."

Lettie clamped her hand over her mouth.

It was terrible news. The library did indeed hold wonders, and the last thing any fae wanted was for these greedy Earthside humans to get hold of them. Bad enough the Brocéliande humans were already there—and all the goblins. *I'll have to go tell Queen Persephone—and leave Nada alone with the humans.*

Aiden and Keera turned back toward the forge.

Lettie followed, staying close to the perimeter, her hands stinging with the burning itch of ivy every time she peeked through the boundary fence. By the time she caught up, the queue of people waiting to use the forge were fawning over Keera or grumbling that they wouldn't get a look in today. The rest of the village cheerfully ignored the sword smiths, too busy minding children, thatching the roofs, gardening and doing all the many chores that made this

A.J. Ponder

unsightly village so awful. That and the stomach-turning stench of smoke and iron coming from the forge.

I've got to be brave. I've got to do something. Lettie imagined Wyrden laughing at her, sweeping in with spiders and destroying everything. And still she hesitated, caught in terrible indecision. Too scared to slip into the human encampment while the gates were open, too scared to leave Nada here all alone and tell Queen Persephone the news. And all the while her changeling became more Ruby than her Nada, and all, doubtlessly, while King Hades and Queen Persephone's rage grew.

FORGING

Keera turned from Alice to see how well the princess was doing with the bellows. A fine job—heat shimmered from the white-hot flames. She grinned her thanks to the raven-haired princess.

Pearl squealed and crawled across the clearing toward them, nappy trailing. She was chasing after Tailor. "Careful!" Keera yelled. "Hot! Hey Aiden! Can you come and help?" *Where is he?*

"I've got them." Alice grabbed Pearl under one arm and Tailor under the other. "Come on, let's give your mum and dad room to think. Thank goodness *you're* behaving, Ruby. You're the only good child here. How about you and I go look for Hazel and Arthur, and see what trouble they're getting up to?"

"Thanks," Keera said, turning back to focus on the steel. It helped not to think about Ruby and Alice for a moment and focus on creating the perfect sword for Pearl.

Aiden sloshed the bucket of river water down in his hurry and set to work with the bellows, taking over from the raven-haired princess. It had been easy to forget the young woman who was now watching with such care, drinking in every hammer-blow. She'd taken over Aiden's usual role so seamlessly.

Keera pulled her thoughts back to her work, and hammered until the sword was glowing with inner heat and magic. Carefully, she pulled out the wooden strips with the silver and gold script and laid them on the blade.

So close now.

"No," Changeling Ruby said, her voice like grating stones. "No—Blood—Fae."

"Ruby, you spoke!" Keera yelled. Half thrilled, half shocked. *What blood? Could it be something to do with the gold and silver I'm laying on the iron?* All the tales she'd heard about fae clashed in her head. Fae hated iron, but their attitudes to gold and silver ranged from covetous greed to hate, depending on who was telling the story.

Alice came running back. "What is it?"

"It seems the child spoke for the first time," the princess interjected into the awkward silence. "Congratulations."

Alice shivered. "What? Ruby spoke? Of course Ruby can speak. What's wrong? Keera. What's wrong with Ruby?"

Keera shook her head. Holding in the flood of tears was like cramming bricks into her heart.

"Hazel! Arthur!" Alice called. "Could you please take the little ones and look for blackcurrants or strawberries in the town garden? The more you find, the more we can have for dessert."

The children out of sight, Alice turned to Keera. "It's not…" Her question hung in the air like thunderclouds before a storm.

"Don't say it," Aiden growled, glancing over at the line of smiths trying their best to pretend an interest in anything else.

Caught in Alice's gaze, Keera found she couldn't lie. "Yes," she whispered. "We've got to rescue her." The enormity of the task weighed on her soul until the dam of tears broke.

Dimly, she heard Alice trying to comfort her and the hiss of water dripping on hot metal as her tears hit the newly forged steel. Now she'd started crying, she was not sure she could ever stop, even as she tapped on the design to fix it, and plunged it back into the fire.

§

If Lettie was brave enough, or strong enough, she'd go in right now and push the woman into the flames…and yet she didn't. Mostly because she wasn't sure how to get through the human's barricades.

I could knock on the gate. Pretend to be an adventurer. A travelling smithy—but without any metal, or even a mallet. But, no. It would not be very believable. All she could do was watch her changeling at a distance.

"No," Changeling Ruby spoke, her voice grating worse than a hob-goblin's. "No—Blood—Fae."

Lettie's breath caught. Her changeling had spoken. It was like a dream come true. She imagined the magnificent coming-out ball, the ceremony, the praise—and despite the miserable thorns and the rotten hiding place—she felt like her heart would burst.

But only if she and Nada could rise to their task.

No. Everyone in FaerLand needed to know how special her changeling was. She'd waited too long, risked too much. Queen Persephone would know what to do.

This whole thing was a test. A test her benevolent queen would set right. Persephone would come in here with her army and devastate the humans and their stupid village with its stupid forge, and bring Nada back triumphant.

With one last glance behind her, Lettie sprinted out of the clearing, all the miles to the FaerLand border where fae soldiers were amassing alongside an army of spiders.

They're going to attack. Soon. "Quick," she demanded. "Where's the Queen? I have urgent news."

One pointed in the direction of a giant oak tree just inside the border of FaerLand.

Lettie straightened her bedraggled dress, reached for her lost hat and zipped toward where Queen Persephone was shading herself under the giant oak.

Zadie, still in flutter form, shot out from among the branches, reaching Lettie just before she made it into the clearing under the giant oak. "My goodness, what a sight," she clucked, grinning madly.

"Zadie, Zadie, you'll never believe it. Nada talked. We have to save faer," Lettie babbled, deliriously happy.

Zadie's grin dropped.

"Don't you understand?" Lettie hated the pleading tone of her voice. The triumph that had surged through her faded as fast as morning dew. *Surely Zadie's betrayal was one of her short-lived piques of anger.* "Nada is fae. Properly, fully fae."

"I'm so worried," Zadie said. "You have to go back before Queen Persephone sees you."

"But—" Lettie objected.

"Abandoning your post. The punishment will be dire. And abandoning a fae will only make it worse. Hurry, and I'll cover for you. No, wait a moment. I have an idea." Zadie flitted away through the giant trees around the edge of the clearing, leaving Lettie confused.

In moments, Wyrden emerged from behind a trunk, walking toward them with his white cane and a grin splitting his white-whiskered chin. "Ah, there she is. Just like you said, Zadie."

Zadie nodded and fluttered back up into the trees. Lettie sighed, wishing she wasn't going to be going straight back into Brocéliande.

"Listen up," Wyrden said. "We're going to attack. Provide a distraction. Don't worry, the spiders will get you in over the iron, and then you can kill the Sword Master and her husband with this." He held out a silvery blade.

Lettie examined the shiny edge and whispered. "Titania silver."

"Of course it is."

"But isn't that sacrilege? Isn't silver only for our soldiers?"

"It's for whomever the queen says it's for. Do you question her?"

Queen Persephone must have her reasons. Lettie shook her head earnestly. She wanted no part of this.

"Traitor." Zadie snorted from up in the branches.

"I'm no traitor," Lettie said. "There's never been anyone more loyal. And I'm going to prove it by doing what needs to be done." *All I have to do is kill the Sword Master to rescue Nada and get everything I ever wanted. How hard can it be?*

A.J. Ponder

TEARS

Keera leaned into Aiden as he wrapped his arms around her. The pungent smell of sweat and fire and steel bringing her back to the moment, she threw the hair from Pearl's brush into the water. Then, with Aidan's hands over hers, she pulled the blade from the fire and plunged it into the water barrel. With a hiss, the water erupted in an explosion of steam.

This was the moment.

They pulled up the blade. As the steam cleared, the sword glinted silver and gold in precise, intricate swirls.

It was perfect. Triumphantly, Keera declared over the roar of the fire. "Forged in the fires of King Arthur, I name you Wisdom of Pearl, Demonslayer and Protector of the Innocent. You are Pearl at your heart and will respond to none other."

Alice applauded. "Your swords are so beautiful. I wish I was half as talented."

"Thank you, Alice. That's very sweet of you to say, when it is in fact your talents that we'll most need—as soon as we're sure about Pearl. I know this is a difficult favour, but," Aiden nodded at Ruby, "as you can see, our need is dire."

Alice shivered. "Travel the paths of the dead? It's dangerous. More dangerous than you know."

"The fae are protective of their border. We're not sure if we can get in any other way. You can show us. Please." Aiden held his breath.

"It was a dangerous folly of youth."

"It's everything. Please show us how to do it."

"No. Brian and I will help any way we can, but…no." Alice's body convulsed in shivers.

"It's alright, Alice." Keera's mind spun. The triumph of the flawless sword quickly replaced by the uncertainty of their mission. Still, Alice was right. Aiden should never have suggested the paths of the dead—except it might be less dangerous than walking through the border of the fae kingdom.

"You'll just have to make it through the border," Alice whispered, flicking a furtive glance in Not-Ruby's direction.

"We wouldn't ask if we thought there was another way," Aiden persisted, but Alice didn't seem to hear.

§

Lettie sighed. Here she was, back again, and no sign of the Sword Master or the spiders. *Patience.*

Clutching the silver sword Wyrden had given her, she waited in the shade of the trees for the attack to begin. But maybe there was something she could do while she waited. She grasped a fig tree, begged it for a small branch, and pulled.

The branch came cleanly away.

She whispered enlightening things, so that it would be strong, and settled down to wait. She needed to be ready.

Spiders were quiet creatures, not so much inclined to warfare as devouring unsuspecting prey…there wouldn't be much warning.

A.J. Ponder

No Time to Waste

I've never made a sword so fast." Keera said, tapping away to secure the pommel. A process she called peening the tang. Aiden thought he'd misheard the first time she'd said it.

"It's still a work of art." Unlike the workroom. It was a trash site. Aiden was fumbling scattered tools into cupboards and drawers, and hoping he'd put them back in the right place. His mother would complain…if she got the chance before they left. The blade almost glowed with power. "I think it's a match to her sister's—and that's saying something."

Keera nodded. "I think it'll do." She examined the blade inch by inch. Checking the pearls were firmly placed into the pommel. One a warm gold, and the other a rare black pearl, shimmering purple and green. Together, they symbolised the sweet wee child that had fallen asleep on the couch, fingers in her mouth. *Hopefully.*

"Now for the moment of truth." Keera swallowed, bringing the sword's pommel near the infant's crib.

"I've got it." Carefully, Aiden placed Pearl's sleepy hand on the hilt.

Pearl's fingers wrapped around the leather-bound pommel, a smile curving her wee lips. The sword's black pearl glimmered in the afternoon light.

Keera let out a long breath. "Not fae."

They hugged in relief.

And still my parents are not back.

"We should leave the blade with Pearl," Keera said, throwing things out of her pack and into a day bag. "Do you think the Faulkners will be able to look after her until your parents arrive? We have to go."

Aiden had packed light. A change of clothes, a coat and a couple of torches. Clothes and tools were left strewn across their room like a hurricane had passed through. He wrapped baby Pearl in her blanket and pulled her into his arms. She murmured sleepily, head against his breast as Keera opened the cottage door.

Out in the courtyard, Ruby and Alice's three kids were playing a game that involved hopscotch and climbing a tree while Alice stared out over the gate.

"No sign of them?" Keera asked.

"Not yet."

"Hey, thank you so much for all your help today," Aiden said.

Alice nodded, distractedly.

"We were…"

"You know, I'd rather make swords than look after five children. Where would we have been without you?"

Alice shrugged. "Stuck with a changel—" She glanced over at Ruby and shook her head. "Anyway, I should like to know where that husband of mine is."

All the things that could have gone wrong rushed through Aiden's head. Killed by demons, ambushed by spiders, attacked by brigands on the road.

He shook away an image of his parents being dropped by griffons and dashed onto the rocks.

"I'm sure they've all just had a busy day," Keera said supportively. "Lost track of time." Keera shot him a look. If she didn't know where the library was, he'd eat his hat. Fortunately, nobody else noticed.

"I hope they've found it at last," Aiden said, shrugging on the light backpack and checking his sword-scabbard was strapped on just right.

"The Library of Alexandria? Yes, I hope so, too," Alice said wistfully. "Brian will be sad he wasn't the first, but he would love to visit it." She glanced over at the children playing stop-out behind the town hall. "Damn that Burcham. He stirs up trouble and then he runs off, leaving Brian to babysit his inevitable disaster while he goes on Brian's dream mission."

Aiden nodded. "Imagine all the lost secrets hidden in that library. I think we'd all love to go."

"Lost secrets?" Keera's lips twitched into a half-smile. "Can't be all that lost if they're safely stored in a library."

Aiden raised his eyebrows. "Yes. It does seem odd that we haven't found it yet."

"Mmm," Keera said, taking her non-committal comments to the library to new lows.

"Do you think—?" Alice wrung her hands. "I don't know what I'd do if anything happened to him. I just…I don't want you to go yet."

The sun was dipping on the horizon. Aiden wondered about mentioning the mirror again, but Alice was clearly in no state to take them that way. Besides, who would look after Alice's children, and Pearl? "I'm sorry, Alice. We've got to go." Any later and they'd be crossing into FaerLand in the dark. Any later and Ruby would be stuck there another day—by Brocéliande time.

Keera followed Aiden's gaze out across the forest, and turned back to Alice. "Alice, are you going to be alright? Just until…"

Alice hugged them. "Of course. Go. Save your child."

"Thank you." Reluctantly, Aiden handed over their youngest daughter, trying not to worry that this might be the last time they saw her. "Bye darling. Look after Alice."

Sleepily, Pearl open and closed her little hand in an awkward wave. "Bub-ba."

"Ruby! We have to go," Keera called.

Changeling Ruby ran to hug Aiden's legs…stopped and backed off. Inching herself away from the sword Aiden had unsheathed.

A thin cry rang out. It was coming from outside the fence. They all turned.

Demons? A forest animal? "There hasn't been trouble for ages…" Aiden trailed off, replaying the cry in his mind.

"And there won't be now." Keera pushed her shoulders back, hand ready on her pommel, but not drawing her sword.

"No, of course not," Aiden agreed. There was no point frightening the children. "Are you going to be alright, Alice?"

"We'll be fine." Alice said. "Come on, children. Let's make some dinner. Your father will be in soon and he'll be hungry."

"Can we have sausages and chips?" Arthur asked.

"But…" Hazel protested. "Someone's coming. We saw."

"The watch people would warn us…" Aiden said.

The bell in the tower rang, its metallic clang sounding once, twice—people were coming, Hazel was right. A third ring clanged over the courtyard.

Danger!

Keera drew her sword, and she was not the only one. The ring of swords being drawn echoed around the village.

Alice stood unmoving. "Dammit!" Aiden swore. He gathered Pearl and then Ruby into his arms. "Children, stay close to me. We have to make it to the Faulkner's cottage, okay?"

The boys nodded, and Hazel drew her bow and joined them, moving in close.

A.J. Ponder

Ruby's red hair spilling over her shoulders, the changeling grated, "The Spinners are angry."

§

Lettie shivered, clutching herself tight as she saw Changeling Ruby—Nada. Fae was glorious, faer red hair spilling over her shoulders. A spark of power in faer fingers as fae muttered, "The Spinners are angry." Aiden glanced down at Nada as if puzzled. But Nada's speech was clear as day. Fae was no longer merely a Changeling. Fae had Become. Nobody could doubt it. Not now.

And the changeling was right. Wyrden had done his job, riling up the spiders. They swarmed in the trees around the village, ready to strike. It wasn't like the spiders to come so far into Brocéliande territory. She never really thought they'd attack the humans—and now, here they were.

§

"Earthsiders," Keera muttered. *If that Philips has stirred up the spiders, there will be blood... You can't reverse time. Deal with now.* Satisfied Aiden and the children were headed for safety, Keera headed closer to the gate where a small crowd was forming, swords ready.

Footsteps echoed in the gathering dark, pelting towards them. A small band of humans by the look of it.

Keera squinted at the shadowy group. Two people, with one trailing. They didn't appear to be in a very effective attack formation. *Maybe it's a sortie...or the border guards are mistaken and it's not an attack at all.* They were older...

She rolled her eyes. It was Aiden's parents. They bounded into the clearing with Burcham close behind. "We found it! We found it. You'll never believe it," Aiden's mother gushed. "We found the Library of Alexandria! It was everything we could have wished.

Bigger than a castle with scrolls and books from floor to ceiling." She waved a little gold and black book at the crowd. "There were giants and goblins, and students from thousands of places we never knew existed—"

"Congratulations. That's fantastic, amazing," Alice said through a clearly forced smile. "I can't wait to see it." She peered behind the trio into the dark forest.

Her husband's still missing, and the warning call's gone out—it isn't like the sentries to be mistaken. Something is out there.

"And there's a Room of Many Ways," Burcham said, completely missing the flat tone of Alice's voice, the drawn swords and the acrid smell of danger in the air. "It leads to all corners of the Earth. You know what that means?"

"We might be able to create a non-forest portal," Aiden's father gushed. "It'll mean a new era of exploration. No more tramping for half a day to get to the Three Sisters tree. No more dangerous mirrors. No more…"

A shrill scream cut through into the clearing.

"Coming in hot!"

Corson? Keera didn't think she'd ever heard him so panicked.

Philips, Corson and Faulkner thundered into the clearing—a pack of enormous spiders on their heels. Their matt-black exoskeletons partially reflected the setting sun while their mandibles snapped at Corson's heels.

Corson turned and waved a sword at the beasts swarming near the iron fence.

"Light the lanterns!" Burcham roared.

"Swords ready!" Keera glanced back. Aiden was still in the town square. He must have dallied when he saw his parents arrive—but he was still closer to the Faulkner's cottage than Alice, who was only turning back now. Keera's heart throbbed to see her children clutched in his arms—knowing one of them wasn't her child at all.

Keera waved, but he'd turned away. He was doing his best to get the five children to safety. *To help him, and them, I need to do my job.* She raced out to protect Corson and his small party. "Behind me," she called.

"Stuff that," Corson said. He closed in on Keera until they were standing shoulder to shoulder. "Aiden would never forgive me if something happened to you. Now, let's fight."

§

With a rustle of leaves, and the skitter of hundreds of legs, several fast-moving spiders burst past Lettie. The two jumping spiders in the lead leapt at Keera and her friend as they played defence for the two less athletic figures running through the gate.

Both slaughtered their spiders with brutally careless swipes.

Spiders screamed, and Lettie covered her ears.

Keera and the man used the spiders' hesitation to jump back through the gate.

Four more spiders rushed the pair—three giant, giant house spiders and a cutely striped zebra spider with soulful eyes.

Keera slashed, ripping off several pairs of the giant house spiders' front legs, and then the gate crashed closed, crushing the poor zebra spider with its iron bars.

Furious, another wave of giant spiders dashed up onto the fence and began weaving a silken swathe over the cold steel and treacherous ivy.

More villagers joined the humans' defence, swords stabbing the oncoming spiders. Terrified, some spiders scuttled back to safety, but more were coming, aiming away from the front gates and toward areas of the fence with fewer defenders. Lettie followed the trail of a redback spider just behind the main attack. Hands clenching and unclenching, she waited for it to spin enough web to smother the ivy-covered iron fence. When it was safe, she scrambled over the spiderweb, holding her fig branch and sword under one arm and climbing with the other. Carelessly, she brushed a rivet of cold iron from the fence, and sucked in a cry, her fingers blistering. Not that anyone would notice any sound she made with all the heavy fighting.

Safely over, she darted under a lemon tree and glanced around. *Where's the Sword Master?* She was in amongst the fighting, but Aiden…he was out in the open, Nada and the human child in his arms. He was hurrying toward a cottage with roses in the front garden.

The red-back she'd followed scuttled away from the fence, circling by the bushes at the edge of the courtyard as if unsure who to attack first. Then it darted toward Aiden and the children.

My chance.

Lettie ran. While Aiden was distracted with the spider, she'd snatch Nada into her arms and take her far away from the stupid humans who were so careless as to rile up some of the most dangerous creatures she knew. *Wyrden's doing. The humans and everyone else are just sticks in his hands. Sticks to make fire.*

Stop thinking. Just kill the man and take Nada back.

She held up the blade of Titania silver, and her fig-tree stick, and charged.

"Die, defiler!" she screamed.

Aiden's Bane

Hugging Pearl and the changeling tight, Aiden's relief that his parents had arrived safely vanished.

The spiders were so fast. All he could think about was getting the children inside.

"Hazel, with me. Closer."

"But I want to fight. Can't you hear them? They need me."

"With me," he growled. "We have a job to do. Keep your brothers and my babies safe. Then we'll see."

She nodded and, with the clang and cry of battle ringing around them, helped shepherd her reluctant brothers to the cottage.

A red-splotched creature scuttled toward them, shiny jaws snapping.

"Hurry!" Aiden yelled. "Get to your house. Run!"

The Andersen children fled, Hazel dragging Tailor into the safety of the house, just steps away.

More villagers, their dinners and evenings disrupted, were tumbling out of their houses. Some raced into the fray. Some ran back into their houses. None were close enough to help.

The two children wriggling in his arms, Aiden ran as fast as he could. The spider was faster. It was circling to cut them off from his parents' cottage.

Pearl wailed.

The red-splotched spider flashed in, and Changeling Ruby flung out a hand. Rearing up onto its back legs, it lifted its pincers.

Aiden swivelled. Clutching the children tight, he turned so his body was between the giant red-backed spider and the children he was carrying, and ran.

Help! The word died in his throat.

A fae was running at them, a glowing wand in one hand and a silver sword in the other. "Die, defiler."

Changeling Ruby screamed, hugging Pearl tight. All around, the battle swirled.

"I'm sorry," Aiden whispered to the children, his failure crashing against his chest like a tidal wave. Behind him, the peat-smell of spider rushed in.

PITCHING IN

Keera spared a glance back. Aiden was gone, lost behind the crowd of villagers pouring across the square to help with the defence. There was nothing she could do for him and the children except help repel the threat pouring over the warded fence and into the village.

With a cry, she bounded forward, Corson by her side. Spiders were everywhere; some dripping venom from their fangs, others weaving thick spiderweb over the wall. Twenty spiders swept forward, all larger than a man; brown, furry, giant wood spiders, shiny black death spiders, and a giant white orb-weaver.

Keera stabbed at the head of another one of those fast-moving brown and cream striped spiders with four huge eyes. It jumped back. More rushed to take its place.

"They have the high ground," Corson shouted. "We need more people."

"Ring the bell!" Burcham yelled from behind them. "There must be more fighters."

Smiths appeared, joining Corson and her on the front line.

An arrow streaked over their heads. And another. *There must be reinforcements up in the belltower.* A white knobbly spider fell, an arrow through its abdomen, before pulling its body up and ploughing into the cordon of fighters.

Some of the villagers had pitchforks—they were surprisingly effective at keeping the spiders at bay. Others had hammers, and many had swords, some absolutely beautiful pieces of work, like the one the dark-haired princess was wielding, gleaming silver and orange in the setting sun.

A smith whirled a hammer overhead and threw it at a white spider's abdomen. The spider crumpled under the blow. "Ah got ya, ya bastard," the smith crowed. Moments later, the spider scrabbled to its feet and stabbed him with venom-dripping fangs.

Keera raced to help, but people were already there, slicing the creature to pieces.

More spiders surged over the wall. Too many. And worse, they were using the fence to their advantage as higher ground. "Slow retreat!" she yelled, looking for cover. A few trees, some watering troughs that could be upended…and the houses themselves.

A green and white-spotted spider jumped into the fray. Two steps and it was upon her. It reared back, poison dripping from its fangs.

Keera slashed through the chitinous jaws and the creature's mandible thumped to the ground.

Hissing with pain, the spider retreated over the bodies of its kin.

The bell in the tower tolled with a teeth-itching dong, dong, dong. *More trouble?*

A rumble of water…no…the spiders were making that weird sound.

The creatures retreated, slowly inching back to the top of the fence.

"Hold!" Keera yelled.

Corson, ichor dripping from his sword, stopped mid-step.

The brown patterned spiders with large diamond abdomens spun webs on the thorn bush on the border of the village.

Some of the smaller, nimbler, dark-brown spiders climbed up the trees nearest the fence, looking down on the village with their enormous eyes.

Can they jump from there? Or are they planning their next move?

Archers shot arrows at the few spiders left inside the border. A waste of arrows. All the remaining spiders were dying, too injured to move far.

"Attack!" yelled a young man in a forging smock, an over-excited prince by the look of him. All soft gold curls and soft hands. Waving his sword, he headed for the gate.

"Steady!" Corson called.

A ragged cheer turned into exultant celebrations as fighters punched the air and clapped each other on the back.

"Well done!" Philips said.

"It's not over yet," Keera said. "They've not retreated. They're just regrouping."

Keera wiped her sword and peered out past the spider-laden fence and into the dark forest.

LETTIE'S ANGUISH

Lettie clutched the sword, her heart flickering with hope. With Aiden too busy worrying about the giant spider, she had a chance to complete Queen Persephone's sacred task. And she was so close to everything she ever wanted—to prove herself and Nada worthy.

Queen Persephone was right. The mud-humans deserved death. And all she had to do to get Nada back was strike down one man while his back was turned.

Nada—bundled in the mud-human's arms and clutching her not-sister—screamed. Lettie's silver blood cooled like ice. Nada seemed to care more for the baby than for her.

I abandoned faer. Her heart twisted with the horrible thought. "I won't hurt you," Lettie told the changeling. *Just the mud human carrying you.*

How can I save Nada by killing the one person trying to protect faer?

Lettie took a deep breath. Her people needed her, and sacrifices had to be made. She had to get to him and kill him.

Holding the babies close to his chest, Aiden turned and ran, the spider a step behind him.

Venom dripped from the spider's fangs—fangs large enough to pass through Aiden's chest and hit the babies on the other side.

§

His veins running cold with fear, Aiden flinched. The spider was at his back, and a wicked fae sprinted toward them from the left. Bright green light flared from one of faer hands and a silver fae-sword in the other.

Caught between two deadly foes, he swerved from the oncoming fae—her face a perfect mask of fury as her sword flashed down.

The spider thudded into his back.

Aiden fell to his knees.

§

Lettie's heart cracked as the spider knocked Aiden to the ground.

The vision of the spider's fangs hitting Nada and Pearl hit Lettie like a bolt of lightning. *And my sword could also just as easily kill the children as the man holding them. I can't risk Nada. Surely the queen will understand.*

The queen will not.

Above, the bell tolled. *Dong…*

Lettie pushed past Aiden. Brandishing her staff in one hand, and the sword in the other, she screamed at the oncoming beast. The spider laughed.

Electric anger ran through her. She let it surge through the staff. Its bright green light flared, gaining the spider's attention as she thrust out the sword with her other hand.

…dong, dong.

The spider half-fell in its hurry to get away from her, crashing a leg into Aiden before backing off, along with its fellows, sending out the stridulent message to regroup to the safety of the fence circling the village. Sending out the message that they have been betrayed by a fae. *By me.*

Lettie whipped around, but Aiden was stumbling back toward the houses surrounded by a small crowd of people.

I saved Nada.

I failed my queen.

Dozens of adults now stood guard around Aiden, swords at the ready.

Lettie fled. There would be no easy way past that tight cordon of defence, and so she slipped through the shadowy bushes and fruit trees within the village.

There will be another time, another opportunity. But Lettie had doubts now that she could ever take it. Something inside her had changed. Something was wrong. She'd seen the way the human had cared for her changeling and it weighed on her heart—she'd never be able to look at anything the same ever again.

§

Still alive. Aiden took a deep breath. Light headed with relief, and amazed that he and the two children he was carrying were still alive, he glanced behind him. The spider was scuttling away. The fae who'd protected them ran after it.

More people arrived. Among them, his parents, swords drawn. "Are you alright?"

"Yeah," Aiden replied, trying not to sound shaky. He handed the children over, unable to say what he'd seen. Trying to gather his thoughts. The giant spider had been so fast…and the fae had been faster. He glanced over, but both fae and spider had disappeared.

A fae rescued us. Her shimmery sky-blue dress, her determined face, her wand wielded like a fairy godmother… Now it was over, he had the sense that he'd seen her before. But where? Fae were dangerous, wicked. Everybody said so. That's why he'd always tried to avoid them—successfully, except for when Ruby had been stolen, and he hadn't even noticed. *Was it then?*

Aiden shook his head. However much he wanted to, he couldn't go back in time.

Alice ran up behind them. "My children. Where are they?"

Brian strode along behind her, shaking his sword arm.

Thoughts scattered like confetti, Aiden pointed up at the house where Hazel was sitting on the doorstep, bow drawn, her two brothers hiding behind her.

Safe. I didn't fail them.

"Thank you so much." Alice gathered Pearl into her arms. "Could you take Ruby, Mrs Andersen?"

"Oh, right." Aiden's mother inattentively held out her hand. "Are you sure you're alright, Aiden?"

"I'm fine," Aiden lied, glancing back at the battle. Keera was out there in the thick of it.

"Your father and I could go out instead. Don't you think we should be amongst the fighting, John?"

"Oh, dear me. Mr and Mrs Andersen, thank goodness you're here," Alice interceded before his parents went out and got themselves killed. "I'm going to need your help."

"Good. Good." Aiden's father said. "Aiden, we'll be out as soon as we've assisted Alice. Give these creatures a taste of iron."

"Thank you, Alice," Aiden flashed a tight smile. "Better go." He drew his sword, his hands steady as rocks now the children were safe. Filled with fiery energy pumping through his veins, Aiden felt as if he could take on the whole world.

"Wait!" Alice said. "Take a torch." She thrust a burning brand at Aiden.

He snatched it up and ran toward the gate to where he'd last seen Keera. The fighting was heaviest here. Mostly spiders dashing in from the fence and retreating before they could be surrounded and brought down.

Aiden skirted a severed spider leg, twitching in the courtyard... and there she was with Corson by her side. Keera was in the thick of the fighting, her dark braids flying. Her sword flashed. A giant brown spider lurched; its leg cut away. It stumbled and scarpered back up the fence on a trail of spider silk. A couple of nearby redback spiders retreated with it.

"Enjoy the break," Corson said, surveying the carnage—mostly hacked-off spider legs. "It won't be for long. It never is."

Keera rubbed her biceps and rolled her shoulders, taking advantage of the lull. "I'm not sure how much longer we can hold."

"More villagers are coming," Aiden assured her. "They're just getting their families to safety."

Keera frowned. "We need good fighters, people with fast reactions. I'm not sure the whole settlement has enough. We should be evacuating."

The whole settlement?

"Incoming," Corson yelled.

Torch burning in one hand, sword in the other, Aiden braced for the attack. A pink spider dashed into the line of defenders, and away just as quickly—as if looking for weaknesses—while a furry, grey spider shot a glob of web at the dark-haired princess, who'd been busy showing off her silver and orange sword.

Avondale's two trained medics rushed in to cut her free.

A spindly legged spider at the top of the fence waved its legs, almost dancing as it created a stridulent call that grated in Aiden's ears. Other spiders joined in.

How are they making that sound?

Aiden's stomach turned as he saw the courtyard and its fighters reflected in their multifaceted eyes. They were clever. They were learning. They were fast as lightning, and they had control of both poison and webs. How long would it take for them to deploy these weapons effectively in another attack?

Worse, web shrouded the iron fence and the fae-bane ivy that was the protection against fae and other creatures that inhabited this forest. *Not that it matters now. We're already being attacked by one of the scariest dangers in the forest.*

The strange noise hit a crescendo and half a dozen giant spiders hurtled toward them. They surged over the front gate and toward Keera.

A.J. Ponder

FAIRY COURT

Lettie threw herself under the feijoa tree and peeked out. In the heat of battle, and with so much happening, no one was taking any notice of her. Even Aiden's focus was on the children and the humans running to his aid.

Nada is alive.

And so are the humans. I failed.

Unsure of whether to laugh or cry, Lettie took stock of the battle. The spiders could have had the upper hand if they'd co-ordinated their attacks. But they were timid, hating the sting of swords and flinching away from the burning brands that the villagers waved in their faces. They clearly wanted to retreat again, skittering nervously back and forth along the web-encrusted boundary fence. Fae were cheering them on with applause that rustled through the forest like falling leaves. *Cowards, letting the spiders do their fighting while they hide in the shadows.* Lettie was surprised that the spiders were taking battle orders from the fae. Wyrden must have succeeded in his quest to rile the spiders. The manipulative, conniving skin demon should not be underestimated.

Fae battle-fifes tooted like demented thrushes, sending the spiders back out to fight with promises of help to come.

Obeying orders, they sallied through the front gate.

Why there, in the thick of the defenders?

A leaf rustled behind Lettie. Close. Icy breath tickled the hair on the back of her neck.

Lettie gasped and jumped forward, grazing her knee.

A hand clamped around her heel as she pushed through the low-hanging branches. They dragged her back.

"No!" Lettie cried and turned to see her attacker. *Zadie and two Quips, their silver armour camouflaged and muted with green-dyed spider-web. Queen Persephone must be furious to send two of her elite guard.*

"Let go. What are you doing?" Lettie demanded as the Quips grabbed the sword from her hand.

"Traitor!" Zadie hissed. "We saw your treachery. I've been told to bring you to Queen Persephone and King Hades so you can stand trial for your crimes against fae."

"What crimes?" Lettie demanded. "All I did was save Nada. I've given up everything to serve Queen Persephone. Done everything she asked." Lettie tried to tug her foot free, her heart pounding like it was about to burst.

"Shut it, traitor," Zadie spat. The two Quips grabbed Lettie, each by a shoulder, and dragged her to an uncontested section of the boundary fence obscured by an old apple tree.

"Nada's fae, she really is." Lettie couldn't keep the begging tone from her voice. "I *had* to protect faer."

The Quips were silent.

Lettie fought against their remorseless grip. "Nada!" she yelled.

The grip on her left shoulder eased…

Will they let me go?

The Quip scowled and punched her in the face. The blow rattling her head and sending pain shooting through her eye. "Won't matter what you yell, nobody's going to hear you," the fae muttered, and clutched her shoulder harder than ever, fingers burrowing into her shoulder blades.

She embraced the pain. It was nothing like losing her changeling, her child. The worst thing was that the Quip was right. Nada was trapped with the humans, too far away to hear her over the clash of swords against chitin, the screams of spiders and humans, and all the yelling, crashing and stomping of battle. "We have to go back! Please."

Dragging her fast now, they reached the spiderweb draped fence. This section was empty of spiders and attackers. *An orchestrated move by whoever was behind the battle. Wyrden!*

Lettie kicked out as they went over the top. Her foot banged on the iron barrier, and her flesh hissed. She screamed in pain, and still no human heard, blind creatures that they were. "Damn you all to the Labyrinth," Lettie muttered.

The Quips laughed and pulled her onward through a narrow path in the ivy, resolute as ever. It was no good fighting them. They'd sold their souls for their blood-armour. Surely Zadie would take pity. "Please, please save my changeling," Lettie begged Zadie. "Fae's with the humans. If you wait, there's sure to be an opportunity to save faer."

Zadie ignored her, running ahead on light feet. She seemed happier now, without a changeling to guard. Or a bundle of sticks. *The pretence of looking after it must have been wearying.*

Lettie remembered the fateful day they'd tried to replace the Andersen children in the human woods. Zadie's changeling's tiny limbs barely kicking before shattering in an assortment of precious stones and other oddments.

Zadie's tears. Had they been real, or more manipulation?

A horn sounded. The rustle of stones and the soft clink of padded armour heralded the march of a hundred pairs of feet.

Lettie had never seen so many fae armoured for battle. Their silver armour glowed in the gathering dusk. So much silver. Lettie shivered at the obscenity, wondering how many fae had died to create it. *And still the Queen is going after Keera, when she's doing the same thing. Almost. Keera's also using the tears of the sun. And she's not fae.*

"Wasteling!" soldiers shouted, as Lettie was dragged past. "Traitor!"

"I'm no traitor," Lettie yelled back, furious. She wanted to scream.

Bedraggled and caked in mud, she was in no state to be anywhere near Queen Persephone's Court. And yet that's exactly where the soldiers were dragging her.

The moonlit clearing was beautiful, the whole fairy court in attendance a counterpoint to the silver-clad Quips. Instead of utilitarian silver armour, they were dripping with jewellery like dew-encrusted flowers on a spring morning. And instead of dour expressions and stiff joints, they were dancing merrily, their eveningwear swirling. The gardeners and attendants fluttered around fussing over the plants and flowers—without accomplishing much except being ready for Queen Persephone's every whim. Even here, on the edge of her territory, with the battle raging not so far away, the mossy trees glowed like emeralds. Lettie wanted to sink into their embrace.

Protected by a line of fierce, silver-armoured Quips, King Hades and Queen Persephone sat high on their tree-thrones staring through a large concave seeing-glass set in a bramble bush filled with spiderwebs. When Lettie peered through, the distant battle was thrown into sharp relief.

"There you are, ungrateful wretch," Queen Persephone exclaimed, clapping her hands.

The queen's entourage stopped dancing, their flowing eveningwear becoming as still as their stony expressions.

A.J. Ponder

Worst of all, nearly hidden behind the tall throne trees, was the child, Ruby—her red hair tangled and her eyes bloodshot. She gripped the yellowed bones of her cage—a cage made from the ribs of a long-dead dragon.

The Quips dropped Lettie on her knees in the deep moss before the wooden thrones. The relief she'd hoped for faded as King Hades regarded her with stony-faced disdain while Queen Persephone smiled her porcelain smile.

"I've brought the traitor," Zadie announced. "I only ask you to let me watch her die."

MEDIC

Aiden, standing toe-to-toe with his wife and best friend, struggled to keep up. The bright flash of their blades took down the spiders who dared to get too close.

The pink spider from earlier darted in again. Aiden swung his sword, but missed.

Lightning-fast, Keera intercepted the creature, splitting its jaws in one swift blow. Without pausing, she turned to face the next. Focus and control—that's what made her so good.

She couldn't stop them all, though. Several long-legged brownish spiders and a redback slipped past her and Corson to be confronted by less able fighters.

A small knot of young smiths wielding a trident, a large hammer and a couple of short swords between them were struggling to fight off a long-legged brown spider with a white-tipped abdomen. None of them seemed to have the power to land an effective blow. If it wasn't for the woman holding it at bay with a trident, they'd be dead.

"Damn it," Aiden muttered, dropping back to help them. He swung his sword. And missed. Again. Struggling to find his centre, he pushed his torch forward and readied another blow.

The creature backed off slowly, the light from his torch reflected in its many eyes.

"Medic!" A shout rang out from Aiden's right. A shaggy warrior, fighting a redback all alone.

A jagged tear rent the chest of his leather jerkin.

"Poison!" Aiden yelled, running in to help, flame thrust in front of him.

This spider didn't shy from the flame. It lunged at Aiden.

Aiden reeled back. He couldn't help himself, knowing that even a scratch from its fangs could be deadly.

The shaggy warrior refused to give up. Swaying, he held onto his wounded chest with one hand and staggered forward. With a yell of fury, he thrust his sword through one of the spider's larger eyes. His sword still buried in the spider's head, the man fell over.

The spider wobbled a few shaky steps and fell over, too.

Aiden sheathed his sword and, still holding the brand in his left hand, hooked his right arm around the soldier and pulled him back to the courtyard.

A brown spider scuttled toward them.

Aiden stumbled…and suddenly Keera and Corson were by his side. "Great idea, torches," Corson said, plucking Aiden's from his hand and shoving it into the spider's face.

The spider shrieked and ran away.

A junior medic, a strapping lad, loped in, threw the poisoned soldier over his shoulder in a fireman's lift, and ran him back to the impromptu medic station.

"You ready?" Corson said, handing Aiden's torch back. "We're going all in to push them back now."

"Do you have more torches?" Keera asked Aiden. "Or should we…?"

"I've got some." Corson took off his pack and dug out a couple. He lit them, then handed them around to those who didn't have one. Keeping one for himself, he raised it high. "Are you ready!?" he shouted.

"Always," Aiden replied, eyes watering from the pitch and pine tar laced smoke. "Time to put on a show."

Several nearby fighters cheered while Corson and Keera nodded. They knew what was coming.

"Five! Four! Three! Two! One!" Aiden shouted.

Together, all three of them brandished swords and torches and ran into the thick of the fighting near the front gates, yelling at the top of their lungs. Other fighters joined them, fire lighting their faces.

The spiders fled to the wall and peered down at the humans.

"Well, that worked," Aiden said. "Let's put lit torches around the boundary to keep them at bay."

"Medics are going to be busy tonight," Corson said wryly as he set up the first torch—and jumped back as flame ripped through the spiderweb covering the iron fence. Just as quickly, the blast of flame was over and the spiders had jumped back to the treeline, leaving only the smouldering ivy behind them.

Torches were rushed to secure the boundary. And water quickly followed.

With the fiery brands burning merrily, Aiden brushed a smudge of soot from Keera's cheek. "Do you think the peace will last until morning?" he asked.

Keera shook her head. "Whatever's gotten into them, I don't think they're backing off for long."

"Hmm." Aiden nodded. Something about this fight was bugging him. And it wasn't just the spiders skittering back and forth along the boundary like patrolling soldiers. In the forest behind them, he thought he saw something humanoid in the shadows. "Why do you think the spiders are attacking us, anyway? I mean, I'd understand if we were on the border of FaerLand." He threw out an arm. "But in New Avalon? They've never come near here before."

"And attacking the front gate. Seems weird."

"Hmmm," Keera replied. "If it was an important spiderling that Philips caught, why chase him back here when he'd have been an easy target in the forest?"

Aiden nodded. "And why's all this happening after the fae stole our child?" *If it wasn't for this attack, we'd be at the FaerLand border.*

"It's probably just bad timing," Keera said. "But I know what you mean—every minute here seems like a minute too long."

Aiden nodded. "We can't do much about it now." *Unless we convince Alice to travel by mirror.... That would never fly.* Not with the children and the whole settlement in danger.

"I've got a plan," Corson said. "How about we grab a drink and celebrate that we're still alive while we can?"

Aiden slapped him on the shoulder. "Now, who is it who always has the best ideas?"

CORSON

Corson crashed his tin mug against Aiden and Keera's. "Great fighting so far. Let's hope we're done for the night." He took a gulp to quench his thirst. The cider was watery. Typical Burcham penny pinching—but a good idea under the circumstances.

At least it wasn't dousing the celebrations. Mayor Harder was playing his violin, and a grey-bearded old fellow broke into dance. He flapped his elbows and waltzed around pulling people in to dance with him, while grizzled fighters and young adventurers clapped merrily—encouraging others to join him and strut their stuff.

Corson laughed and tipped back a little more cider. Crisp and sweet. It might be time to get another…

"What's the matter?" Aiden asked Keera.

"They haven't gone," Keera noted, gazing at the fence.

The setting sun lit the clouds over the trees, the view smudged by the smoke from the boundary torches.

Something about the spiders patrolling the edge caught Corson's eye. *They're bunching up near the trees and away from the gates— places where the defence was the weakest. Where the torches were set further apart.*

"Watch out!" Corson called to the celebrating fighters. "They're coming back."

Spiders flooded over the boundary, dropping silk balloons filled with water onto the burning torches.

Arrows sped from the towers into the morass, piercing spiders and sending them to their deaths, or into terrified retreat. It was not enough to reverse the assault.

Fire sizzled and died.

The celebrations ceased, interrupted by the clatter of dropped tin mugs. Armed villagers rushed back to face the tide of spiders spreading out along the boundary fence. Half a dozen scrambled over the huge apple trees near the boundary, avoiding the fighters and jumping onto the roof of the town hall.

Corson glanced back to Burcham, who, despite cowering by the door of the town hall, was now caught in the thick of heavy fighting. He was waving a carpentry hammer as if he thought it was a sword.

Too big. Too clumsy.

A lanky-legged giant brown spider knocked the hammer out of his hand and swathed Burcham in layers of silk, before reeling him up into the web that was being spun over the top of the building.

Cursing, Corson raced back across the square to help, pulling his sword so the silver and gold script flashed in the evening light. His arm, stiff from before, felt like it was hefting weights.

He reached up, slashing at the spider and cleaving a leg.

The lanky brown spider, minus a leg, kept dragging the lawyer up the side of the beige-stoned town hall to the web-encrusted eaves—each strand shimmering with hundreds of droplets.

Above, the archers in the bell tower were also under attack. Stabbing down into the spiders with long knives and swords and firing arrows at point blank range.

No help there.

More people arrived. Unable to reach the spiders climbing the building, they milled around, pointing. Some slashed ineffectually at the web, tangling their swords.

The seven-legged spider hung Burcham from the eaves above and peered down. *Too clever.* Corson shivered, his stomach queasy with the thought of Burcham, or anyone, having to hang like that, completely at the spider's mercy.

A young princeling, kitted out with purple and gold finery, reached up a hand. "How hard can it be to pull it down?"

"Don't touch the web," Philips yelled. "Avoid the droplets and cut it." He used his sword to swipe the strand between two shimmery globules of gluey spiral silk.

Corson followed suit. "Thanks for the tip."

"Any time," Philips said, using a fallen leaf to help stuff the strand of silk he'd cut into a jar.

Corson glared at Philips. The academic shrugged. "If I can get a moment to test it, we'll all be better off."

Fast as lightning, while they were looking in the wrong direction, the spider dropped a single thread of silk on the princeling and abseiled down it, wrapping the lad in layers of silk.

"Let him go!" Corson yelled. Determined not to lose another person to the spider, he jabbed with his sword. It sliced into the spider's front leg. Fluid pumped from the wound, spattering the cobblestones below.

The now six-legged spider abandoned its prize and swung up and away. "You will pay for this," the spider said, its words little more than the whisper of rustling leaves. "Mark my words, pathetic humans. This world is not for you."

Corson flinched. *I should not be so surprised. This is Brocéliande, and those are FaerLand spiders.* He tried to climb after the injured spider, but trails of sticky spiderweb covered the building. *Avoid the sticky droplets.* He had to use his head. Too many fighters were getting caught in the stuff. And he was no good to anyone if he managed to get himself trussed up as a spider snack.

Above, the spider was watching as if it had all the time in the world. Burcham and the other prisoners were still struggling. *Still alive.*

Then, fast as lightning, the huge spider bolted down to get another victim. Taking advantage of its distraction, Corson cut the web clear of the windowsill in one clean swipe, and pulled himself up. He slashed the window free of the sticky threads, sheathed the sword, grabbed Burcham's exposed foot, and pulled hard. Burcham's bundle of silk rocked.

Philips and a leather-jerkin wearing moustachioed swordsmith scrambled to join him. "Hurry," Corson yelled, the six-legged spider was returning.

Philips thrust his hand deep into the cocoon. "I've got Burcham's other leg. Ready, pull!" he yelled. Clinging to the window-frame with one hand, Corson heaved on Burcham's foot with the other.

Muffled yelps came from the spider-silk wrap.

Thank goodness he's still alive.

Corson pulled harder, and someone in the crowd below cheered.

"Almost there," Philips said triumphantly as the bundle that was Burcham sagged toward them.

The bundle of silk rocked and fell—the sole thread of silk holding it stretching faster and faster. *Too fast.*

"Hold on!" Corson shouted. Gripping tightly to the window frame with his left hand, Corson reached out with his right and grabbed hold of the silk-wrapped Burcham. He gritted his teeth against his screaming muscles, but Burcham was even heavier than he looked.

Corson's fingers clutching the window frame slid, his arms spasmed, and the bundle fell from his grip.

"Watch out!" Corson ducked back under the window eave, pushing Philips back with him. "Damn," the moustachioed swordsmith cursed, as they watched Burcham's cocoon drop into the town square with a thud.

"I thought it would be stickier," Corson muttered.

"Yeah," Philips said as a strapping junior medic rushed to tend to Burcham. "Wrapping silk isn't as sticky."

"Bit late to tell me that now," Corson said, feeling guilty about dropping his boss to the ground.

"I'm sure he's fine," the moustachioed swordsmith muttered. "Us, not so much."

"White tail." Philips pointed to a dark grey-brown spider with brown-and-orange banded legs belting around the side of the building. It didn't have a tail at all, but the tip of its abdomen did look like it had been painted with a white spot.

With so many people dangling high in the eaves and protected by patrolling spiders, Corson wouldn't flee. Gritting his teeth, he used his off-hand to hold on to the window frame and reached for his sword.

The creature was almost on top of them. He could see himself reflected in two of its eyes. He pulled the sword and flattened himself back against the window.

An orange and brown banded limb quested toward them. He slashed, and the spider pulled back. Corson could hear it manoeuvring directly above them, but only saw flashes of grey, orange and brown.

Philips shook his head. "This is suicide. We can't stay here." He turned to clamber down. Legs dangling, a nimble jewel-green spider the size of a small pony dashed across the courtyard to attack them. It was being chased by half a dozen soldiers with brands, but none of them were going to make it in time.

Philips landed in front of the spider, bare fists raised.

Dammit.

"Got it," Corson yelled and launched himself at the beast, landing on its head and kicking down at the waving palps. His foot connected.

The spider snapped, grabbing Corson's ankle in its jaws. Pain flared up his leg as he was dangled upside down.

Blood rushing to his head, Corson gritted his teeth and twisted in mid-air, flailing with his sword. It struck the spider's mandible. Blue blood spurted from the wound—the tang of copper heavy in the air.

Released, and half falling, Corson reversed the blade and slashed again. A loud crunch reverberated up his arm. Spider-gore sprayed. The spider's mandible crashed to the ground with a dull thud, and the spider sank, legs collapsing under it.

Corson waved a triumphant fist. "Got the blighter. Now, where's the next one?"

Philips pointed up to the rafters. "They've got that poor swordsmith, now. And who knows who else."

Corson reeled and glanced up again. The roof of the building held seven people bound in silk. And along the eaves of the adjacent building, more ensnared people were hanging like salami at a deli. The enormous orb weaver spider, with a big fat abdomen and spindly long legs, dropped down one of its silken threads to scoop up a fire-fighting villager.

I've failed.

"No." Corson set his jaw. He flashed his sword in a tidy figure of eight, while the spiders watched, their multi-faceted eyes gleaming in the torchlight. A stick-like spider with spindly legs drew his eye. It was creeping along the path toward Keera and Aiden, holding a thick sheet of spiderweb as if it were a blanket.

"Watch out!" Dr Philips said. "That's a net spider!"

But the net spider wasn't the only one scuttling toward their position. A giant spider with furry grey palps, and a vivid blue abdomen decorated with bright orangey-red stripes, leapt over the courtyard. It might not have been quite as big as the others, more the size of a wolf than a pony, but it was fast.

"Look! Maratus…" Dr Philips pointed. "I mean a peacock spider. So pretty,"

The spider stopped on a dime, and its head turned. Four of its eight eyes reflected Philips.

Corson levelled his sword and closed in to help Dr Philips.

The scientist stepped backward. "They're usually so small they're barely visible," he said to nobody.

But before Corson could make it, a huge matt-black spider scuttled behind Keera. It raised its front legs, a drip of venom clinging to each fang—and leapt.

JEALOUSY

Ruby wailed and rattled the bone bars of her cage. "Lettie, Lettie! Please? Please, home. Take me back."

Queen Persephone glanced over at Ruby, and her moue of disappointment and lidded eyes were easy to read.

The queen is jealous that the child likes me. The realisation hit Lettie like a thunderbolt. *It cannot be true.* "Sorry, Ruby," Lettie mumbled, unsure if Ruby could hear her over the whispers of the surrounding fae and the rumble of distant fighting.

"Silence, traitor. Thou shalt pay for thy crimes." Persephone's voice was like the crack of thunder on the bluest day. Points of red flushed her cheeks as she glowered at Lettie, all mirth gone and only hatred in her eyes. A hatred that burned as brightly as the lightning crackling through King Hades' hair.

The gathered fae flinched. Several fled, taking off in flutter form to hide in the depths of the forest. Lettie tried to follow, but Zadie and the soldier's hands pulled her back. In the ruckus, Lettie's dress caught on the bramble bush that held Queen Persephone's large concave seeing-glass. The magical device wobbled. *Glass wobbling?* Lettie tried to right it, and it collapsed—not glass at all, but made of sticky spiderweb and dew.

"Reckless fool," Queen Persephone snapped.

A distant cry and the clang of swords interrupted the gathering.

"Giveth us one moment." Queen Persephone reached over to a rambling rose and plucked a flower shimmering with dew. Carefully, she tipped dew into a spiderweb bigger than a crow's nest—one of many decorating the bramble bush. The dew spread, shimmering and forming a clear concave lens.

King Hades peered through. With a tiny flash of aura, he adjusted the curve, all the better to see the battle being fought in the human village.

Queen Persephone's hands tilted and she clapped daintily; as if the battle was a performance just for her. Her court joined in, rustling with excitement and barely knowing where to keep their attention—their queen, or the battle.

Lettie ignored the sycophants and stared, horrified, at the wide grin on the face of her beloved queen. Spiders were dragging humans up into the eaves of their main building. *Could the spiders do the same thing to fae? Have they already?*

Queen Persephone also clapped when one of the humans cleaved a leg from a spider. Those cheers were muted—as if she didn't want the spiders to hear. *As if the battle is a game, nothing but entertainment.*

Someone coughed.

Wyrden.

The traitorous skin-demon scum stepped out from the shadows and sketched a bow. "We really should sort out this underling issue before the demons chase the humans toward our position."

Underling issue?

"Quite right," King Hades said. "My dearest, what is your most wise plan for your little traitor and the other one?"

"Ah yes, the traitor and the brave hero. Firstly, congratulations, Zads? Zadsum?" Persephone waved a bored hand at Zadie. "Thou hast done well. Thy loyalty shall not be forgotten. And for thy boon, thou head shall remain where it belongs on thou shoulders."

Zadie made a series of pretty bows and elegant flourishes. "Thank you, most beneficent queen."

She was rewarded by a smile as bright as silver.

Queen Persephone turned to Lettie. "Now, little traitor. What shall we do with thou?"

Lettie prostrated herself on the soft, cool moss. "What have I done, oh great queen? Why am I here? I brought the child as you commanded and gave up my changeling…"

"Enough lies. The human desecrators we sent you to kill are still alive. Zadie's changeling is dead. Dust. And all because of you. This war," Queen Persephone waved her hands toward the distant battlefield, "is all on you."

"You know that's not true," Lettie hissed.

Zadie wrapped faer arms about faerself and smirked like a boggart who'd stolen the cream. But when Queen Persephone's retinue ignored faer, Zadie's smile cracked.

"And now we are fighting for our very lives." Queen Persephone continued in a voice that carried across the crowded clearing. "Your treachery threatens us all."

"No!" Lettie cried, unheard over the gasps of the gathered fae.

"For thy crimes, traitorous wretch, thou shall be sentenced to the catacombs. Return my treasured silver axe from the centre of the labyrinth and thou may return to my court. Fail, and thou shall be banished forever."

Nobody leaves the catacombs alive. Lettie slumped, unable to summon up the horror she knew she should be feeling. Her heart was empty. There was a changeling-sized hole in it. Mercurial Nada, the changeling whose preferred form was a butterfly or a bird—all the better to flit about merrily, or cuddle close. Her charge for a hundred years was gone—traded for this small, imprisoned creature with snot and tears running down her face. *Yet another child I've betrayed.* Maybe dying in the darkness of the maze was not so bad. Staying here and being mocked, knowing she'd destroyed the one thing she loved—and this other trusting soul—that would be worse.

Queen Persephone waited for the gasps and whispers to die down. "Take her away!"

Two Quips grabbed Lettie's shoulders, hauling her to her feet.

Little Ruby banged her fists against the bones and screamed as Lettie was dragged away. "But I like Lettie. Where's Lettie going? Bring Lettie back!"

"Silence, child. Lettie is going to the catacombs, like all the other traitors."

"Lettie, no!" Ruby wailed. "No go to cat-a-toms."

Lettie fought to say a final goodbye to the wild-eyed youngster, but the Quip's hands were as implacable and unrelenting as iron.

"No, my dear, dear, child." Jaw clenched; Queen Persephone gazed over the clearing. "Any other fae you choose. But this traitor will pay for faer crimes."

She, her, Lettie thought. But stayed silent.

"Zadie? Queen Persephone? All the good Fae of FaerLand?" Lettie begged. "Please know I am innocent. I swear it."

"The rest of my soldiers!" the queen yelled. "Hear me."

The Quips saluted, hands to chests, their silver armour glittering as they marched to face their queen.

"Thou art mine forces elite. Show thou my foot soldiers the way, not to cower in the shadows, but to prove that we are a match for the puny mortals who threaten our very lives and our precious forest. Then, once we have uprooted the humans and sent them far from our realms, I will seal the borders. So, do not get left behind. Go hence, and do not disappoint, or thou wilst join Lettie as food for the creatures of the catacombs."

All the soldiers, except the ones holding Lettie, strode from the clearing.

"I'm sorry, Ruby," Lettie muttered to the small girl in the cage. "I hope you find your way home."

"See. I told you she was a traitor!" Zadie spat. "Did I not tell you, Oh, Great Queen?"

"Thou didst," Queen Persephone said. "Start the music! It's a busy night and we have no more time for games."

A melody of wind instruments rippled like running water. Their scales and arpeggios flowed ever faster, like a stream picking up speed.

The soldiers pushed her on. More and more fae joined them. Swarming in close, they shoved Lettie's back. Her arms. Her shoulders.

Faster and faster the crowd tumbled along, pushing and shoving her to the underground labyrinth of twisting passages and nightmares.

The melodic gusts of flutes, pipes, ocarinas and other wind instruments rose to become a river, a flood, a waterfall of sound—discordant and merciless in its crescendo as Lettie was pushed along faster and faster, caught like flotsam in the current. Her silver blood ran colder than ever, every push a betrayal.

And then the world stopped.

Her arms half numb from the grip of the soldiers, Lettie found herself standing on the outside of the wood and iron door of the labyrinth. The forest suddenly as silent as death.

Wyrden opened the rust-streaked iron-bound door with a mocking grin and a flourish, unfazed by the tooth-aching screech of its hinges.

A lingering smell of death and mould, dank air and deadly iron wafted over Lettie as she peered down into the rough-cut stone tunnel. Beyond a tiny patch of bone-covered earth floor, there was only unfathomable darkness.

A thin howl split the night—a howl more terrifying than hellhounds—it rocked Lettie back on her heels. *The people down here are traitors and murderers. The kinds of evil not even Queen Persephone would tolerate.*

And now, me.

FROM THE FRYING PAN INTO THE FIRE

To protect Keera, Corson ignored the jumping spider for the moment it took to lop off the matt-black spider's leg. It wheeled back, away from Keera. *That should give her enough time.*

A yell of pain rang out behind him. "Help!"

Corson turned back to find the vivid blue and orange jumping spider had Philips in its jaws. It dragged the scientist backward in a swift, darting movement.

"Philips!" Corson yelled, running to catch up. Mayor Harder joined him, rushing to attack with his two-handed sword in one hand and a brand in the other.

The spider darted backward again. Keera was also trying to follow—but the spider, even with its burden, was too fast. Displaying amazing strength for its size, it leapt over the fence and disappeared into the forest.

The net spider from earlier blocked their way. Holding up its reconstructed net in its legs, it flung the sticky mass at them.

Corson backed up, sword ready to slash.

The mayor thrust out a brand, and the net went up in a puff of smoke.

Relieved, Corson changed direction, running back at the spider carrying Philips. Aiden arrived, backing him up, and the net spider scuttled off. But Philips and the jumping spider had disappeared into the forest.

Heart heavy with failure, Corson tried to figure out where to go next. Behind them, half a dozen people had been hung from the roof of the town hall, two huge orb weaver spiders industriously picking them up, binding them in web and then swinging down for more victims.

We're losing. The thought was sickening. *I should have tackled the first orb web earlier. Being strung up and eaten alive by spiders is no way to die.*

The largest one picked up Mayor Harder from behind, jaws sinking into his back so that he dropped his sword. In moments, it had wrapped the mayor in spiderweb and dragged him up to the eaves. Searching for a free spot, the spider hung him over the front door, above the burning lamps.

Mayor Harder thrashed his legs, his booted foot catching a lamp and smashing the glass. "No!" Corson yelled as the lamp tumbled to the ground, dripping oil and sparks over the spiderweb trailing the building. Black smoke rose. Sparks flickered, and Mayor Harder's cocoon burst into flames.

There was no time to grieve when others needed rescuing. Up in the eaves, the fire was running along the trailing threads of spider-silk and setting the damp thatch alight. The people encased in silk did not have long.

Corson pulled himself up to the window ledge as below, people yelled, "Fire!" and the bells on the tower rang incessantly.

The fat orb weavers threw up their front legs and howled like the wind before fleeing, scuttling over the roofs and trees in a mad dash for the boundary fence.

A.J. Ponder

Thick black smoke tearing his eyes, Corson welcomed Aiden's help on his left-hand side. Together, they ripped the cocooned bodies down and into the arms of the people helping below.

There was so little time. Fire crackled through the thatch, growing in intensity with every moment. More people rushed in to help, throwing water on the flames from below. With each bucket-load steam hissed from the burning thatch—the regular splashing all that was keeping the fire at bay.

His arms cramping, his lungs aching with the thick smoke as the fire blazed, he helped pull the bodies down one by one, until he could barely see Aiden through the smoke.

He looked up. *One to go. High up to his right.*

Corson snatched at the silk-wrapped body as fire flared up behind it. The wet, thick layers of silk smouldered. That and a whoosh of heat from the burning thatch nearly pushed him back. But Aiden was there, pulling the silk-wrapped body just a bit further.

"Got it!" Corson croaked, clinging to the silk parcel and pulling the body down. Above, the building's thatch caught and burned as merrily as a yuletide fire. Muscles burning, Corson half-climbed down before releasing the body to the medics below and jumping away from the licking flames.

Dazed, Corson watched New Avalon's two medics, backlit by sparks from the burning thatch of the buildings behind, tend the injured people below. They were working furiously, offering various salves and medicines and binding wounds, but no matter how fast they worked, the line of patients continued to get longer.

It's not just the town hall. Half of New Avalon's on fire.

"I'm alright." He pushed the medics away and pulled at the sheets of silk surrounding the person he'd just rescued.

"We've got it," the strapping young medic said, gently pushing him back.

There has to be something I can do. He glanced about, but the flames and smoke were proving too much for the spiders, and they were fleeing back over the boundary.

"More water!" someone yelled. "Pump faster."

"There's some by the forge," Aiden yelled back. He dashed through the smoky gap between the town hall and the village buildings.

Corson ran to join his friend, already little more than a shadow through the fumes. Throat raw and eyes watering, he forged through the narrow path under the eaves of the burning hall. And almost crashed into his friend.

Corson peered over Aiden's shoulder. The barrel and pails were there—right next to six demons! A seventh pulled itself out of the smouldering forge-fire. A huge granite demon, still glowing from the heat. "Get the humans," they growled. "Kill them if you must. Bring them to the demon-mines if you can."

"No! Kill the demon-killers," a grey-streaked marble demon shouted. "Kill them all!" It picked up a sword that had been left lying on the ground and waved it like a toothpick. "Today is a good day for Earthsiders to die." The marble demon charged, and the other demons followed, thundering toward Aiden and Corson.

ABANDONING NEW AVALON

Sparks floated in the air, dancing on the hot wind of the fire limning the oncoming demons. Aiden's stomach dropped like a stone. The village would soon be overrun.

He pelted back along the side of the town hall with Corson at his side, and not one bucket between them.

"Where's the water?" Burcham demanded.

Aiden struggled to speak between gasps. "Demons. We. Have. To. Go."

"Demons? Here?"

Corson waved a hand back the way they'd come. "Through the forge. You need to go! Protect the children and get out of here." The demons strode on through the smoke, slow but implacable. "I'll hold them."

"Corson!" Aiden yelled. "Stay with us."

"No." Fire glinted off Corson's blade as the demons strode closer.

Corson pushed them both away. "Get the children and the rest of the village safe." He glanced behind at the spiders swarming along the front wall. "Take the back gate across the bridge. I'll follow."

"We've got his back," a swordsmith assured them, pushing Aiden away and stepping in with her friends to help Corson.

The village square was filling up, the villagers crammed into a smaller and smaller space. Some emerged from buildings with rescued possessions, others retreating from the boundary fence.

Where's Keera!

She was not so far away, with the Faulkners and their children and his parents.

"What about the mirror?" Keera was asking Alice. "Couldn't we escape through there?"

Alice shook her head. "Too many people. Besides, it's in there." She pointed at the burning building.

The bell tower creaked alarmingly and toppled, its bell clanging deafeningly as it smashed to the ground. The one remaining bell tower dinged forlornly.

"We're off!" Burcham roared. "Leave everything. We need to go."

The crowded courtyard erupted into a flurry of activity as people ran about desperately looking for people and possessions they didn't want to leave behind. Many of the returning fighters dove into houses. Keera among them.

Aiden grabbed her hand. "What are you doing?"

"The swords! You stay with the children." Keera peeled away and ran to his parent's cottage. Fortunately, it had escaped the flames—so far.

Aiden glanced after Keera. Burcham was following her into his parents' house.

A SWORD

Keera scrabbled to wrap Pearl's sword in a cloth and pack it next to Ruby's.

"Good. I'll take that." Burcham grabbed at Pearl's sword. "Ow." He snatched his hand away fast.

Keera glared at him, and, using a rag wrapped around her hand, pushed Pearl's sword back into her pack. "I've told you a million times, my swords can only be used by the people they're forged for."

"But—"

"Earthside isn't here. Brocéliande has its own rules. Now, go."

"Dammit." Burcham spluttered, shaking his burned hand. Keera ignored him and rushed out to find her family.

Above, the remaining bell tower's bell was ringing again. A relentless *dong…dong…dong*.

§

Trying to ignore the thick black smoke from the burning buildings, Corson turned back to face the grey-streaked marble demon and its companions. He flashed back to the battered sword he'd lost when he and Aiden had faced the demons at the crossroads, and thanked his lucky stars that he had one of Keera's swords in his hand.

The marble demon slowed its advance, and so did the others. Step by step, Corson gave ground, giving other fighters a chance to join in: mostly smiths who wanted to try their new weapons out on a demon.

A young lady with dark hair and a tiara led a handful of the younger smithies. She yelled and swung her blade at the marble demon. The weapon clanged off its skin, leaving barely a scratch.

She was picked up in its fist and flung into the wall. Her tiara jangled to the ground.

Corson roared with anger and charged in to help. He wasn't the only one rushing to the woman's aid. Two of her young companions darted in to protect her. The best thing he could do was buy them time. The others clearly thought so, too. Ducking close and then darting away, they threw slabs of metal at the oncoming demons, taunting them. They were skilled fighters; it was a shame their swords were no more use than soft sticks against the oncoming demons.

Corson stepped forward as if pressing his attack, buying time for the wounded young lady and her companions to flee. More iron nuggets flew through the air.

The demons took a step backward. And another.

Arms wrapped around each other's shoulders, the three girls made slow progress.

The slate demon grinned and crowded in, balled its fist and threw a punch. Corson dodged the blow and chopped, his sword slicing right through the arm. The limb clanged onto the stone pavers; the stench of sulphur competing with the choking black smoke. Molten demon-blood hissed as it cooled in the night air, while the hand on the severed arm continued opening and closing—as if it was still desperate to grab him.

A.J. Ponder

The demon grunted, and Corson removed the slate demon's head with a sweep of his sword.

The creature dropped, crashing to the ground like an earthquake, its head tumbling after.

His relief was short-lived as two grey-marble demons jumped up to take its place on the narrow path between the burning buildings. They grinned fiercely even as the young ones fighting next to Aiden valiantly hacked at their arms and chests.

And then the remaining tower-bell rang. *Dong…dong…dong.* Corson glanced behind. The village was evacuating.

"Run," he told the young people helping him.

They held on until their swords were twisted scraps of metal. "I said, run!" Corson bellowed. He listened to their retreating footsteps with some small satisfaction and turned his attention to the pack of stone demons.

Alone, he had no hope of stopping the demons, only slowing them.

§

"Keera!" Aiden called. She'd been gone too long.

"Keera will be fine," his mother said, dropping Pearl into his arms. "She doesn't need you getting underfoot. We need to get across the bridge with the children."

Mum's right, Keera should be fine. Goodness knows she can look after herself. Still, he'd worried when he saw Burcham emerge from his parents' house. *What had he been up to?* Maybe asking for Keera's expertise, but it couldn't have gone well, because for all his efforts to wrangle people to safety, he didn't appear to know where to wrangle them to. Any hope of an orderly escape ended when Burcham, Aiden's father, and a few others began arguing about the safest route out. And if they needed to retreat all the way back to Earth or not,

Pearl sucked her fingers and leaned against his chest. "I know how you feel," Aiden murmured.

"Fae incoming!" someone shouted, pointing into the gloomy forest.

"No, they're demons!" Aiden yelled. Except it wasn't demons they were pointing at through the swirling smoke. Outside the village, through the web-encrusted iron bars, silver fae armour flickered eerily in the moonlit woods.

Aiden's heart constricted. Fae were moving to climb up the spiderweb-draped gates, and more still were headed toward the river.

Wooden arrows sailed into the village square. Fae archers. They must be hidden behind the warriors.

A flurry of arrows from the remaining bell tower pattered down harmlessly as the fae hunkered down behind their silver and wooden shields, inching toward town hall.

They'd take the last bell tower and the village...

And the demons were coming from behind the town hall. He hoped Corson could slow them down a little longer. Long enough to evacuate over the river.

The bells rang relentlessly. *Dong...dong...dong.*

"Keera better hurry," his mother said. "I don't want to be waiting for her at the bridge. It's too dangerous for the children."

"She's coming."

"Quick!" Burcham yelled, ushering people around the other side of the town hall and toward the suspension bridge. The stocky man held a knife in one hand and a small hammer in the other. He'd already proved he was about as useful with them as an umbrella in a tornado. At least he seemed to have his self-confidence back as he rallied the township. "I said, bring only weapons and torches. Everything else needs to stay behind."

Few paid attention to his missive, their heavy bags laden with precious possessions. But they were moving toward the bridge. Aiden's party, caught in the exodus, were moving faster and faster. "Keera!" he yelled, waking little Pearl, who pummelled him with her legs and fists and sobbed into his shoulder. *Damn.*

And there she was, running toward them, carrying her large pack, stuffed to the gunnels.

The gap was widening as frightened people swept past them. Alice hurried her two eldest along, clinging to the sleeping Tailor. And Aiden's father appeared and snatched Ruby up into his arms. "Stay close. Let's go," he ordered. "We have to keep up with the others."

Keera, still light-footed, only took moments to catch up. "Sorry." She glanced behind. The fae were close, their silver armour ghostly in the smoke-dimmed moonlight.

"Keera!" Aiden grabbed her hand. Faster now, they passed the smoking ruin of the town hall. And then suddenly they'd caught up with the stragglers—not so far from the snarl-up of people desperate to cross the overloaded bridge. Mostly wounded, encouraged by the two medics and their friends and families helping them.

Hazel fired an arrow toward the forest. "I can protect you." She fired another.

"Hazel, stop, or you'll hit someone," Alice ordered.

"Close up. Close up. Protect the children!" Keera yelled over the hubbub. Swords and other weapons drawn against the slowly approaching fae, the people of New Avalon jostled for the exit. Some had lanterns, some had swords, but many had nothing to protect them if spiders and fae were waiting for them in the woods on the other side of the river.

A volley of arrows flew overhead. A group of roving archers were holding the fae back with carefully targeted attacks.

Aiden thought he saw the nearest fae hold their hands up to shield their faces against the torch-light before they ducked for cover. Maybe spiders weren't the only creatures who abhorred flames.

"Wait!" Aiden yelled to Keera. He handed Pearl to his mother again and emptied his pack hurriedly while keeping an eye on his parents and the children. He needed to get this done before they disappeared into the bush on the other side. The contents of his pack tumbled to the cobblestones, a dark mass of shadow. He pulled out two brands and left random clothes, and goodness knew what else, scattered over the ground.

A burning arrow flew overhead, arcing along the river. The fire glinting on silver armour. *Damn, half the fae are moving downriver.* "Quick!" Aiden yelled to Keera, pushing to catch the rest of their family on the bridge. "Before we're cut off."

Behind them, the clang of swords reverberated around the square. *Corson!* He was fighting a slate demon near twice his size and holding a marble one at bay under the flaming eaves of the town hall. He must have retreated half the way around the building. And then Aiden saw why. A small army of demons was dogging him, waiting for him to slow down so they could overwhelm him. Near Corson and the demons, a tough group of smithies was shielding his flank from two grey spiders.

Corson bent his knees and levelled his sword, creating a moment of stillness before he sprang into action—slashing with precise strokes in a whirlwind of activity. The slate demon dropped to the ground, and immediately another took its place. Corson was an excellent fighter—but he wouldn't be able to hold them off alone.

Aiden hesitated—torn between protecting his friend and his children. *The children have my parents, the Faulkners and all the other villagers.*

"Dammit," Keera muttered and ran toward Corson and the demons.

"Dammit," Aiden echoed, and followed.

§

Step by step, Corson was pushed back—the heat from the burning building near baking his left-hand side. Still, he had to stay. He blinked away sweat, too tired to wipe it from his face. He needed every ounce of strength to keep on fighting.

Only the villagers were moving too slowly. *Hurry and cross the bridge!*

Three huge demons rushed toward him. A granite demon, a marble demon and a slate-green demon with sparkling crystals on its elbows and shoulders. Corson held his ground and swung at the marble demon.

Focus. He levelled his sword threateningly, and they hesitated.

Good. Time to move. He lashed out and sliced the slate demon's arm and whirled to the next one. And the next. They both dodged away, then lunged in to attack again.

He had to keep moving. Had to ignore the kids fighting the spiders…so close. Protecting him from that threat, at least. He whizzed through half a dozen training sequences, not really hoping to hit anything. Just to stop them from coming closer and to focus on the discipline he needed to keep going.

He struck the marble demon's shoulder, and pulled the sword free, whirling to attack the granite demon—but someone else was there already. *Keera!* She sunk her sword into its chest.

It grinned back at her, sulphurous steam rising from its breath.

"Damn it!" Keera kicked its chest, freeing her sword, and swung again.

"Thank goodness you're here!" Corson whirled aside to give himself a little room and hacked at the granite demon. A hit gouged through the rock-muscled chest. The impact juddered through his body, and he failed to dodge the demon's sulphurous blood. It spattered his arm, burning and hissing.

Corson squared his jaw, determined to block out the pain screaming down his arm, and willed himself not to step aside.

The creature knocked Corson's hand. More pain flashed through his hand and up his arm. He tried to regain control of his sword, but his hand wasn't working as intended, allowing the demon to pull the weapon clear of its chest and cast it aside with a disdainful flourish.

Damn.

Aiden arrived, protecting Corson with his body. *Good man in a fight, Aiden. Trustworthy. But he shouldn't be here.*

"Go!" Corson yelled, retrieving his sword with his off-hand and jumping up to block the path to the bridge. "Let me defend. You two crazy kids go look after your babies."

Aiden swung his sword in reply.

"Dammit." Corson waved the sword at the demon awkwardly.

Next to him, Keera was poised. Not making stupid mistakes, but still unable to best the marble monstrosity attacking her. *I need her balance.*

Which gave him an idea to try his old trick. He swung his sword wildly, hooked his leg around the creature's, and pushed.

The demon lifted an arm and smashed a giant fist into Corson's shoulder. Sword flying from his grip once again, he fell, gravel skittering under him as he rolled with the punch. *So, that worked about as well as when Aiden tried.*

More demons sauntered just beyond, seemingly in no hurry to push past the fight. *What are they waiting for?*

The marble demon backhanded Corson. Bones crunched and fiery pain lanced through his face.

Keera swung hard, hacking it through its chest. It looked up, grinned, and fell to the ground.

"Yes!" Aiden yelled. "One down."

"Several more to go." Corson sensed movement and ducked away, the wind from the granite demon's hand cooling his face as it flashed by. *Dammit. Focus.* Ignoring the burning pain, he kicked out, grabbed his sword, and twisted to safety.

The slate-green demon burst through the burning wall of the building, blindsiding Corson.

"Watch out!" Keera yelled.

Corson ducked its flying fist and swerved away, only to find the granite demon winding up a punch. He swerved again, too slow, and its grey knuckles cracked into his jaw. Red pain exploding behind his eyeballs, Corson tumbled back. *This can't be happening.* Breath rasping in his throat, Corson wiped away the hot tears streaking down his cheeks.

"No!" Keera screamed. Hacking and slashing, her sword glowing in the light of the fires, she rushed to Corson's aid.

"This is going to be fun!" the slate-green demon growled and stepped toward them.

Aiden swiped at its flank, careless of the danger. Hot lava-blood boiled and steamed out of its wound, spattering the cobbles and carrying with it an eye-watering stench of sulphur.

Unperturbed, the demon stepped forward.

A glance confirmed two other demons were trying to flank him. The granite one, and a new lumpy greyish one.

Damn. Corson's vision swam, his right eye swollen shut. He held his soot-blackened sword out. He needed to dispatch this slate demon and help Aiden.

"Fighters. We have to slow them down." It was the injured woman from earlier. Battered and bruised, but jaw set in a determined smile she was calling out to two young friends she'd brought to help. Princesses by the look of them.

Aiden's two demons turned to face the oncoming threat.

The princesses' swords clanged ineffectually on the granite demons' hide and sank into the lumpy greyish ones'. *A mud demon? But damn, they're brave, dancing in and out like that.*

Corson and Keera quickly re-joined Aiden, the slate demon falling back under their concerted attack.

A scream. The granite demon had pulled a sword out of one of the young fighter's hands. Grinning, the demon closed its fist around the blade. It produced a hideous shriek of graunching metal as it crumpled into something resembling a giant paperclip.

"Princess Eirlys!" Her companions yelled, surging into danger.

"Get back," Keera yelled. "If your sword's not effective, get back. Everyone else, listen up."

"One," Aiden called.

Keera thrust her sword into the lumpy greyish demon. Then she pulled back, hard. The sword squelched, but didn't come free. *A clay demon?*

"Two."

The clay monster grinned. "Got you, now," it said, reaching out to grab her.

In a fluid motion, Keera let go of her weapon, ducked low to avoid its fists, then regripped the sword and yanked it clear. Hot mud gooped from the wound.

"Three." Aiden yelled, grabbing hold of Corson's sleeve. "Time to go."

The three women cheered and ran. "Go! Go! Go!" they yelled. A call echoed by the archers and fighters waiting for them by the bridge.

"But…!" Pulled along by his two friends, Corson decided to stop complaining and start retreating. Barely able to see out the eye he could open, defending any longer would be the stupidest kind of self-sacrifice—Keera and Aiden were right not to let him throw his life away. And so he ran with them, down the path toward the river. More warriors joined them, pulling back from their battles to join a clot of stragglers trying to push trolleys of possessions across the overladen swing bridge. With one last backward glance, Corson yelled at the people mooching around. "Move. *Now*. How many have to die so you can carry your pillows? Let's go."

Lending urgency to his words, another volley of arrows shot toward them, piercing Keera's backpack and grazing his arm.

"Run!"

Far too many people surged over the bridge at once. It creaked alarmingly. "Slow down! Don't all cross at once." Corson shook his head and turned to face the oncoming foe. Fortunately, the long-lived and quick-footed fae were reticent to fight. Even so, he would have loved the women who'd come to his rescue during the demon attack to stand with him, Keera, and Aiden, but they'd melted into the crowd. Maybe it was for the best.

It was the demons trudging closer that worried him. Slow and steady, while the fae darted here and there, never taking the lead.

They backed up, retreating step by step, all too aware that, once again, he and Aiden and Keera were the last line of defence. A fae arrow zinged past his ear. More arrows from the other side of the river sent the fae archers ducking back behind cover.

"Run!" Aiden yelled.

Corson ran. In two strides he was on the old bridge. Hades, he hated this thing. It bounced with every step. Still, it had its advantages, the large metal cables deterrent enough for many of Brocéliande's most dangerous creatures. A torrent of water crashed over the boulders below.

They were running, and nothing was chasing—except the slow-moving demons. Another arrow whizzed past his ear.

"Keep low!" Aiden shouted.

Corson ducked to the height of the handrail cable. "Where are the spiders?"

"Heading for the crossing upriver."

"They won't cross."

"Hopefully not," Aiden muttered.

They passed knot after knot of people on the road, and still Aiden's parents and the children were nowhere to be seen. From the lights flickering ahead, it looked as if the village had split in two directions. Half continuing upriver toward Market Town, and the Three Sisters, and half heading downriver to the sea.

"Which way do you think the children went?" Keera asked, looking down the two tracks.

"Out through the Three Sisters," Aiden said. "The Society and all the Earthsiders will be trying to get back to Earth. Besides, Alice knows that way's our best chance of getting to FaerLand."

Corson scanned the far bank. No spiders or fae…not that he could see.

"Wouldn't the circus-town by the coast be safer?" Keera argued. "That's where they found the library. We could get to FaerLand through there." *Not get caught in an ambush.*

"Really?" Aiden said. Even in the moonlight, Corson imagined he saw his friend's eyebrows raised.

"Didn't Burcham say it had a room of many ways?"

Corson took a couple of steps back; he didn't want to be in the middle of a decision like this. Instead, he kept his eyes peeled, and listened to the night. Screams echoed in the distance. Downstream, not so far away, people were being ambushed by spiders or fae. Exhausted as Corson was, he kept his sword drawn, and his senses on high alert to every wind-blown leaf and every scream.

Not going toward the sea had been the right idea.

Footsteps echoed behind him. Villagers who'd been downstream, now changing their minds and running past, their possessions—if they'd brought any—abandoned.

Like we're being herded upstream—into a trap. Another trap.

"Stop. This is wrong," Corson said, pausing. His stomach roiled with foreboding as he peered around.

Moonlight pooled on the slow-moving section of the river to his right. Nothing there. Then something flickered to his left. The silver of an armoured fae. Faer appeared out of the forest and flourished a sword.

Corson defended, flicking away the sword casually. "Fae!" he yelled. "Protect the villagers."

A blow thunked into his back.

Fiery pain sliced through him as bone grated and a sword burst through his chest. Blood bubbled from his mouth. "Look after the children," he burbled, gasping for air.

A beautiful face leered over him.

§

The fae laughed and turned toward Keera and Aiden. "Run, little humans, and don't come back."

LETTIE

Lettie stared at the bones strewn about the labyrinth floor, unsettled by the mad howling coming from within. The stench of death and her own fear rising to meet her, she fought to be free, then tried to change into flutter form. But the soldiers had her locked fast, their hands squeezing Lettie's upper arms so tight her fingers tingled. The crowd of fae pressing close, pinching and tugging and pushing.

"Zadie!" she yelled, only to be met by crazed giggles. "Please. I'm not a traitor. You know I'm not!"

"It was your fault," Zadie screamed in her ear. "A hundred years, and what did I have to show for it? A handful of twigs and leaves?"

"It wasn't my fault—"

"Don't lie. You had everything you wanted, and all I had was failure."

"Enough!" Queen Persephone roared. "I don't want to see the wretch again."

There was a deathly pause as someone whispered words Lettie couldn't hear. *Maybe it's King Hades. Maybe, beyond all hope, he will grant me a reprieve.*

"Yes, yes, of course. Return my treasured silver axe from the centre of the labyrinth and thou may return to my court," Queen

Persephone said, her voice a slowly building crescendo of fury. "Fail, and I shall banish thee forever. Now send faer in!"

A hundred hands shoved her into darkness.

Feet crunching on bone, she stumbled across the ground. Tripping on a ribcage, she slowed and took stock of the darkness. Behind her, a small child wailed, the sound thin and reedy and echoing. "Lettie, come back!" Ruby cried.

Lettie turned and called, "I'm sorry," guilt dragging at her limbs.

The door slammed and the darkness was absolute. Dulling her white-hot fury to a heavy bruise on her heart. Smothering her.

She fought for breath. Damp earth and animal musk assailed her nostrils.

Slow down. Where's the door?

Inside the darkness something was moving. A heavy scraping and the rattle of falling dirt and rocks was accompanied by snuffling breaths and the thud of the creature's heavy hoof steps—every noise echoing in the dark confines of the passage.

Lettie reached out, fingers touching the crumbling rock that was the cave's edge, and felt—wood. The door!

"Let me out. Please let me out," she banged on the iron-bound wooden door, her fists burning from the iron.

Muffled laughter floated through.

Lettie was going to scream, even though she'd promised herself she wasn't. She'd heard the screams of the victims thrown into the catacombs before. Imagined the horrors they must be experiencing. Heard Queen Persephone's cruel laughter and thought it nothing less than they deserved.

Don't scream. Don't scream. Deep, calm breaths.

Lettie turned and stared into the darkness. Somewhere within, a creature was approaching, its heavy footsteps implacable. It was close now, its snuffles echoing through the corridor. And still, she couldn't see a thing, the darkness deep and thick and stinking like a pigpen. *I thought the minotaur would smell more like a bull.*

The creature charged, hooves clattering loudly on the stone floor.

Her heart fluttering like a sparrow's, Lettie turned to run from it, blindly pelting along the rough corridor, one hand on the wall. One step. Two. Three…

Something thumped into the small of her back. Two sharp somethings.

Lettie screamed.

LAST BATTLE

Aiden slashed at the fae. A half-hearted effort intended to scare her so he could break through to Corson, lying unmoving on the rocky path.

The fae responded with a circular attack. Refusing to give in, Aiden pressed closer, flashing a parry riposte at the fae's shoulder and catching a drip of silver blood on his blade.

More silver-armoured fae were closing in around Corson's body. *Too many to fight.* The fae he'd tried to attack stepped back to the others. Together, they turned their cold eyes and sharp teeth on Aiden.

Keera held her sword out, threatening the fae, and they shied back. "We've got to go." She pulled him away.

"But—" Aiden could barely see through the tears streaming down his face.

"Don't let Corson's sacrifice be for nothing." Keera wiped the back of a hand over her eyes and reached out to tug his shirt. "Come on. We've got to get to the girls."

Still reeling, Aiden backed slowly away. *They'd never hurt a child, would they? His mind shied away from the question, and he began to jog. He couldn't imagine losing any of the children. Or Keera.*

Moonlit silver flashed through the trees. *"Run!"* Keera shouted.

"Okay, but only till we get the others to safety. Then we have to go back save Ruby." *If the fae don't kill us first. Aiden* belted down the forest path with Keera, the fae's silver armour flitting through the trees not so far behind.

As they got closer to Market Town, Aiden struggled to keep up, soon gasping for breath and near tripping over stones, tree roots, abandoned backpacks and other possessions strewn across the track. Ahead, the flicker of torches showed much of the village had taken the path, not out of Brocéliande, but toward Market Town. In the midst of the shadowy crowd ahead, he caught sight of his father only because Changeling Ruby was riding on his shoulders.

"Stop!" Aiden called, sucking gasps of air through his raw throat. "Shouldn't we be getting everyone to safety?"

Aiden's mother was the first to turn back. Snuggled in her arms, Pearl was little more than a shadow against her chest. *Safe.*

"Aiden, my boy, what's wrong?" his father asked. "Where's Corson? Don't say the rumour I heard was true? Was Princess Eirlys right?"

Aiden shook his head. Unable to say the words. Not now.

Changeling Ruby waved, and Aiden smiled at her. Weird how the changeling was becoming more lovable with every breath. He wanted to protect her with his life—as if she were his own daughter.

"Pearl, Ruby, thank goodness you're alright." Keera rushed to Pearl and enfolded the baby in her arms.

Changeling Ruby held out her hand—her mouth moving as if she wanted to say something, but the words were too difficult.

"Come on, Ruby." Aiden plucked Changeling Ruby from his father's shoulders. "We have to get out of here. We can't risk more people getting hurt."

"Nonsense," Burcham said. "We'll go to the trading village. Set up there. Everything will be fine. You'll see. It's what Corson would have wanted."

"Is it?" Keera strode toward him, towering over the man.

Burcham coughed. "Yes, yes, of course. It's the safest option. The Three Sisters is too close to the FaerLand border. We'll go to Market Town. Get help there. Surely, it's a big enough settlement to scare away a handful of fae and spiders."

But at the edge of Market Town, there were no lights and no sign of life. The signpost rattled in the wind, the village eerily silent as leaves and other forest debris blew through empty dirt lanes. An owl called, its thin hoot echoing into the night before disappearing.

Wordless, Burcham and the remaining villagers trooped on, trying to ignore the distant fae racing along under their giant trees, like a silver river, not trying to cut them off—just stopping them from setting foot near FaerLand.

"Aiden, look." Keera pointed ahead. The barest sliver of a crescent moon hung in the sky over a tree with only two trunks.

The Three Sisters—was now only two.

Alice strode ahead and peeked through the trunks. "It's alright," she said. "Earth's still this way." She pulled her three children through the gap.

More villagers hurried through, scrambling between the two trunks to Earth.

Keera and Aiden waited, the fae inching closer as more and more people disappeared through the tree.

A lanky fae bellowed to his companions, "Raise your weapons."

"Damnation," Keera swore. She pushed Pearl into Aiden's mother's hands. "Go."

"On my mark, fire at will." The fae raised an arm.

The remaining people rushed through the small gap. They slowed as they were caught in the crush between the trunks, and had to scrabble for safety. If fae started firing, there'd be a bloodbath. Instead, the fae seemed to be having a whispered argument.

Arrows were nocked. With one last glance across at FaerLand and the arrayed forces, Aiden ran at the now empty gap in the trunk, carrying changeling Ruby through the portal as arrows zinged past.

Keera?

There she was, stepping over the threshold and onto the leafy forest floor, her dark hair shimmering in the moonlight. His heart lighter, he ran to her.

A crack echoed around the clearing.

Changeling Ruby screamed and pointed to the Three Sisters. The tree that should have had three trunks, now only had one.

We're trapped on Earth.

A tear leaked from Ruby's eye. Silver. And it wasn't just the moonlight.

Don't let Burcham, or anyone, see. Aiden wiped away the tear. "Don't be frightened. We're going to get you home." *Somehow.*

Keera sheathed her sword. "How are we going to get back in, now?"

"What do you mean, get back in?" Aiden's father demanded.

Aiden took a deep breath. "Ruby is…not Ruby, she's a change-ling. We need to go into FaerLand to get our Ruby back."

Aiden's dad scowled. "What is this nonsense? Kill the abomi-nation and break the faery pact. What are you waiting for?"

"No," Keera said.

"I'm serious," he continued, ignoring the terrified child burying her face in Aiden's chest and drawing his sword. "You know this is the only way. Do it."

LETTIE IN THE LABYRINTH

Her back throbbing from where the minotaur-creature's horns had stabbed her, Lettie was thrown to the rocky wall of the tunnel. She bounced off the rocks and fell, grazing her hands on the stones below.

Wincing, she tried to jump up.

A hoof stomped on her back, right where she'd been stabbed. *The minotaur is playing with me. How long before it tires and eats me alive?* Lettie sucked in a breath—and the creature screamed. A harrowing cry that split the air above her head. It overpowered her own scream and echoed through the underground tunnel, terminating in a falling death squeal.

Lettie wiggled, half expecting the creature above her to be dead. *No such luck.*

Muffled fae music struck up. Lettie recognised the piece. A celebratory woodwind number that would soon have everyone whirling and capering about as they lost themselves in the music. No, they couldn't be dancing again. Queen Persephone had said they were fighting for their lives and their forest. *What court would be dancing during such a threat?*

"Sorry about that." The creature snuffled and removed its hoof from her shoulders. "I really should introduce myself. I'm Will, Will Burr."

Lettie blinked into the dark. Pinpoints of light on the ceiling danced to life. Enough to show a vague outline of the creature standing on two legs. It didn't have a bull's head, but a pig's snout with curled tusks on each side. And, if she wasn't mistaken, it was covered in woolly fur.

"Who…. What…." Lettie stammered out before pointing a finger at the strange creature. "How dare you?"

The glow worms winked out, and they were thrown back into darkness. Suddenly, Lettie remembered she still had her fig-tree stick. She pulled it from her dress, summoning the green light.

"Come on," Will Burr snorted. "That stick's too bright. You're upsetting the glow worms. They don't like noise or light, but if we speak quietly and don't move too fast, they should light the way."

Lettie rolled her eyes, but she staunched the light from the stick and put it away. "You attacked me, and now you're acting like you think you're my friend?"

"Sorry," the creature grunted, not managing to sound the least bit contrite. "Can't have the queen think we're letting people live, or she might stop sending us recruits."

Maybe it's concussion. Or I'm dreaming. "What?" Lettie asked, rubbing her head.

"What's hardly a question. What-what?"

"Uh?"

"Wonders never cease to amaze… You see what I did there? Maze? Amaze?" He shook his head, his tusks scything from side to side. "Never mind. You're just not ready for it yet. You see, I'm wasted in these tunnels—nobody gets my sense of humour." Sniff. "I don't suppose you thought to bring a match? I've rather run out. Also, the lack of hands, you see. Or rather, you don't, and I suspect that's the problem."

Lettie's mind spun. She'd imagined all kinds of horrors festering in the dark, but a half-mad pig creature was not one of them. "Yes, that's all very…funny, but I need to get back to the surface."

"Everyone says that at first. And they're always wrong. Did you know that needing and wanting to go to the surface are two very different things? Unless you need your head removed from your shoulders, of course. You're not suffering from stone-head or anything, are you?"

"No, what? Of course my head's not infected with stone blight. Also, Queen Persephone isn't into chopping off heads, so that would never happen."

The pig-creature laughed. "That's hilarious, that is." He paused. "Oh, you're not joking. What exactly do you think *will* happen if you go back?"

Lettie frowned. "I don't know. Nobody has ever escaped."

"Ugh, ugh," little half-choked grunts echoed from the annoying creature. "Updweller nonsense. You run around with your eyes closed and don't know what's happening right in front of your noses."

Lettie's head was still spinning. Talking to this annoying creature wasn't exactly what she'd been expecting. She reached out and touched its fur to check that she wasn't imagining things. It was sparse and coarse. Definitely real.

"Do. You. Mind." He snorted.

"Not at all," Lettie smiled. "Besides, if you're all so very nice, how come nobody ever returns from the labyrinth?"

"How do you know they don't? To be honest, most of us prefer it down here, anyway. It's much safer, you know."

"And what about the minotaur?"

"That big softie? A head like a bull. And what do bulls eat? Do you see bulls running about tearing people limb from limb unless they're being run at with red capes? No, you do not."

Lettie frowned. "Isn't he a bit territorial? And isn't this *his* territory?"

"That's why it's important that you're introduced. Come on, let's go find my dad. I think he's going to like you. You're funny."

Lettie sighed and followed the trip-trap of the creature's hooves.

Stuck on the Wrong Side of Everywhere:

Aiden clutched the child to his chest. "Kill her? Never. We want Ruby back, but no."

Burcham nodded. "It should work. It's one of the reasons the fae signed the Myrddin pact."

"What? Because people were murdering changelings?" Aiden snapped.

Burcham nodded.

"And what about Pearl? What if she's a changeling, too?" Aiden's father demanded, glancing at Pearl, who was sleeping wrapped in his wife's arms. "I said this whole thing would end badly." He waved his hands at Aiden and Keera.

"Take that back," Aiden hissed, but his father barrelled on.

"I said it from the beginning. And now you won't even follow my advice to get your own children back. What's wrong with you?"

"Pearl's fine. We tested her, and she's fine. Besides, I'm not a murderer," Aiden replied. "That's what's wrong with me and Keera." How his wife was keeping her temper, he didn't know. But if she could, then so could he—it wouldn't help anyone to yell at the bigoted old fool.

"Just the one changeling?" Aiden's father's voice was sharp-edged.

Aiden nodded.

Burcham let out a whoosh of breath.

It seemed the lawyer had a heart, after all. Unlike dad.

"Good. Kill it," Aiden's father was insisting. "It's the only way."

Ruby clung tighter.

"Then what?" Keera demanded. "What if it doesn't work? You think we can go back to the fae with a dead body and demand our child back? You think Ruby will magically appear here, alive?"

"But, my grandchild..." Aiden's mum sputtered.

"Will be dead if we kill the changeling. That's how we'd get her back—dead," Keera told him. "Is that what you want?"

"Mmm, you may well be right. You have to read between the lines of the old texts." Aiden's mother backed Keera up. "I...I think the children—I mean, Aiden and his wife—are right. If we want Ruby back alive, we need to get them into FaerLand so they can swap the changeling for Ruby."

"Don't listen to me, then," Aiden's father snapped and stormed off.

"He'll be fine," Aiden's mother whispered. "It's just a shock." She turned to go, Pearl still sleeping in her arms. "Also, take this." She pressed the gold and black book she'd found in the Library of Alexandria into his hands. "Take this as a good-luck charm. I have a feeling you'll need it."

"Keep her safe," Aiden said, tucking the book into his pocket and trying not to worry about his father's tantrum. Hopefully, Mum was right and he'd be over it soon. "We'll get this child home, and your sister back," he told the sleeping Pearl. Fighting tears, he turned away. In his arms, Changeling Ruby flashed her chubby fingers open and closed in a sad goodbye.

Keera raced over to bid her baby goodbye, too. Then she ran back to Alice, who was juggling her own three small children, the smallest one asleep in her arms. "Alice, we have to get into FaerLand. And you're the only one who can do it."

"Of course I'll help you get your Ruby back," Alice replied. "But we needn't hurry, time passes differently across the fae border. If we wait…"

"It's been days," Keera said.

"Yes." Alice nodded. "Yes, of course it has. Burcham, I need to get to my silver mirror."

"Ah." Burcham wiped a hand across his forehead. "It's very late."

"Believe me, I know." Aiden grated. "And if I go back in and it's too late to save Ruby—" He left the threat hanging in the air.

"Of course, it's no trouble." Burcham nodded. "No trouble at all."

Alice kissed her children goodbye, handing the youngest over to her husband, Prof Brian Faulkner. "Get them home to bed, will you? Night children, I've got to go, but I'll be back soon. I hope." The last two words were barely a whisper in the breeze.

"Mum," Hazel said. "Let me come with you."

"I'd rather you were safe at home in bed." Alice cuddled each of her children again and waved goodbye.

Brian Faulkner kissed her. "Be careful."

"I will."

"Brian, will you hold on to my forging equipment and Pearl's sword?" Keera said. "If…"

"We'll be back soon," Aiden said. Any other alternative was unthinkable. "The sooner we're gone. The sooner we're back."

Keera shouldered Ruby's sword. "Good. Then, let's go."

Burcham stepped into the conversation. "I'm not so sure I'm up to it, after everything."

The young medic interrupted. "I'm sure you're fine, sir. But if you'd like, I'll keep an eye on you and make sure you get home safe afterward."

Burcham huffed. "Fine. I'll come right out and say it. I'm not so sure I want them to use my mirror. The risk of being possessed by demons is too great."

Alice put her hands on her hips. "Like I said, it's *my* mirror. You have it for safekeeping, remember?"

"Really, you don't want to do this. There must be another way," Burcham insisted, arguing about the danger of travelling into FaerLand all the way to his office.

"Burcham, you are not my keeper," Alice snapped. "I know the dangers, and I know how to avoid them."

Burcham finally relented and let them in, but only after Aiden threatened to break down the door.

Alice pulled the sheet off the silver surface. "Are you ready?"

Scenes flickered across the mirror.

Alice took a deep breath and put her arms around Aiden's and Keera's shoulders. "I'm only going to get you to the FaerLand forest border. It's up to you from there."

"Mercy be on your souls," Burcham muttered as if Aiden wasn't freaking out enough already.

Keera nodded bravely, her hand reaching out to him. Changeling Ruby gripped Aiden tight again.

"Ready?" Alice said.

"Ready," Aiden and Keera confirmed. Together, the three stepped through the liquid-silver surface into the Silver Paths of the Dead.

§

The sensation of drowning rushed over Aiden.

Keera? He grasped her hand and she smiled back. Between them, Alice was stoic. *She's been here before. How bad can it be?*

Endless reflective corridors of silver and darkness. Black wings battered him. Aiden glanced down at the squirming bundle in his arms. *Are you alright?* He tried to push the words out, but he couldn't speak. The air was so thick, his lungs felt heavy, like he was trying to breathe underwater.

Changeling Ruby turned into a bush monkey, then a possum and an owl—its sharp claws scratching him.

He screamed soundlessly. Stopping only when he saw Keera's wide-eyed concern echoed.

Trees, taller than the highest building he'd ever seen, towered dizzyingly all around them. Reflections of the fae world outside. Alice clutched his shoulder hard and pulled them toward the ancient forest. They bounced away, off the unyielding mirror-like surface and fell through the Paths of the Dead—spiralling down, down, down into a sparkly abyss. Aiden, with no breath left to scream, clutched the squirming changeling who turned into everything from a tea set to a pack of cards to a butterfly.

LETTIE'S AMAZED

The further Lettie walked, the more she felt as if she was being drawn into a trap, the winding tunnels branching and branching again.

I'll never find my way out. Unless…I leave a trail. That's what you're supposed to do in a maze.

Lettie had no handy balls of string. No breadcrumbs. Just her dress…spun from the finest spider silk. She picked at an edge, smiling now. *Now I can find my way out, I'll only have to bring Queen Persephone the silver axe she so desperately wants…or survive her wrath. Surely, surely, she'll realise I'm no traitor.*

Will looked sideways at her. "Wouldn't bother," he said. "Almost everyone has already done it. See?"

Lettie peered closer in the dim light. Sure enough, the floor under her slippered feet was a tangle of string and other markers.

"I mean, nobody is going to stop you leaving a trail. And so long as it's not food, it'll stay right where it is—nobody will touch it. Believe me, food disappears here, sure as eggs are eggs and mushrooms are mushrooms. Talking of food, I'm starving. Do you have anything on you?"

"Sorry." Lettie shook her head. "I gave my emergency supply to the child."

"It's hungry work waiting for victims," the creature said. "But sometimes they're already dead, so that's why I do it. For the *just in case*."

"Ew," Lettie held a hand over her mouth. "You eat dead bodies?"

"Can't waste good food. There's not a lot to eat down here except ant food and fungi. But I guess you'll find that out soon enough. And the only way out is... Anyway. Time you met the boss, Asterius."

"A star what?" Lettie blurted.

"Yes, bit of a terrible joke. He hasn't seen the stars for years. But he says the glow worms are his stars, so maybe that's good enough."

Oh, he's wittering on about the minotaur, Asterius.

She shook her head. "If it's all right with you, I'd rather not meet this Asterius. Maybe instead, you could show me the way out."

Will Burr snuffled with laughter. "Good one..." His laughter trailed off. "Oh, right, you really don't know how things work here. Well, everyone who comes in must be brought to Asterius. It's kinda a big deal. You know what he did with the last fae who came here? The gardener?"

Lettie patted her head, remembering the old gardener and his daisies. A hundred years ago, when she still missed being a changeling, he'd made daisy chains for her and made her feel special. And he'd always had a kind word. "No! Asterius didn't kill the gardener, did he?"

"Not at all. The boss gave faer a position making the official labyrinth garden pretty as a picture. He's decided on getting everything looking just so. Like a palace garden. Wait until we get there, then you'll see what all us feyr-folk are made of." He said the word feyr, a little like fire, and not like fair or faer.

After hours of walking around and around the wickedly complex maze, a bright light beckoned. They walked toward it for a time. As they approached the dazzling cavern, Lettie squinted into the brilliance, to find it not as bright as she first thought. Indirect light flooded in from above, reflecting off a silver trove of jewels and other treasures. Shining daisies studded the ground all around like living gems.

"Where are we?"

"Under the island of the fairy godmothers."

The minotaur—half man, half bull—sat on a throne of silver faery bones dripping with gold as if in mockery of the fae belief that gold was the literal tears of the sun.

Seated in a semicircle around the throne, like they were in a stadium, were creatures of the night and of the forest. The creatures Queen Persephone deemed too ugly for her court. Terrifying spines and googly eyes were everywhere, along with all manner of creatures. Gnomes, cave dragons, golems, boggarts, goblins, leprechauns and satyr, trows, mole people and more. Big furry monsters she didn't recognise and a handful of sturdy no-nonsense trolls. They crowded themselves into the seating up in the stands around a roped-off dirt pit. Creatures Lettie had rarely seen, and until now, had deeply feared, were sharing drinks and food and having a ball–well, not precisely a ball, but they appeared happier than the queen's courtiers at an all-summer party.

Lettie took a calming breath. All in all, the creatures in the crowd were not nearly as scary as they first looked with their dark clothes, piercing eyes and shaggy hair. She couldn't say the same for Asterius, though. The famously dangerous minotaur sat on his gruesomely sparkling bone throne, with gems and silver treasure gathered at his feet and a gold crown on his broad head. The axe was lying on the ground in front of him—like a challenge.

As Will Burr pulled Lettie closer, there was a rumble from the stands about how Queen Persephone needed to look after her own. Shrill voices rose over the ruckus.

"Persephone has broken the overland pact twice this year! That's two times too many."

"We should teach Persephone and Hades a lesson."

Lettie quailed, shuffling back in an attempt to hide in the dark shadows.

"Don't worry. It's all talk," Will said. "They'll never do a thing. Been ranting about King Hades and Queen Persephone since I was a nipper. But all we've ever done is hide and talk about the overland pact, even though Queen Persephone breaks it every time she throws someone down here."

"How can you all hide down here?" Lettie asked, finding her nerve. "Queen Persephone has stolen my child. She's stolen a human child and broken Myrddin's pact. What makes you think she'll keep any of your other agreements?"

"We will revolt," Will said. "We are revolting." He paused. "Come on. That was funny."

"It…was…not…funny," Asterius growled. "Fae. Have you come to offer your fealty to me?"

"Not really," Lettie said, digging her fingernails into her palms to stop herself from shaking. "Well, it wasn't the plan." She wrinkled her nose at the nauseating aroma of wet-hair and sweat emanating from the minotaur's body.

Asterius stomped a cloven hoof. "You. Make it your plan."

Lettie glanced at the silver axe. "I have to escape."

"You've come for the cursed axe, haven't you? You know the queen only wants it so she can chop people's heads off."

"And what do *you* use it for?"

Asterius grinned, picking up the wickedly sharp axe and tossing it from heavily muscled arm to heavily muscled arm. "Why don't you come here, little fae, and find out?"

A winged pegasus flew in through an opening high in the ceiling, trailing a silver-birch-wood carriage. It was decorated with ornate protective silver spells not so different from the scrollwork on Keera's swords. "Thank goodness you're here," a flutter-form fairy in a blue ball dress called through the open window. "Lettie, you have to go back, or both Rubys will die."

LIBRARY

"Mirror, mirror, on the wall
"how do I destroy the most evil one of all?"

"Silver-etched writing rippled across the surface:
"Evil? How can you tell?"

—Records and Papers:
"How to Destroy a Farie Queen."

A howl echoed through the Silver Paths of the Dead. The primal fear of a wolf echoed through Aiden's bones. The bundle in his arms twisted and turned. Silky scales wrapped around his arm. Unable to scream, Aiden quashed his fear and his impulse to throw the changeling in his arms away.

Changeling Ruby is holding on tight, the only way she knows how.

Flickering in the mirror-scape were forests and meadows, clouds and castles and many vistas, both achingly beautiful and terrible to behold. Crystalline forests, ice-sculpted canyons, blazing golden deserts where scrawny plants dripped with rubies, sapphires and diamonds, Aiden even thought he glimpsed a dragon skimming low over a vast ocean.

A murder of ravens battered past, shrieking and cawing. Something large howled, the echo bouncing around the fractured mirror-landscape.

The changeling turned into an owl. It grasped Aiden's arm so tight, blood welled where the claws jabbed into his skin.

How much longer? Will we suffocate? He thought about his family, the last glimpse of Ruby, and the book his mother had given him.

A stately old room full of books, and lit by moonlight, flashed in front of them.

Is something wrong?

Alice pulled them through. The silver sucked at him as he stepped out onto the library floor, coughing and spluttering. As they passed the barrier, the changeling transformed back into her Ruby form. She clung to Aiden, sobbing while he gasped for air.

Keera and Alice were also doubled over wheezing. Only Changeling Ruby seemed unfazed by the lack of oxygen. Silver tears drying, she stared around the gloomy old room full of books, scrolls, and parchment. It looked more like a weird wine cellar full of layers of compartmentalised shelves of ancient paper, than any library he'd ever seen before. Maybe that was partly due to the poor lighting, leaving many of the shelves in deep shadow.

"Oh, Alice, that was awful. I'm sorry we put you through this," Keera said.

"That's alright," Alice brushed down her brown circle-dress. "I'm sorry. I'm not sure what was stopping me, but I couldn't get us in. And I'm not sure how we got in here either, but it's lucky we did, Cerberus was on our path. You heard his howl."

"Can he get in here?" Aiden asked, thinking about how lucky they'd been that his mother had given him the book, but focussing on the dangers ahead.

Alice shuddered. "I hope not." She looked around, taking in her surroundings for the first time, her jaw dropping. "I think we're in the Great Library." She ran to the shelving, mumbling. "How did I find this place? I could never get here before."

A siren whined from the stairwell. A pair of heavy footsteps thundered through the building, coming their way.

"And it looks like Cerberus isn't our only problem," she said. "That sounds like a giant."

"Well, well, well, who is this in *my* library?" An enormous voice bellowed from the darkened corridor.

Aiden fumbled for the tinderbox to see better. A spark flashed before his eyes. It quickly died, and the room seemed all the dimmer for it.

A wheelchair appeared in the door. The shadowy occupant, her foot swathed in plaster, rolled fast toward them and stopped on a dime, plucking the tinderbox from Aiden's fingers. "Bad enough you brought swords," she bellowed into a speaking brassy flower-like trumpet before pushing it away. "We have a strictly no swords policy. But a tinderbox! What were you thinking?"

"Um," Aiden mumbled. "Ah…I'm Aiden Andersen, and this is my wife, Keera, and our friend, Alice. My wife and I are trying to get to FaerLand."

"Yeah, I'm Abigail Lawson, Head Librarian. As you can see, this isn't FaerLand. The way is closed. I heard some annoying mud-humans had riled up the spiders." The librarian adjusted her winged glasses and peered at them closely. "Ah, sorry. I thought you must be…someone else. Why are you here? It's such a nuisance, you know. Visitors are perfectly acceptable during the day. But at night I have to take you to processing. And you'll never be able to come back again." She sighed.

Poor Alice clapped her hand over her mouth. "But…"

She and Brian had talked about discovering the wonders of this library ever since they knew it existed.

Aiden stepped forward. "We have to save our child. But let Alice go…"

"But that's not a chil…ah, it's a changeling. I see. Queen Persephone has found a red-headed babe and doesn't want to part with it. Happens about once every few centuries. I could get the texts if you like? No, sorry, you probably don't have time."

"We need to find a way into FaerLand?" Alice said. "A way that's not closed."

The librarian nodded toward the door that led back into the room with the mirror. "I couldn't really say. But as the path's warded, you'd need something from FaerLand." The librarian wheeled their chair round to better look at Changeling Ruby and sighed. "Seems to me you never asked. The child's not a talisman or a book, you can't assume…anything. Now, please take the hint and leave. That way I can say that due to my poor injured leg, you evaded me. But let me warn you now, if you come back into the library again without going through the proper channels, I'll not be so forgiving."

"Alice, do you think you can try one more time?"

Alice took a lingering glance down the corridor stuffed with books and sighed.

"You remember the faery rules?" The librarian prompted.

Aiden and the rest of the party nodded. No doubt the rules flashed through their minds, too.

Don't eat the food, or you'll be
trapped in Faerland forever.

Don't touch what is not yours, for it all belongs
to fae, and the fae have no mercy for mortals.

And don't stand still—time
disappears in FaerLand.

Aiden remembered one more from the book Wyrden had given him:

> *If you invite yourself to the dance—*
> *not even the queen herself can hurt*
> *you until after the dance is over.*

What if Ruby has already broken the rules?

UNDER GROUND KERFUFFLE

Asterius stood up and shook the axe at the fairy godmother. "How dare you interrupt my court!" he bellowed.

Lettie quailed, but the audience loved Asterius' outburst. They rose to their feet, clapping and stamping.

"Fight!" a young satyr shouted, stamping her hoofed feet.

Hundreds of the underground dwelling miscreants cheered and took up the call.

The minotaur waved for silence, turning to Lettie. "Are you sure this is what you want? If the fairy godmothers like you, you can't be all bad. So why are you thinking about taking my axe to that awful upstart of a queen?"

"Ah…" Lettie glanced around. She'd thought the cavern was full before, but more of Asterius' feyr-folk were snuffling and trotting and even swooping into the grandstand.

The pegasus-drawn carriage circled overhead, swooping past Lettie to reveal half-a-dozen fairy godmothers in flowery garments—each magnificent dress containing layers and layers of petal petticoats. Lettie grinned to think what Queen Persephone would think of poofy petticoats and outrageous dresses—but still, her heart leapt at the thought of wearing one herself.

A.J. Ponder

The floofy fairy godmother in the blue ball dress called out to Lettie again. "What are you doing? Run!"

It was far too late for that. The exits were full of feyr-folk. She couldn't shove her way through. They pushed her into the arena.

"Go on, take the axe, see what you can do." Asterius threw the axe so it landed in the centre of the sandy arena.

Lettie took in the charged atmosphere. She strode into the arena, picked up the axe and tried to run. The crowd gathered close, joining hands so she could not push through. "Stand and face me," the minotaur roared.

Lettie backed off. "I'm not a fighter."

A fairy godmother tutted. "We can see that. You're a fae, though. Not a very old half-human pretending to be fae. So, use that."

Lettie frowned. *I can change?* The thought flicked through her mind, and the next thing she knew she was in flutter form. Whatever Persephone or her soldiers had done, the effect was over.

The axe clattered to the dirt floor.

In flutter form, it was easy to duck Asterius' blows. Landing any was another matter.

A heavy blow caught her shoulder and sent her tumbling, pain ricocheting down her arm.

The crowd roared with approval.

Time to get out.

"Lettie," Will said. "Just swear fealty to Asterius and you can stay safe here."

"Take the axe and run." Someone yelled from the stand. The old gardener. "Go save your Nada!"

Lettie fluttered away from Asterius and waved to the old soul. She only wished she'd appreciated him more when he was above ground. "I would," Lettie said. "But I don't think Queen Persephone really wants it. It was just a pretext to get me to do something stupid—like fight a minotaur."

Take the axe and run back to the queen. Or stay and pay fealty to a minotaur. There had to be another way. She glanced up to the fairy godmother's carriage.

She fluttered high into the air, out of the minotaur's reach. "Stop! Listen. I don't need the axe. I'm going to rescue Ruby and Nada, and then I'm leaving FaerLand." *Leaving everything I ever knew or wanted behind.* "Is anyone brave enough to follow me?"

The crowd roared with laughter.

THE CHANGELING'S
HOME & CERBERUS

Keera turned to Changeling Ruby. "Can you take us to your home?"

Changeling Ruby bit her lip, then nodded. She took them by their hands and dragged them into the mirror.

Keera held her breath. A howl echoed through the silvery-denseness that was the paths of the dead. She glanced behind.

Three enormous dogs were chasing them. *No. One. Cerberus.* Keera caught a glimpse of its three heads yapping. And along with the dog, a thick black swarm of crows rushed toward them. *Could Hades have sent them for us? Surely, we're not so important as all that.*

Her stomach lurched.

We're going to die.

Instinctively, she reached for her sword.

A tiny room with a cot in the centre was in front of them. Changeling Ruby dragged them closer.

Keera flinched. Would they bounce off as they had before? This time it would be right into the jaws of the slavering Cerberus.

Crows battered them, their claws raking Keera's shoulders and sending searing pain running down her back. In the onslaught, it was all Keera could do to keep holding the changeling's hand.

A crow rebounded from an invisible surface, tumbling crazily in front of the tiny cabin. Panic they'd never make it through washed through Keera the moment before they burst through the invisible barrier, leaving the birds to rebound off the surface. *They weren't invited.*

On this side, the portal they'd come through wasn't a mirror, so much as a spatter of silver smeared across the wall.

An enormous dog's head emerged from the splatter. Keera drew her sword, hand still tingling from the burning sensation she'd felt in the Silver Paths of the Dead.

Through the smear, Keera saw Cerberus cock another one of his heads, as if listening to something far away. Snapping one last time at empty air, the huge creature retreated.

Keera heaved a sigh of relief.

Moonlight filtered in through the wall slats of a tiny wooden room. A cot in the centre was strewn with cushions and draped with a gossamer-like fabric. The one fancy feature in the plain wooden cottage—no, treehouse.

Changeling Ruby smiled beatifically and released their hands. In an instant, the child was gone, and a butterfly fluttered above them. Then an owl. In a flurry of beating wings, the flying creature hovered over a little nest of feathers and trinkets.

She circled the room and transformed back into Ruby... well, almost Ruby. The changeling had Ruby's red hair, and Ruby's chubby arms and determined scowl—but with wings in the fiery hues of autumn.

"Ruby. Changeling." Keera said. "We need to go and rescue our Ruby."

"No. Stay home, now. Waiting for Lettie." The changeling's voice was clearer now she'd had some practice. *If she'd talked like this earlier....* Aiden shook the thought away. If she'd been able to talk earlier, they would never have known their child was stolen. The changeling climbed into the cot, turned into a hedgehog and snuggled into the cushions.

"Sleep sound." Aiden covered her with the gossamer fabric.

Keera hesitated.

Alice clasped and unclasped her hands. "I don't like this at all. I can't go back. The mirror's too small." She sighed. "I guess I'll have to stick around. Help you get home in reasonable time."

"Thank you so much," Aiden said. "I don't know where we'd be without you."

Alice flashed a tight smile, worry hiding in the crinkles.

Past time to leave, Aiden thought. He peeked around the cottage door and gasped at the ancient forest that spread out below them. They were hundreds of feet above the ground and halfway up an enormous tree with tree-fort like cottages scattered along its branches. Wood-and-rope paths were strung around the trees and between houses, each with wharf-like structures leading to empty air.

Along the many branches, fae appeared at their doors. Some looking like people with tree-coloured skin and butterfly wings, others tall and willowy and regal.

"We have a changeling. She...fae is sleeping." Keera sheathed her sword in a gesture of good will.

A low rumble of muttering rose from the nearby houses. Tiny fae flew like butterflies before alighting on the platform outside Lettie's house and transforming back into full sized fae.

Sharp teeth and wide curious eyes loomed closer. "Humans!"

"Humans, what are you doing here?"

"How *dare* you?!"

"*You* don't belong here." The accusing voices got louder and louder.

"Let's go!" Aiden grabbed Keera's hand, and they ran out onto the walkway over the forest...but there was nowhere to go. No stairs down. Only the forest floor hundreds of feet below.

Alice shook her head as if she knew better, while Keera and Aiden skidded to a halt, grabbing onto branches.

More and more fae crowded toward them. Urgent voices demanding they leave.

Sudden laughter peeled out. "It's a miracle! You brought Nada back. Thank you, thank you," a green-limbed figure with a peachy pink dress—and a head to match—fluttered over to Aiden and Keera. "I'm Rose, Lettie's neighbour. May the good queen bless you."

Changeling Ruby put her head out the door. "Can Nada please sleep?"

"And Nada is fae! We really need to celebrate!" Rose insisted, eliciting a round of cheering. "I know, a dance!"

"Stop!" A striking green fae dressed in bright yellow petals flew up to the platform and levelled an accusatory green finger at the humans. "It be a trap. A trick. Lettie be a liar and a..."

"Oh, shut up, Zadie," the neighbour said. "That's enough. I'll hear no more against poor Lettie. She was a treasure. And you, you are nothing but a jealous streak of sunshine, ready to burn anyone who dares to venture into the forest. The mud-humans who brought our treasure home are free to stay or go so long as... so long as the queen doesn't say otherwise."

"Queen Persephone knows what they deserve," Zadie yelled, fluttering green-speckled yellow wings and landing on the branch that served as a railing. "She knows all about them—*and* Lettie's treachery. That's why Queen Persephone sent Lettie into the labyrinth."

The neighbour gasped. But not everyone was surprised. A tiny fae, dressed all in green, nodded furiously. "Yes, she's gone into the Labyrinth. No, there's nothing we could do. The queen wills it, and so it must be right."

"What?" Keera interjected. "The fae we're looking for was sent into the Labyrinth? What about the child?"

"Child!" Zadie shouted. "*Child*? You mean the monster who has stolen the heart of the queen. We all know how this goes, don't we?"

Aiden pulled Keera's sleeve. "We should go."

The tiny green fae jumped up next to Zadie. "We must obey Queen Persephone. Anything else is treachery."

"Hear, hear!" Zadie yelled. "And I am the voice of the queen. Obey me!"

With the bridges blocked, and unwilling to jump down to the ground a hundred metres or more below, Keera, Aiden and Alice backed into the hut. Changeling Ruby greeted them by the door. She pulled at Keera's shirt and pointed away from the growing cluster of fae to what appeared to be a wharf sticking out of the rickety balcony and into mid-air.

Swiftly, they raced to where Changeling Ruby was pointing, but just as swiftly it became clear this was another dead end, leading only to the forest floor below.

Keera pulled back. "We can't."

Changeling Ruby didn't say a word, merely flicked out her wings and turned into a red-feathered bird the size of a lion. She picked up Aiden in one giant claw and Keera in the other, then dragged them to the edge.

"Let me go!" Keera shouted, struggling to break free. But the giant bird the changeling had turned into was more than a match for Keera. The footpads were strong and wiry, and the huge claws wrapped around her chest like steel bars.

"Stop," Zadie cried, flying over and trying to get in Changeling Ruby's way.

With a rush of air, the changeling jumped off the edge.

"Keera!" Alice yelled. Catching hold of a startled Zadie, she jumped after them, her brown skirts catching the breeze like a parachute.

Keera's stomach lurched sickeningly as they plummeted toward the forest floor. Behind them, Zadie screamed all the way down until Alice let go of her and dropped into a thick carpet of moss. Moments later, they also hit the forest floor—the landing jarring every bone in Keera's body.

Above, Zadie took off into the forest, whistling loudly. A flock of fae took off after her, like a pastel squad of fighter pilots. They didn't hang around, but flew off through the enormous trees.

Aiden staggered to his feet and clutched his limbs, as if checking them for damage. Keera followed suit, almost surprised to find nothing broken.

Alice tried to dust the green moss stains from her knees and failed. "You alright?"

"Still breathing," Aiden muttered.

The changeling shook herself, transforming from the bird creature and into a giant iridescent-blue butterfly. Rising just out of reach, she fluttered impatiently, darting to and fro over the path, as if unsure whether to wait or follow Zadie and the others.

Keera and Alice took off after her.

"Wait." Aiden cast about, trying to peer down the path in each direction.

But the trees crowded close, and the path twisted and turned. All he could see in the thin twilight that pierced the forest was a wall of rich, leafy and mossy greens in both directions. Even the famous Fae moon was almost invisible through the foliage in this strange twilight land of green.

A.J. Ponder

If the fables were true, the fae would have taken Ruby to one of Queen Persephone's famous balls. There'd be hundreds of glorious dancers, dazzling in the twilight, artfully lit in the glow of a million glow worms that shone like stars in the sky. The heady scent of roses and the sweet taste of ambrosia would permeate the air.

"Which way?" Aiden asked, his voice swallowed by the silence.

Keera took out Ruby's sword and balanced it on her fist. It twisted, swivelling so that the pommel pointed deeper into the forest.

Rustling to the side of the path caught her attention. A shiny black head with half a dozen eyes appeared from behind an ancient tree—a giant spider the size of a wolf! It skittered closer.

Keera, Aiden and Alice ran. Keera sucked in lungfuls of the heavy forest air, determined to outrun it. She'd seen enough giant spiders for one lifetime, and this was even bigger than the ones they'd been fighting. Their only hope was that it would be slow.

The spider matched them stride for stride. Its long spiky legs easily keeping up with their hectic pace through the towering forest, never once faltering over the roots that snaked over the mossy ground. With fangs the size of arms, and spinnerets producing silk as thick as her arm, Keera couldn't help but be intimidated.

Then Keera's injured back prickled. As if the spider wasn't bad enough, she felt an eerie certainty that they were being followed.

Glancing back, Keera was aware of other strange people following them. The more she looked, the more of the unusual fae she saw creeping through the trees.

Maybe it's a trap. Keera felt for her pommel. *If I'm going to die, I'm going to go down fighting.*

Arachne's Daughter

Aiden glanced behind at the elegant spider, its long legs and even its face subtly different to the ones that had attacked them in Brocéliande. Less arachnid, and more human, perhaps. Surprised to be still alive and not dragged off to hang from the closest tree, Aiden's memory of fairy tales and mythology prickled at his memory. If only he'd paid more attention to Faulkner, who loved that kind of stuff.

Alice was also slowing. "Do I know you?" she called over to the terrifying creature. "Arachne? Daughter of Arachne?"

The spider said nothing. It seemed more fascinated by the changeling than by any of the humans. There was one small mercy though, she was kind enough to keep her distance. There was no reason to think this daughter of Arachne, or whatever it was, would be hostile—except for the recent Brocéliande attack. But FaerLand was not Brocéliande, and this spider was not one of the ones they'd been facing.

Aiden's right side stabbed with crippling pain. He clutched his flank. Stitch, nothing more, but he couldn't force himself to keep running fast enough. Out of choices, he turned to face the creature, putting himself in front of Keera.

"You smell of death," the spider said. "Why are you here?"

"I've come for my child." Keera answered, hand hovering near her sword. "The fae stole her."

"I see. Up to their old tricks. They sent my foolish children out to die, too. But I wish you hadn't killed them."

"Not by choice," Aiden said. "We…" He shook his head. "So, the fae were behind this. Their soldiers—"

The spider turned to go.

"Wait!" Keera called. "Have you seen her? A little girl. Red hair…"

The creature pointed along the path and turned away, disappearing back into the forest.

Alice frowned. "Are you sure we can trust a spider? After…"

"She didn't kill us. Seemed like an act of good faith to me." Keera pulled out the sword she'd made for Ruby again. It swivelled and settled, the handle pointing the way they were going. "See?"

Rustling in the ferns alerted Aiden. Someone was watching them. More than one someone. Their small party was gaining a following, creeping along the edges of the forest. With snub noses and pale hands, these creatures were hardly elegant like the fae Aiden was used to seeing. Aiden kept turning back in the hope to catch a glimpse, but the shimmery FaerLand light made it hard to spot the followers creeping through the velvet-green shadows beneath the giant trees.

Two silver-armoured soldiers approached on the path ahead with two rainbow-winged gossamer butterflies trailing behind them. The soldiers trudged toward Aiden and Keera.

The giant butterflies' hind wings fluttered like coattails as they flew nearer, their giant curled proboscises unravelling into sharp-tipped straws.

Their legs reached out.

Keera drew her sword.

"I wouldn't if I were you," one of the fae butterflies said.

"This is the Fae Kingdom. It is not for mortals," a silver-armoured soldier barked. "Why are you here?"

Aiden raised his sword. "We have come to return this changeling and reclaim our daughter. Do you stand in our way?"

"Not at all." The soldier smirked. "We've come to kill you."

Meanwhile, Back in the Labyrinth

Asterius charged Lettie, horns down.

She fluttered out of the way, but not before the minotaur caught her dress on his horns and sent her tumbling to the dirt.

Asterius posed, a hand raised to the ceiling. Expecting a thunderous roar of applause that didn't arrive.

The crowd turned to stare through the door Lettie had entered.

"What's happening?" Asterius roared. "Is this not enough entertainment for you?"

A boggart soldier saluted. "Something's happening back at FaerLand. Despite the sealed borders, Earthsiders have entered the kingdom of FaerLand. The fools have claimed the rite of the dance."

"They're not running? Well, this will put the boggarts in the cream." Asterius hefted his axe over his shoulder and adjusted his crown. "This is our time. The fae is right. Down with the half-gods Queen Persephone and King Hades!"

He turned his back on Lettie and followed his boggart soldiers back along the path. Fae of all kinds jostling along in front, beside and behind them.

"Come with us," the blue fairy godmother called, pulling Lettie up and into their carriage and jumping onto the pegasus' back.

Lettie was crammed inside with five other fairy godmothers. She squirrelled her way onto the bench-seat, half-buried in their massive skirts.

"Welcome to the Sewing Circle of Fairy Godmothers. Do you want to join?"

"Let me think about it," Lettie answered. On one hand, the fairy godmothers were a topic of gossip and scandalous rumour of their human-loving ways. On the other, they seemed a lot more fun than either Persephone or the elderfae.

A fairy godmother in a blue dress patted her hand. "You should join us, you know. Fairy godmothers don't need to answer to Asterius or Queen Persephone." Lettie nodded and watched out the window as the pegasus shot up through the hole in the ceiling, dragging the sumptuous little carriage across the tiny island, flying like the wind itself. Lettie, crushed up next to the ample fairy godmothers, marvelled at the blur of colourful flowers beneath them, the sea and then the forests in the heart of FaerLand. Too soon, the fairy godmother's carriage hovered above a tree just outside Queen Persephone's royal theatre.

The Rite of the Dance

"**W**ait!" Aiden told the fae soldiers. Their lustrous hair falling around faer shoulders as they drew their swords. "We, ah…claim right of the dance."

The soldier barely blinked. "You can dance all you like. It won't do you much good." But he stood aside and let them continue on their way, albeit with two silver-armoured guards and two enormous butterflies following in their wake.

The clearing was brighter than the deep forest they'd left behind. It glittered with lanterns and giant glow worms. Threads of lights, like clear Christmas tree decorations, dangled from the branches.

A red-headed beauty in a stunning pomegranate evening dress sat on a high-backed throne of elaborate living wood and draped in blousy roses. Aiden hardly needed to see her crown of silver and sparkling jewels to be confident that this was the famous Queen Persephone.

The throne next to hers was empty.

Queen Persephone rose, elegant and terrifying. Eyes blazing, she roared, "Thou dare to enter my kingdom? Thou dare to barge into my court? Thine wretched kind is not wanted here." She waved her hand. In the distance was Brocéliande, and the charred remains of New Avalon.

Wyrden drifted in. "What a lovely surprise seeing you here. I think you'll find there's a human saying that fits this occasion: you can check out any time you like, but only fae can leave."

At least Hades isn't here. Without his power, and his demons, we still have a chance.

Ruby was clutching the giant ribcage of bones that surrounded her—like a museum exhibit of a long-extinct creature—or an evil witch's idea of a playpen. Her hair was tussled, her face grimy, but the gossamer dress she was wearing rivalled those of the fae swirling around. Keera raced toward Ruby, and almost barrelled into a giant three-headed dog—Cerberus. The hell hound's snake-tail swayed from side to side as if to get a better view. The cobra-like tail then hissed and spat venom at them over Cerberus' head. The toxic mess spattering to the ground at their feet.

Behind the terrifying three-headed dog was a human figure with fiery hair. *Hades!* He laughed and pulled on the creature's leash. "Later."

Aiden's heart sank as the King of the Underworld sauntered over to the fae throne.

"Mama," Ruby called, her little hand reaching through the ivory bones. "Mama!"

The fae stopped, glancing to their king and queen.

Keera and Aiden used the distraction to rush over. "Ruby!" Keera called and held the sword up to her daughter. Ruby's fingers brushed its hilt and the red stone flared. One of the enormous butterflies swooped over Ruby's cage, its evening coat tails brushing the ivory bones.

"Thou made it after all," Queen Persephone said. "Soldiers, what did I say? And you again, Alice. Why, the pleasure is all mine. Or at least it shall be."

A soldier whispered in her ear. "They claimed the right of the dance."

Her lips curled upward. "Well then, thou may dance. Then thou shall pay the price."

The book had said nothing about a price.

Aiden swallowed. *What have I done?*

Wyrden waved his white cane, his lips curled in a triumphant smile. "I can't wait to see you both dance."

"Musicians!" Queen Persephone called.

"Wait. I shall tell you a story first," Aiden said, picturing the words he'd read in the tome. Treatise On Fae. It was taking everything he had not to look to see what Keera and Alice were doing while he distracted the fae. "A story of a bargain between you and Myrddin Wyllt, signed in the year five hundred and seventy—"

"I don't want to hear it," Queen Persephone replied. "The child is ours. A child for a child. That is our way. And now the dance." She clapped her hands, and a discordant cacophony of wind instruments began.

"A child for a child," Keera shouted over the rapid music, sidestepping the fae who tried to pull her into the dance. "Now take her."

Aiden pushed Changeling Ruby toward Queen Persephone.

Queen Persephone held out a green-tinged hand. "No."

The fae jumped at Persephone's, no. Some even stopped dancing to watch.

Aiden raised an eyebrow, refusing to bow to her authority. "That's against the terms of Myrddin's Pact."

"The pact be no more. Wake up. Myrddin be long gone, while we fae continue on longer than any mortal pact."

"Surely, your word is binding?" Keera demanded over her shoulder even as she and Alice were whirled away into the dance.

Persephone clapped. "Lawyers, where be my lawyers? They should be here when I'm dealing with Earthsiders. Fetch them immediately, Wyrden."

Wyrden bowed. "Very well, my lady. At once. I shall see what is taking them so long."

"In the meantime, musicians, louder! We shall have some fun. Dance. Dance."

The clearing was filled with swirling fae as the musicians' cacophony reached a crescendo. Ruby wailed again, and they matched her wails with harmony and syncopation.

Aiden was pulled into the dance and thrown from one fae to the next, his hiking clothes out of place in all the finery. He angled his way back toward the cage.

"Ruby!"

"Dada." Ruby hiccoughed and wiped the tears from her face. "Dada! Dada! Maaaamaaaa…"

Where is Keera?

Aiden couldn't see her in the mass of dancing—the chaotic music crashing through the sparkling woody grove as he whirled around and around. He thought he caught sight of Alice's brown dress as she danced with a blue Edwardian waistcoated fae with long hair. *There.* An electric-blue butterfly caught his eye, its wings edged with darkness. Aiden wasn't even sure how he knew the butterfly was the changeling, but something about faer was familiar. And faer was dancing above Keera's head as fae pushed her from partner to partner with wild abandon.

"Run, little changeling," Aiden called. But the changeling didn't run or fly away. Swirling over the celebrations, the changeling dipped toward a familiar fae, transforming into a dozen different creatures as if in sheer excitement. A fae in a blue dress so grubby she looked as if she'd been buried in a dungeon…

"Lettie!" the changeling cried out.

The blue-capped fae stood, enraptured, her mouth moving— but Aiden couldn't hear her over the music. The delight on her face dropped as Wyrden strode toward her, his white cane swinging jauntily. He clapped his hands. "Oh, Burcham, would you be a dear and bring out the dancing shoes? This is going to be fun."

Burcham?!

Aiden blinked as Burcham appeared through a large silver mirror. He was holding a pair of sparkling red dancing shoes awkwardly by the straps in one hand, and his briefcase in the other.

What in all the worlds is Burcham doing here?

LETTIE'S DANCE

The roil of uplifting music moved Lettie to dance, but she refused to surrender to the music. Ducking between the dancers, she half ran, half waltzed toward Nada. Her beautiful changeling was no longer trapped in the shape of a child, but fluttering above the dancers in the shape of a long trailing-winged butterfly. The gold spots and dark blue edges of faer wings rippled in silent repudiation of Queen Persephone.

"Nada! Nada, you're safe!" Lettie caught Nada up in a hug, but Nada shimmied free. Circling Lettie, fae transformed into creature after creature in a dazzling display.

"And I can talk!" Nada said. "Am I fae now?"

Lettie grinned with delight. "See, everyone. See! My changeling is everything we could have wanted, and more."

Nobody even turned to look—except the humans, their bulging eyes taking in the scene with the lack of decorum for which humans were so famous. On the other hand, the queen's retinue acted as if the sight of Nada dancing was distasteful. They shivered in their elegant spider-silk gowns and whispered behind their hands about the gauche mores of flutter-form.

"So showy."

"They have no shame."

"Sad."

Zadie walked up to Lettie, her fists curled into balls. Lettie stepped away meaning to avoid her once-friend, and almost ran smack bang into Wyrden.

"What a lovely surprise seeing you here." He clapped his hands and said, "Oh, Burcham, would you be a dear and bring out the dancing shoes? This is going to be fun."

A large, ruddy-faced man—Burcham—hurried over. He was holding a briefcase in one hand and a pair of sparkling red dancing shoes awkwardly by the straps in the other. Vampyric dancing shoes.

"Ah, this is irregular. I thought I was here for a contract," Burcham said, eyes wide. "And to return this property from our vaults." He waved the soul-sucking shoes.

Lettie took the opportunity to flutter backward, and watch the conversation from a safe distance.

The crowd parted for Queen Persephone, who strode through the clearing like the goddess she was. "Who's this? Where's Silvertongue?"

Wyrden licked his lips. "Dear Queen Persephone, I'm so sorry your favourite lawyer, Silvertongue, was nowhere to be seen. Fortunately, Burcham is here, and he's quite able and willing to carry out the obligations of his law firm—aren't you, Burcham?"

"Of course, my, ah... Queen Persephone," Burcham said. His eyes were wide. His face ashen.

"Yes, quite." Wyrden turned his attention toward Lettie. "Alette, I'm so pleased you made it back. You're just in time to see what the Queen does to your precious Nada and all the mud-humans. No offence, Burcham."

Burcham glared.

"Come, Lettie," Queen Persephone ordered, angry enough for lightning to crackle around her pomegranate dress. "Obey thy command, and I'm sure we can work something out to allay thy wilful disobedience."

Lettie shied away, her eyes fixed on the shoes. No matter the queen's sweet tone, asking Lettie to step into those shoes was literally ordering her to dance to her death. A fate reserved for those who dared to think they could fill Queen Persephone's metaphorical shoes.

"I have never wanted to be you. And now I am no longer yours to command. You threw that away when you threw me into the Labyrinth." Lettie looked up to the fairy godmothers in their pegasus-drawn carriage and her heart surged.

They cared for younglings and bowed to no queen. Or king. Seeing them in the minotaur's cavern, she'd finally understood her calling. They were waving their arms, their voices unable to pierce the queen's music, but their meaning was clear. "Come with us."

"Nada! Let's go." Lettie swirled up toward the silver godmother's carriage, up and up. Nada transformed and flew after her.

In a rush, the queen's Fae-in-Waiting transformed and fluttered into the air, grabbing at Lettie and Nada.

Avoiding the hands grabbing at faer, Nada transformed into a sleek purple bird and spiralled up into the sky, and to freedom. Lettie let loose a cheer for her youngling, who flew as fast and strong as a swallow.

It was glorious. Lettie revelled in Nada's accomplishment, and the freedom of finally knowing who she was. And what she wanted. Flying toward the cheering fairy godmothers in their pegasus-drawn silver-birch-wood carriage, she couldn't wait to escape Queen Persephone's court. Strange to discover too late that Zadie had been right all along when she'd said Persephone was not the wonderful queen Lettie had always imagined. Just a thief and a bully.

Almost there. The dancers below were so caught up in the music that most had failed to notice Lettie's flight. Only Zadie was close, fingers stretching out to grasp at Lettie's feet. Lettie kicked out and flew fast as an arrow. The swirl of the waltz below could hardly drown out her heart's call to freedom.

Below, courtiers gasped.

Hades reached out and grasped Persephone's hand. Lightning arcing between them, they shot a lightning bolt out of their free hands. It flashed past Lettie, and up to the silver-birch-wood carriage, engulfing it in light. Caught in the blast of wind, Lettie reeled, arms flailing, dimly aware of the fairy godmothers inside the carriage booing Hades as Nada plummeted.

"Nada!" Lettie cried.

Nada righted herself.

Ears ringing, Lettie pushed toward the carriage.

"You never learn, do you, Aidoneus?" A green godmother yelled down to Hades. "We'll never endorse you, and you can't catch us, or our pegasus with your lightning."

Zadie rushed forward, caught Lettie by the heel and pulled her down.

Lettie kicked. "Let go, Zadie! Nada, keep going. Go on, the godmothers will save you."

Zadie pulled again, wrapping her wiry arms around Lettie's leg. Lettie kicked out, Zadie's grasp loosening—then Lettie's other leg was grabbed. A fae from the queen's retinue held on with wiry tenacity.

Lettie's wings ached. She kicked and struggled against the relentless hands pulling her down.

Nada hesitated. Then, wings shimmering, she zipped toward Lettie, dive-bombing Zadie's face. *Too close.*

The fae that had been attacking Lettie grabbed Nada. In a flash, Nada turned into an eagle.

Nada is brave and bright and free. Faer will not be pulled down so easily.

More fae piled on.

The plucky youngling fae changed forms from giant bird to pegasus, to dragon. *Surely, she'll win free.*

"Stop this!" the green fairy godmother shouted. "This is against the fairy pact. You cannot break…"

No matter Nada's form, the fae pulling at her did not let go. They clutched tight to Nada and underwent their own transformations into elegant form. Slowly but surely, they pulled the youngling down. Lettie swiped away a silver tear of frustration as she and her youngling were fae-handled to the ground at King Hades and Queen Persephone's feet. Quips hurried to grab them both, piling on until Lettie could barely move.

"Let our subject go!" The fairy godmothers demanded. "You break your own fae law, and you will pay the price."

"That is why we have brought in the lawyer," King Hades said smugly.

"Lettie, my darling child. These shoes shall look so good on you!" Queen Persephone said.

Lettie kicked and squirmed. "Let me go!" It was no use.

"Zadie, will you do the honours?"

"Yes, my queen." Zadie took the ruby slippers and smiled as she began wrestling Lettie's feet into them. It wasn't a fair fight. The soldiers made sure of it, but still Lettie kicked for all she was worth.

"I'm not so sure…" Burcham started to say.

"You will notice the subject is one Alette, fae is…"

"*She,*" Lettie said, struggling against the silver-armoured soldiers holding her.

"*She* is *my* subject and must obey *me,*" Persephone insisted.

"No!" Lettie protested. "Let me go!"

Hades inspected his nails. "This is all in accordance to fae law."

Lettie crossed her arms. "It is not true fae law, and I do not recognise it."

"I'm sorry, but that's no defence in the eyes of the law." Burcham pulled out a stack of papers from his briefcase. "You will note it clearly says here, 'FaerLand is under the provenance of Queen Persephone. The Underworld is the Provenance of Aidoneus Hades. And Asterius has claim to the Labyrinth.'"

"That ugly minotaur only has the Labyrinth so he can keep those vile peoples away from my door." Queen Persephone muttered, "if for no other reason than they're the most terrible dancers I've ever seen."

Lettie kicked Zadie one more time.

"Ow!"

The elation at that small victory died as Zadie tied the final lace, and the shoes on her feet compelled Lettie to dance.

ALICE IS WRONG

*A*iden, swirled around by the many dancers, struggled to keep an eye on Keera and Alice. He turned his head this way and that, while fae loomed in and swung away, always perfectly poised, their uncanny faces smiling to reveal sharp teeth. Keera, normally so light on her feet, was struggling. She whirled close, and Aiden reached out, only to be pulled away.

Alice was on the outskirts of the dance, talking to some of the less courtly fae as if they were old friends. She seemed in control of her dancing, and not nearly so confused by the dance as either Keera or himself. *Maybe she's organising our escape?* He whipped his head from side to side to get another glimpse. Alice peered up at Queen Persephone and ducked back under cover. *She's been here before.*

The changeling and the fae in the mud-spattered blue dress were pulled back down to earth and taken to the cage where Ruby was crying.

The queen's soldiers attached a silver chain around Nada's ankle—and to the bone bars. Fae was trapped. Fae kicked out and changed half a dozen times, but could not escape the enchanted shackle.

The changeling sighed and patted Ruby's shoulder. "Both stuck."

Intent on the tender moment, Aiden tripped over his own feet and landed face-first on the churned moss.

Alice turned blank eyes on Aiden. Watery darkness roiled in the whites of her eyes like an oily shadow, or a weird trick of the light. Alice frowned and blinked.

"What's the matter," Aiden asked as he was picked up and whirled past.

"I surely don't know what you mean," she replied.

Whatever had got into Alice, he couldn't say. But that didn't change the mission. Send Ruby home. It's just that unless the Three Sisters Tree appeared again, it would be hard to avoid the danger of being stuck in one of the fae's seven-year time warps. So they were relying on Alice's navigation of the Silver Paths of the Dead. And to keep them safe from possession by demons.... *No!* The thought hit him like a tonne of bricks. *What if the oily shadow wasn't a trick of the light, and Alice is succumbing to the Silver Path's biggest danger?* If that were true, he could only pray she held on a little longer.

DEAL

Lettie's breath was coming in gasps. Her legs ached as the red shoes whirled her across the green. If nothing happened soon, she'd collapse dead in the midst of all the dancers, with Nada watching.

Poor Nada, chained to the cage. *Whatever will happen to my darling, sweet child?*

Banging on the iron-wrought door disturbed Lettie's thoughts and the rhythm of the dance. The music quickened to match the syncopation, a speed that only the finest of the dancers could match. A wild frenzy. A whirl. Lettie's shoes kick-stepped with wild abandon, adding twirls and sashays until Lettie was spinning so fast the world was a blur.

With a soul-shattering shriek, an axe chopped through the silver metal protruding from the wood. It glinted in the moonlight for an instant before the door toppled. Lettie toppled to the grass with it, the spell collapsing as the cacophony of music stopped with a discordant shriek.

The huge minotaur, Asterius, strode through. All bull head and rippling biceps, he charged into Persephone's arena.

Ominous music, breathy and dissonant, struck up, and Lettie was forced to dance again. Her legs rubbery, her face hot, she was grateful for the slower speed.

"Intruders!" Zadie screamed, turning to Queen Persephone, as if expecting to be congratulated for being a guard dog.

A Fae-in-Waiting stood and glared at the newcomers. "How *dare* you!"

Lettie, her feet whirling, cheered with happiness. "Asterius, you made it."

"Yes." Queen Persephone smiled glassily at the minotaur. "How lovely of you to turn up after all these years, Asterius."

"It is rather nice, isn't it?" The huge minotaur took a deep whuffly breath and strode into the midst of the dancers. The elegant fae scattered—near falling over their feet to do so. "I have come to take what is mine."

Back and forth, this way and that, Lettie danced over to him. The shoes had a mind of their own, but gradually she forced them to move closer to the minotaur and his entourage.

Queen Persephone glared at Asterius. "Could thou watch where thou art stomping? You're quite ruining the dance, *and* my precious dance-floor."

"Go away," Hades muttered, head-to-head with one of his de-mon body-guards. "We're rather busy at the moment. Can't you see we have unexpected guests? Not that my soldiers couldn't best your little force, but surely you could let me deal with these annoying mud-humans before barging in like this?" Hades smiled a smile that sparked in his eyes and lit his hair blue. "Unless you also want to visit the demon mines."

The demon nodded. "To be fair, that minotaur would be strong enough to shift a good amount of stone. Better than the humans, who will likely break. They are so pathetic."

Asterius bellowed. A roar that had the musicians change their music to match. Soon, they were playing an energetic waltz from notes that mimicked the minotaur's roar and had the fine dancers snickering behind their handkerchiefs. *This is the intrigue many come to court for,* Lettie thought, the shoes on her feet throwing her this way and that as the dance picked up pace.

Asterius ignored them all as he cut a path to the queen, like a sword through silk. His people trailed nervously behind him with an assortment of weapons, from swords and axes to spoons and stones and wooden serving bowls. "My people may not look like much, but, unlike your fancy ornaments, they know how to fight."

Battle lines were being drawn, even while the waltz continued to play and Lettie danced on, unable to stop, her whole body burning with pain. Still, now the queen was distracted, and no doubt itching to exact her revenge on her soldiers for letting the minotaur get too close, she had a chance. All she had to do was find someone willing to take the vampiric shoes off before they had her dancing dead on her feet.

Lettie determined she'd triple-step her way to freedom. Will, the pig-creature, seemed like a good bet. Lettie spotted him in the crowd backing up the minotaur. He was chatting to a boggart and a trow. "Yeah, it's a revolution," Will said. "We're going to live on the surface, like kings."

"Oh, I hope not." The trow shielded his eyes. "It's too bright up here. And there's so much noise. Give me a nice quiet crypt any day."

"Join us," Queen Persephone's old gardener called out to the crowd of fae. The dancers hesitated and backed away from Asterius' subjects, ruining the beautiful flow of the fairy dance.

Will Burr threw up his trotters. "Shake off the shackles of this false king and queen. They're not even fae. A human and a demigod ruining our summer with their nonsense."

A.J. Ponder

And he wasn't the only one imploring people to stand against Persephone and Hades. Lettie's gardener friend ran around imploring the gardeners and serving staff to stand strong. "We should be dancing free, not tied to these malignant half-humans. Look at my poor daisies. Such little respect."

Asterius roared. "Persephone, let us get to business. I've had enough lurking in the shadows. I want better food. Ambrosia and wheat-grass smoothies, mushrooms in a nice white wine vinegar. You know, food fit for a first-class vegan. Stop treating me like a rabid carnivore."

Lettie gasped. She should have known he was only out for himself. Acting not so much as an independent party, but as a goaler for those subjects Persephone didn't quite dare kill.

Zadie grabbed Lettie's waist as she tried to dance close enough to get Will Burr's attention. "Don't even try," Zadie hissed. "I know what you're up to. I should have known you'd find your own level with the traitorous Labyrinth scum."

"You'd love it, Zadie," Lettie shot back, and gasped for air, lungs burning. "Actually, you would. You always hated Queen Persephone, all your life. You're just too frightened of change to think things could be better."

"Naïve fool" Zadie spat.

Lettie tried to pull away, but Zadie whirled her closer to Asterius and Queen Persephone. Close enough to hear them bargaining.

"Fine, I'll deal with thou, Asterius," Queen Persephone said.

"I could deal," Asterius smiled smugly. "What have you got?"

§

Aiden was breathless and thirsty. He wanted nothing more than to swipe up a flower goblet of ambrosia as he was swirled into the arms of yet another elegant fae, one whose blue skin faded to white around her shoulders. Ruby, whimpering in her cage, held out her hands. "Mama, Dada. Mummy, Daddy. Help."

Queen Persephone, King Hades, Wyrden and the minotaur and the traitorous lawyer, Burcham, argued about territory and food and prisoners.

Aiden's mind spun. *How far back does Wyrden and Burcham's treachery go?*

The poor fae, the one called Lettie, was dancing around in red shoes that appeared to have a life of their own, while the orchestra played half-heartedly, and Queen Persephone and the Minotaur haggled over their territory.

Alice was sneaking around toward Ruby. Hopefully, she had a plan. Hopefully, she was still Alice.

The minotaur kept looking back to his motley collection of boggarts and other underground-dwelling creatures. For all his raw power, the minotaur appeared to have the weaker hand. His followers gripped their weapons nervously and glared at the revellers and Queen Persephone's silver-clad warriors.

Queen Persephone yawned, displaying her elegant hand, fingers smothered in emerald and silver jewellery. "I know I sent Lettie to you, Asterius, but I want faer back."

Jostled this way and that by other curious dancers, Zadie and Lettie did their best to stay close to Persephone and Asterius' conversation. The dance slowed to a mere shuffle as they jostled for position.

The minotaur waved his calloused hand. "I don't need trouble-makers like faer in my kingdom."

"Her," Lettie called over her shoulder, trying to make sure the fairy godmothers could hear. "I'm a fairy godmother. That means I am no longer your subject."

Persephone rolled her eyes. "We'll see about that. It's past time I laid claim to those pesky godmothers." Queen Persephone smiled. "Even though I'm sure they're more trouble than they're worth."

"No, I'll keep them," Asterius said. "Or to be more accurate they'll keep themselves and me safe. Don't think any of my court are going to fall for your nonsense." He waved a heavily muscled arm. "Don't think me and my people can't destroy all this."

"That'll do," Persephone purred and turned to Burcham. "Lawyer, do you have all that? Amendment 20b, the split of FaerLand Territories includes the new rule that any Labyrinthine dweller or other being trespassing on the Queen's lands shall be sent to the Underworld. Oh, and any of my citizens who upset me. Hades and I can't have them going to the Labyrinth, when we both know you can't keep them under control, can we?"

A gasp echoed around the clearing.

"What!" Aiden demanded.

"Shut up, Earthsider." Hades glowered. "You're part of the reason the law was so necessary."

"Lawyer, do you have my amendments, too?" Asterius said. "Will Burr, go and check." Will Burr, who appeared to be a smaller pig version of the minotaur, but with tusks instead of horns, grunted. "Yes, it's exactly as they said. Only..."

"Only what?"

"Of course, my amendments are exactly as stated." Burcham's crisp, no-nonsense tone caused some of the closer fae to flinch back. Burcham ploughed on. "That's why Burcham, Steadfast and Silvertongue are the most trusted lawyers in every realm. We're the letter of the law, and our letters are binding."

Queen Persephone glanced at the document and nodded. "It be satisfactory to me. Stamp it with thine seal, and be done. I have other matters to attend to."

Aiden inched over to the poor dancing fairy in the red shoes. She whirled away to dance near a small bunch of the minotaur's creatures—all listening carefully to the conversation the rulers were having with Burcham.

"Ah, but we have some loose ends," Burcham was saying.

Hades nodded. "Yes. The humans. They invited themselves, claiming the right of the dance. It's foolish and annoying and look at the mess it's caused."

"Hmm," Burcham said. "So, bear with me. The right of the dance is the curse where they must dance until they have worn through the soles of their shoes. Hmm. And yet, they are barely dancing?"

"I could put the vampyric shoes on them," Queen Persephone replied.

"A brilliant idea, my Queen." Wyrden rubbed his hands together. "I'd love to see it."

"I would not. The uninvited Earthsiders are about as elegant as potatoes."

Burcham bit his lip. "Maybe we could try another way?"

"I don't want another way," Hades screamed. "Unless you want to spend the rest of your pitiful life tormented by demons, too."

Aiden was swept away. By the time he'd fought his way back—after treading on half a dozen pairs of feet—Burcham was licking his lips nervously. "So then, it's decided, just as you sealed into this document. The caregivers must fight over the child. If Alette and her companion win, they can keep their changeling. If Keera and Aiden…"

"The mud humans?" An elegant fae spat, hands smoothing their autumnal brocade vest. "Are you really giving concessions to mud humans?"

Burcham nodded. "Yes, the forms are clear. If the humans win, they keep their child."

"Ew." The fae covered their mouth as if to retch. "They really want the snotty, disgusting, mud child back?"

Queen Persephone frowned at the fae who'd bad-mouthed Ruby. "You will treat the child with respect, and you will like it, or you will die."

The fae bowed slightly—although faer brocade vest did not so much as crease—and turned away.

Burcham shuffled papers. "You could let the human child go, and take the changeling in exchange—as they have offered."

So calm. And yet in his own way, he was fighting for them. Maybe there's hope...

"I think not," Queen Persephone said. "I told you, I'm tired of all the flutter fae. They're always fluttering here and fluttering there. It's so...unrefined. I want a human child. Another elegant companion. Damn your rules, lawyers. Am I, or am I not, Queen? Queen of this realm and the whole of the Underworld?"

Hades' hair flamed. "Oh yes, and it's very important the new clause 27 part B is actioned."

Burcham gulped. "So, if they lose, they will be sent to the demon mines."

"Indeed."

Persephone clapped. "Orchestra halt."

Aiden doubled over. He felt like a marionette whose strings had been cut, but Keera didn't waste an instant. She rushed over to Burcham. "Um," she whispered, putting Ruby's sword into a backpack and handing it to Burcham. "This is my will. If we do not survive, take this sword and give it to Brian Faulkner. He will know what to do. *You* know what to do."

Burcham nodded, and they both turned to Persephone, whose anger was not about to be quenched. "...and that fae, Alette." Persephone shook her head, watching the poor fae. "Faer dancing is not amusing; it will be so much better to send faer to the demon mines after fae disposes of the Earthsiders. But even that is not punishment enough for faer treachery."

Hades whispered something to his demon entourage. At last, he nodded. "Certainly, my dear. Remember when you were younger and said you wouldn't even send your worst enemy there?"

"Oh, yes. The wailing was excruciating and…you're right, it's perfect. If only they could all be sent there." She glanced over at Wyrden and Burcham. "But I suppose the forms must be followed."

She nodded over at Lettie, who was doing her best to avoid kicking a pig-like minotaur's tusked face while he unbuckled one of the brutal shoes.

With a triumphant cry, Lettie pulled her foot free, then tugged the other shoe off. She threw the shoes under a giant tree and lay down on the greensward, pale and delicate as an orchid.

"Zads…Zadie!" Queen Persephone called. "Since thou failed to keep Alette in line, you can join her. If thou fight well enough, I'll forgive thou crimes."

"But," the fae in a yellow dress spluttered. The one that had tried to ambush them outside Lettie's house.

"Zadie!" Lettie shouted. "And all you fae who support Queen Persephone, can you not see that she hates you? All you need do is not obey her commands, and you would be free."

"Shut up," Zadie said. "Save your energy for beating the pitiful Earthsiders."

COLD IRON

Lettie's feet hurt. The vampiric shoes had rubbed them raw. And now she had to fight for her child—against the man who'd fought spiders for Nada and, against the odds, brought her beloved changeling back home.

Nada!

Lettie rushed to her changeling. Faer was at once achingly beautiful, and perfectly fickle, flicking from one form to the next. Never quite able to escape the magical silver cord Persephone had placed around faer foot.

A quick hug was all she could manage before a Quip dragged her to the queen. A sword was placed in her hand—the same one the Quips had taken from her when she was thrown into the labyrinth. An abomination of silver, far worse than the tiny amount the human had in her swords. "This is so wrong." She gazed across at what had been a dance-floor. The centre was now clear, with boggarts and other Labyrinth citizens on one side of the circle, and Queen Persephone and her court on the other.

Zadie screamed at Lettie. "This is your fault. It's always your fault. Why did you ever come back?"

Lettie shook her head. "You would never understand."

"Well, Zadie is right," Wyrden said. "You should have killed the humans earlier. Saved everyone a lot of trouble."

"You should've stayed buried under a million barrels of rock," Lettie answered.

"Draw your swords," Wyrden said, pushing Lettie into the centre of the circle to join the humans and Zadie.

The humans put their hands to their hilts. "Not those swords!" One of Persephone's entourage shouted at Keera and Aiden. Too late—the air rang with the tang of iron.

"How dare you pull cold iron in a faerie glade?" Zadie screamed, staggering backward. Persephone's courtiers had also backed further away, giving them a wider circle in which to fight.

Lettie couldn't blame them. The shiver from cold iron physically hurt, burning like ice. She hardened her heart. She had to do this for Nada. She raced forward, whirling the sword, Zadie by her side.

The woodwind in the orchestra accompanied her every move.

Keera stepped in to meet them, moving in time to the strings in the orchestra. Lettie danced back again. The shrill notes of her movements contrasting with the moody passion of the violins.

Testing herself, Lettie danced back and forth across the greensward, teasing her clumsy human foe, and trying to tire her out. Any time she got close; a cheer rose. It lifted her heart.

Keera's gold earrings jingled. She moved like a cat, saving energy.

Lettie darted closer to elicit a reaction, and Keera's sword flashed out. The combination of fae silver, gold and cold iron slicing the air made Lettie's teeth itch. The blow hit, more painful than a brand, searing her skin. The crowd gasped as Lettie danced away, her dress slashed, beautiful blue spider-silk trailing from the cut. That was close. So much for clumsy human. She'd underestimated her foe.

"Watch out," Zadie warned, swirling in with gusto and thrashing faer sword. A few onlookers clapped. Several tittered. Zadie had clearly never held a sword before. This would be up to Lettie alone.

"Get behind them. Threaten their backs," Lettie said, stepping in.

"Good plan." Zadie smiled. "I could have made something out of you, but you were always too soft."

"Soft?" Lettie said. "You're just a bully."

She slashed at Keera.

Keera parried and slashed back, drawing blood again.

Pain flashed through Lettie's sword arm. *Damn I'm as good as dead.* She gritted her teeth and gripped the sword harder, fingers tingling. Her vision narrowed.

Keera stepped in close. Lettie dashed away, colliding with the boggarts at the edge of the circle. Helpfully, they pushed her back into the ring—before she lost her nerve and fled. *I cannot abandon Nada.*

"Quick, she's on the ropes," Keera said.

Aiden pulled Keera back and whispered something. "But Ruby!" They both looked to poor Ruby trapped in her bones—so close, and so far away. "Love you," Aiden yelled at the tousle-haired child, face streaked with dried tears."

But Ruby didn't respond. Maybe she couldn't hear over the screech of the orchestra and the roar of the crowd. *There has to be a way.*

Aiden put up a hand. "Truce. Parley." He put his sword down in a show of good faith.

"There's nothing in the rules against it," Burcham said, as the crowd howled in dismay.

Wyrden scowled. "I'm going to get Silvertongue. You're useless."

Might as well figure out what they're after. Lettie placed her sword in her corner and stepped in to see what Aiden thought he had to offer.

Music blasted, loud and sudden, so that Aiden could barely hear himself think, let alone talk. He was trying to tell the blue fae that he understood. That this whole thing was not her doing and, like her, all he wanted to do was save his child.

The fae turned to the children, then smiled at him, her wickedly sharp teeth gleaming in the moonlight. One of her eyes twitched weirdly as she lifted a hand clutching a short stick.

"Human fool," Lettie shouted, green light flashing from her wand as she ran past. Aiden ducked away so the attack only glanced his shoulder. The searing pain running up his arm. He shook it and steadied himself for another attack. But Lettie wasn't following up. She was running toward Queen Persephone's side of the circle.

Why attack like that and not follow it up?

The cage. Ruby! Aiden raced after Lettie to protect his child.

He slashed at Lettie and she rounded on him, the green light from her wand surprisingly painful as it raked across his chest. The other fae was keeping Keera occupied. Unable to land a blow, she darted here and there with the lithe-fleet-footed grace that came so naturally to her.

This is not the sort of fight you win by fighting. It's not the sort of fight you can win at all.

Aiden ploughed toward the cage.

As he was unarmed, none of the soldiers raised their swords. They just stepped aside.

The fae in the yellow and green dress grabbed Lettie and pulled her away from Ruby and the Changeling.

"No!" Lettie let out a howl of anguish.

§

"No!" Lettie screamed in frustration. She'd been a finger's width away from her Nada before Zadie had ruthlessly pulled her away. It had been a clever ploy from the human to get them so close to the children. Damn it to Hades that Zadie had noticed. She'd failed her changeling once—she wasn't going to fail again.

Easier said than done. Silver blood pouring down her shoulder, Zadie pulled Lettie back toward the fight. "Stop it, Lettie." Zadie scowled. "What are you doing? We should be making Queen Persephone proud."

Lettie struggled, thrashing her arm against Zadie's grip. "Look!" she whispered. *Zadie has to know this is wrong.* Lettie pointed to Ruby and Nada. "Free them, and this fight will be over."

Zadie threw Lettie aside. "Be like that." Fae darted past Aiden and the soldiers rushing to intercept him and plucked the human child from its cage. "Put down your swords.

Keera and Aiden both stopped. Keera threw down her sword, raising her arms in the air—slowly, so slowly.

"Die, human!" Zadie yelled. Fae ran at the woman, a child in one arm and a sword grasped in the other, as if it was a javelin to be thrown.

Keera stood motionless.

Lettie didn't need to imagine how it felt to know your child was in mortal danger. Of wanting to do everything to protect them.

All around the court watched the drama. The musicians played breathy notes in a minor key, hinting at a move to a major chord, as if expecting celebration any minute.

"Please, Zadie." Nada's voice rang out clear as a bell.

The court gasped and Lettie's heart swelled. There was no mistaking it. Nada had a will of her own. Lettie darted over to her charge.

"Dammit. Damn you all." Zadie swerved. Releasing Ruby and faer sword, Zadie changed into flutter form and swooped out of the circle past Asterius' forces, and into the deep dark forest. Lettie could only hope the elderfae would welcome faer after all this time in Persephone's court.

Silver plates crashed, a harsh percussive accompaniment to the frantic battle music.

Zadie wasn't the only one stepping away from Queen Persephone's court. Many of the crowded fae followed her—throwing off their elegant forms and cheering with delight as they winged their way into the forest—slipping away into the darkness to where Lettie could only hope they'd find the elderfae untouched by Queen Persephone and her monarchical madness.

Lettie yanked at the chain holding Nada.

Nothing.

Lettie glanced around at the angry fae.

This fight was only supposed to go one way. Now, without Zadie, Lettie had no doubt…she was going to lose.

But the parents weren't attacking her. Aiden had gathered up their child, protected by Keera's slashing sword. "Alice!" he yelled.

"This way!" Alice yelled back. Hand outstretched, she was waiting by Queen Persephone's mirror.

Not that way! That way lies the Underworld! Lettie opened her mouth to yell. She let out a strangled wail as Hades stepped in close to Alice and shoved her through the silvery mirror. It rippled and Alice was gone, the reflected greenery wavering in her wake.

§

"Alice!" Aiden yelled again, his heart sinking.

Hopefully, she'd find her way home. But now that she was gone, they had little hope of rescuing Ruby. Even if they could reach Queen Persephone's mirror, without a guide they would be lost. A terrible fate—but they had to try. There had to be hope.

The fae were closing in, all sharp teeth and long-legged grace. But one was worried about the changeling. Pulling at the silver chain. Slashing at it with the sword.

The changeling moved from form to form. Despair written in every shape it took from tear-drop butterfly wings to a bird with blood-splashed feathers.

Aiden might not be able to save himself or his small family, but he could at least rescue this one small creature from the grips of this mad court.

§

Lettie screamed as Aiden's sword stabbed at her beloved Nada. She threw herself at the vile weapon.

With a clink, Nada's silver chain attaching her to the dragon's rib cage was sliced clean through. Lettie pulled back—too slow. She screamed, the sound interweaving with Keera's shout of disbelief.

Burning pain pierced her shoulder as the sword hit. Silver blood cascaded down her chest, shimmering in the fae-light. Lettie fought back tears of excruciating pain as her heart lifted. *Nada's free.*

The breeze from the soft wingbeats of a snowy owl figure brushed her face. Nada was swooping down to check on her. "No! Fly!" Lettie yelled, aware of the Quips closing in on them. "Please, for me."

Nada's soft wingbeats changed to a heavy thrum as fae shifted into an eagle to free faerself from the clutching hands of the Quips. Lettie's heart sang to see her beloved Nada soar up to join the fairy godmothers and freedom.

Lettie struggled to shift into flutter form to join faer. But she'd lost too much blood. The world spun.

"I'm so sorry," Aiden was saying, standing over her. He shouldn't be sorry. He'd saved Nada. Glancing down, she dipped her finger in the silver fluid and thought of their world. The place she'd met Wyrden meaning to kill the humans—the park bench tattered, the paint peeling. That would be a good place…to take the humans. *I'm really going to do this?*

They saved Nada. A life for a life.

Persephone shook with anger. "You are the most *useless* of fae. But I will not kill you. No, I will let you contemplate how horribly you failed before you die. It shall be as you deserve."

What? How?

Best to ignore the queen. She focussed on Earth. On the Andersen's house. The silver blood at her feet shimmered and rippled with inky darkness.

Earth!

Dizzying pathways split and split again. She thought she recognised the park before the scene shifted to a dimly lit corridor.

Aiden and Keera scrambled toward it. "Ruby! Go!" Aiden pushed Ruby through the portal and tried to follow.

The Queen's elegant fae grabbed their shoulders and held them back.

"Wait!" Queen Persephone yelled. "Alette. Thou art banished from Faerland. Thou will stay…"

A low hum could be heard from the fairy godmother contingent.

"…on Earth until you are dead, or Ruby is of age."

Some of the fairy godmothers even cheered. It was alright for them, flying around in their carriage like royalty.

"What? No! Never!" Lettie yelled. "You can't send me to Earth."

Queen Persephone smiled wickedly. "Or thou could join these two in the demon mines." She waved dismissively at Keera and Aiden.

The demon mines or Earth. There was no contest. Lettie jumped.

§

Aiden struggled to free himself, but wiry hands dug into his flesh and pulled him back from the portal shimmering at Lettie's feet.

Keera was caught, too. Held back by fae in silvery armour and unable to follow Ruby as she fell through the shifting silver pathways created by the puddle of blood—the blood of the fae who kept on rescuing him.

Frantically, they tried to make it to the threshold, through the pathway.

Ruby held her hand up on the other side. Her mouth moving so fast it was a blur.

Behind her, a little girl was running down the corridor, long, dark hair swirling around her shoulders.

"Ruby!" Aiden cried as his little girl disappeared from sight and he and Keera were wrapped in spider-silk and dragged away.

§

"Who are you?" Ruby asked the girl with long glistening-black hair. "What are you doing in Mummy and Daddy's house?"

"I'm Pearl," the little girl replied. "Who are you?"

§

Once upon a time, and happily ever after. That's how the story is supposed to go. But mine ends here, on the banks of the river Lethe.

Ruby. If you get this. Take my tears, hear my story.

Find me.

THE END

P.S. I love reviews! Readers are my life blood, and a line or two on Amazon, Bookbub or Goodreads will help readers discover Lettie, Keera, Aiden, Corson and the world of FaerLand.

Thank You for Reading

BLOOD OF THE FAE

2

INTO
BROCÉLIANDE

USA TODAY BESTSELLING AUTHOR
A.J. PONDER

CHAPTER 1: SKIN WALKER

Lettie sighed. *82 days, 11 hours and 57 minutes to go until Ruby officially turns 21 and my exile is over.*

Every moment I'm stuck in this world, I regret that I didn't run from Queen Persephone long before I was exiled. My changeling, Nada, and I could have joined the elderfae in the deep, dark forest. We could have searched for the fairy godmothers. At a pinch, we could have explored Brocéliande. Even that would be better than Earth. Here, I feel as if I'll turn into an autumn leaf and blow away.

My heart aches. I want my changeling back. Ruby is no substitute. Although she was an adorable child, she is human. And humans not only sundered my world, but they peck away at it like magpies.

Every day I wonder how my changeling is...no I mustn't think of Nada as a changeling—Nada is fae. And fae will have grown. Mastered elegant form and faery form, become someone amazing.

The fairy godmothers will have looked after Nada and spoilt faer with balls and dresses and parties.

And I am not there to see it.

I am here. Where the wind brings not the scent of leaves, but the stench of smoke, tarmac, and death.

Ruby wiped a cloth over the last expanse of library shelving and shoved the books into place. All the returns were shelved and standing at attention for tomorrow.

"All done," Ruby said, trying to ignore her tiny fairy godmother, Lettie, fluttering around her head in one of her graceful blue ball gowns.

"Thank Chronos." Lettie sighed dramatically. "It's five thirty. Let's go."

"You okay?" Ruby asked and stopped as the head librarian rushed from the office. The woman gave Ruby a sharp glance. "Just make sure the doors are locked when you leave." She hitched her purse over her shoulder and sped out the door.

"Sure thing." Ruby grabbed Agatha Christie's newish book, They Came to Baghdad and settled in, shucking off her shoes and tucking her legs to the side on her favourite oversized reading chair.

Lettie sighed. "Don't tell me you're going to sit around and read. I've been waiting for you for hours."

"Might as well. Pearl's been kept late to cover the afternoon shift. We'll pick her up at seven."

Lettie reached for a blue, flower-shaped flask hidden in her dress. She tipped it back, then peered into the murky blue depths. "Worse luck," Lettie muttered.

§

Pearl hurried out the hospital doors, thankful to be out in the fresh air and away from the funk of antiseptic and illness.

"Hey Pearl," Arthur Faulkner said. The dark-haired athlete drew away from his brother and sister and strode up to Pearl. "You ready?" He flashed his magnetic smile. He looked dashing, as always, in his Teddy boy jacket.

She nodded. In truth, she wished she'd changed out of her nurse's uniform for the Faulkner's Literary Society meeting, but then Ruby would have twigged. It wasn't worth the stress. Not when Gran and Grandad were always warning them away from the Faulkners. Gran would wag her finger and say, "You know that the Faulkners and their Society are the reason your parents went missing."

And that was exactly why Pearl needed to go and see what The Literary Society was all about. Also, there was the fact that Arthur was gorgeous. Arthur's dark eyes were the perfect complement to his chiseled features. And he was tall. At least 6 feet. Pearl's chest tightened. *I wasn't swooning over him like Ruby said. But there's no denying he has looks.*

Pearl tried to think of something suitably witty to say to Arthur. Nothing. *If I'm not careful, I'll put my foot in my mouth.* She tugged her nurse's uniform. "It's been a long day."

"Yes, it certainly has," he replied with a grin.

Damn, did I really say that aloud? But his smile was infectious. Pearl found herself smiling back.

Hazel and Tailor caught up, Hazel looking stunning in her green shirt-waist dress that brought out the green-gold in her eyes.

"We should get moving, or we'll be late," Tailor said. "It's going to be so much fun having you along," he continued, as if he was the one who'd asked her to the society meeting.

If he had, would I have accepted? Pearl smiled politely. "So, tell me more about this literary society," she asked. "I thought Arthur was more into football and fencing, not books."

"You're about to find out," Hazel said. "Though today is more of a lecture."

Tailor nodded. "When you know what we really do, you can decide what to tell your grandparents."

Pearl flinched. "Why do you think there's a problem?" She scurried to keep up with their long strides.

"Ah, I guess they always seemed really strict," Tailor replied, jumping up onto the low stone wall that ran along the outside of the university.

Arthur lengthened his stride. "Come on, we don't want to be late."

Hazel ran along the echoey corridor beside him. "Last one there's a rotten egg."

"How old are you?" Arthur asked, sprinting to catch up to her.

Pearl followed suit and Tailor grinned, matching Pearl step for step as they raced after the others up the university steps and through an echoey corridor.

Arthur stopped at a door and Hazel put her finger to her lips. Together, they all crept into the lecture theatre and founds seats at the back.

"The thing with fairy tales," Prof Brian Faulkner was saying, "is it's not so much the truths they hold. It's the possibilities they unfold and the limits they create. Don't think of..." he trailed off, glancing at Pearl with a slight nod. "...the world of fairy tales as static, but as a living, breathing place of interconnected mythology."

"Look, Mum's here," Tailor whispered, pointing at Alice Faulkner. She was talking to an old gentleman leaning forward on a chair, a white cane planted in front of him. The old gentleman glanced back, his eyes shielded by dark glasses.

"That's odd," Hazel said. "Mum hates these meetings. Complains that Dad treats everyone like students at a lecture."

"And who's she with?" Tailor whispered.

"I don't think it matters," Hazel replied as the old man stood and made his way back down the corridor. "Looks like he's off, anyway."

A.J. Ponder

Pearl's skin crawled as he strode past with an unexpectedly fluid grace and slipped out the door without hesitating or using his cane once.

"He was odd," she said.

Arthur nodded and placed an arm around Pearl's shoulder. He smelled so good, like spice and sunlit apples.

"Now, where was I?" Prof continued. "The story of Snow White and Rose Red. Traditionally, it's the story of two well-behaved girls who live happily ever after." He opened a huge gold-bound book with the title Hidden Tales embossed on the cover and started reading the tale Pearl knew so well.

Pearl's eyes slipped closed. It had been a long day.

§

Ruby raced up to the hospital carpark, late as usual. The only car here was a beat-up old Cadillac. She pulled in and parked three spaces over from it.

"Where's Pearl?" Lettie asked from her favourite spot on Ruby's shoulder. "I need to get home and have a drink."

But there was no sign of Pearl. *She should be waiting on the park bench, under the wrought-metal electric lights. Or at least, making her way there.* The gardens on the other side of the carpark were filled with long shadows. The heady scent of late summer roses and freshly cut grass failed to stop Pearl's absence from being ominous. *Whatever could be keeping her?*

Ruby hopped out of the car. "Pearl!?"

Something rustled in the bushes.

"Pearl. It's not funny." Ruby peered into the darkness.

Lettie swiveled around on Ruby's shoulder, her blue spider-silk dress shimmering in the lamplight. "Watch out!" she called.

"Where?" Ruby asked the fae, spinning around and squinting into the darkness.

"Here." A silver-haired gentleman with a white walking cane and eyes like pools of midnight emerged from under a statue.

He moved fast, stepping rather than running, malice emanating from his wiry frame. A pair of dark glasses was perched on the top of his head.

Lettie fluttered up into the sky, and Ruby stepped back.

She considered getting into the car—but not with Pearl out there. "Stay away!" She pulled the back door open and fumbled for the fencing swords on the car seat as he loped closer. She could hear his breath. Smell his aftershave.

The practice swords were right here.

The moment felt like an hour. He was a stride away, his hands reaching out to grab her when she found the blade and training took over. She gripped the pommel and whipped around, cracking the metal down on his hand with a force hard enough to break a finger, or at least leave a serious welt.

He didn't flinch. He knocked the practice sword sideways and wrapped his hand around Ruby's wrist, drawing her closer. Ruby flailed at him ineffectively with her free hand, while his stone-like grip crushed Ruby's bones together until her épée fell from her numb fingers and clanged to the ground.

"Wyrden! Skin demon, get away," Lettie yelled, flying at the man.

He smiled, ignoring Lettie and flashing white teeth below his eyes so endlessly empty of light they were like pits to hell itself. "It's time you returned, Ruby."

"Returned?" Ruby asked. Not that she cared what he meant. She only wanted to distract him. *Where is Pearl?*

Ruby kicked him hard. Her toe flamed with pain, but the man seemed more bothered by Lettie as the wee fae zipped back and forth, barely beyond his grasp. "You shouldn't be Earthside. Do King Hades and Queen Persephone even know you're here?"

"Pearl!" Ruby elbowed her attacker. It was like hitting steel. Electric pain zinged along the fragile bone, worse than pins and needles.

"I'm just doing your job for you." The man whipped out a hand to catch Lettie.

She darted away. "My job?" she yelled. "My job was to raise a changeling, but faer was stolen away on a whim of Queen Persephone. Then, for my troubles, I was banished from FaerLand to mind this human. I'll be sent to the Underworld before I lose Ruby. Leave. Her. Be!"

Ruby struggled, battering this Wyrden skin demon person with her free hand. It was like hitting stone.

"Come. Queen Persephone has been waiting for you." Wyrden dragged Ruby along the gravel path through the park and toward the shadows of the forest behind.

Ruby dug her feet in, trying to wrench herself from his grip. Fiery pain coursed through her arm. She screamed.

"Foolish human," he spat. He tossed Ruby over his shoulder. Stomach crushed, she gasped for breath.

Lettie threw a last punch at his head and disappeared into the night.

The demon moved fast. The dark forest loomed. Any second they'd be hidden under its branches, where no amount of screaming would bring help.

Where could Lettie have possibly gone? And where's Pearl?

"Pearl!" Ruby yelled, battering the man's back with her arms and kicking his rock-solid gut. "Help!" The forest soaked up the noise, and the man, or skin walker, or whatever he was, strode on, slowly and steadily eating up the miles until they reached a tree with two trunks.

Through the gap in the trunks, and illuminated by a silvery moon, the deep velvet green of the woods of Brocéliande enticed Ruby. *Brocéliande? How do I know this place? When?*

The skin walker strode into the gap between the two trunks. Ruby almost willing him on past the barrier. There was something here she'd wanted to do. If only she could remember.

Red-hot pain lanced through Ruby along with old, long-forgotten memories, as she smashed into an invisible barrier with a force that rattled her bones.

She screamed.

§ § §

Blood of the Fae continues in
Into Brocéliande

A.J. Ponder

A Secret World
Hidden Demons
An Impossible Mission

Fifteen years ago, Ruby's parents rescued her from FaerLand, but then disappeared, leaving nothing but a blue-glass vial of her father's memories.

Determined to find them, Ruby defies her kick-ass but bumbling grandparents and enters the legendary world of Brocéliande.

She's up against a dangerous literary society, vengeful fae, and vicious demons with no one to help her but her alcoholic fairy godmother who has passed out on the sofa in the mortal realm, and the enigmatic and treacherous witch, Baba Yaga.

Time is running out. If Ruby doesn't rescue her parents before the equinox, they'll be trapped in the Underworld forever.

Blood of the Fae continues in
Into Brocéliande.

ACKNOWLEDGEMENTS

There are so many people I need to thank, without whom this book would never have seen the light of day.

Firstly, I'd like to thank Lee Murray and Chloe Wright for awarding me the Wright-Murray Residency for Speculative Fiction. The residency was an amazing opportunity to be immersed in writing and creating this series that encompasses worlds of fairy tale and mythology. I also loved having the opportunity to contribute to the writing community in Tauranga, Young New Zealand Writers, and to explore the beautiful native bush north of Tauranga—soaking in that ambience for my world.

I'd also like to thank my fellow authors. Charlotte Jardine, for her careful editing of this book and amazing ability to make every story better. Eileen Mueller, for encouraging me to tell people my books exist. And Peter Friend for his encouragement and for kick-starting me on this crazy writing journey.

Lastly, a special thank you to all my volunteers. Yes, when I asked who'd like to die heroically in a book, so many people put up their hands I had to spread them over two books!

The people in this book include my husband, Philip Sirvid, who was very keen on a spectacular death, but I couldn't quite manage to do it, so his fate is somewhat more reserved. His character was based on the fact that he's an arachnologist. It was a shame that as the scientific person entering a mythological world, he was always going to get everyone into trouble! But it was also fun. And he has a great sense of humour. So, thank you, Phil.

And a thank you to the hero of the story, Schuyler Corson, whose character was inspired by the fact they're a "...big fan of terribly bad movies." And an "owner of a copy of the movie where Chuck Norris is knocked out by Dean Martin."

Not to forget Craig Harder, whose name graced the mayor of New Avondale. I salute Craig for bravely volunteering, and his character was based somewhat on my recollections of David Gemmel's old-hand last-stand warriors.

And as for next book, I can't wait to introduce you to more wonderful volunteers. Let all my volunteers names live on in mythology and in the world of Brocéliande for as long as stories are told!

ABOUT THE AUTHOR

USA Today bestselling author, A.J. Ponder (BSc, Dip Teach) is the author of numerous novels and short stories including the award winning Frankie and the Netball Clone, Dying for the Record, The Sylvalla Chronicles, Wizard's Guide to Wellington and more.

A.J. lives in a hundred year old house overlooking Wellington harbour with three cats and a family all obsessed with games, books and dungeons and dragons. A.J. has a head full of monsters, and recklessly spills them onto the written page. Beware dragons, dreadbeasts, taniwha, and small children—all are equally dangerous, and capable of treading on your heart—or tearing it, still beating, from your chest.

Find me at ponderbooks.com,
A.J. Ponder

Also By A.J. Ponder

Sylvalla Chronicles

Quest
Prophecy
Omens
The Secret Child (prequel)
The Secret Story (short story prequel)

The Dragon Society Papers

The Dragon Transport & Pacification Society
The Society for the Prevention of Cruelty
to Dragons & Magical Creatures

Blood of the Fae

Into FaerLand
Into Broceliande
Into the Underworld
Into Treachery

Dragon Shifters' Hoard

Snow and Red
Zephyr and Snow
Dante and Red

Other

Miss Lionheart and the Laboratory of Death (11+)
Wizard's Guide to Wellington (8-12)
Attack of the Giant Bugs (8-12)
The Frankie Files (7-11)
The Great Weta Robbery (6-8)
Save the Moa (6-8)

THE SECRET STORY

A horde of rats
A coven of witches desperate to stay hidden
A ball to die for, and a ball that must remain secret at any cost

Smithy's daughter, Amarinda's daydreaming must end when her father is injured and she discovers her family is in debt to Lady Dragonheart. Amarinda must take extraordinary measures to pay back the debt.

To save her father, she must infiltrate castle Avondale and steal a 'cookbook' with secret recipes everyone wants to get their hands on.

The harder she tries, the more Amarinda is drawn into a hidden world of witches and power—not to mention Lady Dragonheart's schemes to infiltrate the Avondale ball and seize the kingdom.

Will Amarinda's father survive the night? Will she get to dance with the prince? And who will be turned into a rat? Find out by reading this secret story of a not-quite Cinderella, whose closest thing to a Fairy godmother is, alas, old Granny Earwax. For magical mayhem that flies off the page faster than a witch's broomstick, get your copy of The Secret Story today!

THE DRAGON TRANSPORT & PACIFICATION SOCIETY

After Mandy's family Troll Bridge is attacked and destroyed by dragons, Mandy finds herself alone. Her parents and her two little brothers have disappeared. Suspecting the dragons, she embarks on a desperate quest to find and rescue her missing family, or avenge them.

On the way, she swallows her new resentment of dragons long enough to rescue Beeble, a tiny fae dragon. With the cute dragon's help, and help from unexpected friends within the walls of the Dragon Transport and Pacification Society itself, the pair unravel a plot bigger than the destruction of her beloved family troll bridge.

More lives are on the line than Mandy could have imagined, including those of her new friends. Can she stay true to herself and help everyone, or will she throw her new friends away to save her family?

www.ingramcontent.com/pod-product-compliance
Lightning Source LLC
Chambersburg PA
CBHW020304200626
46814CB00006BA/2084